D0758762

Barawa and the Ways Birds Fly in the Sky

An Ethnographic Novel

Michael Jackson **BARAWA**

and the Ways Birds Fly in the Sky

Smithsonian Series in Ethnographic Inquiry
Published by the Smithsonian Institution Press
Washington and London
1986

The paper used in this publication meets the requirements
of the American National Standard for Permanence of Paper for
Printed Library Materials Z39.48-1984.

Library of Congress Cataloguing in Publication Data

Jackson, Michael, 1940–
Barawa and the ways birds fly in the sky.

(Smithsonian series in ethnographic inquiry)
Bibliography: p.
1. Kuranko (African people) 2. Ethnology—Sierra
Leone. I. Title. II. Series.
GN655.S5J33 1986   306′.0966′4   85–43406
ISBN 0-87474-536-5

Edited by Jane McAllister
Designed by Alan Carter

To the memory of George Devereux, 1908–1985

Pathfinder, Mentor, Friend

 # Contents

Acknowledgments   ix

Barawa and the Ways Birds Fly in the Sky   1

Notes   205

Sources   209

Glossary of Kuranko Words   211

Acknowledgments

I hope that this book will be regarded as an acknowledgment of my gratitude and esteem for the people of Barawa and of other Kuranko chiefdoms in Sierra Leone. I hope also that it will justify the faith of friends who read and commented upon earlier drafts and helped it on its long journey toward publication—Mariama Ceesay, Caroline Ifeka, Ivan Karp, Cheleen Mahar, Sewa B. Marah, Keith Ridler, and Michael Young. At the Smithsonian Institution, Paula Roberts, William L. Merrill, and Daniel H. Goodwin gave me invaluable advice.

Finally, I wish to remember here with love my late wife, Pauline, with whom six years ago the idea of this book was born.

In recent years there has been a new turn, one which amounts to a deep rupture. The writer has discovered that invention based on life can have its point of departure in the real existence of men situated in quite specific circumstances—atypical or anomic—and acquire the value of a symbol or myth.

Jean Duvignaud (*Change at Shebika*)

Meaning is not in things but in between: in the iridescence, the interplay; in the interconnections: at the intersections, at the crossroads. Meaning is transitional as it is transitory: in the puns or bridges, the correspondence.

Norman O. Brown (*Love's Body*)

I never had, and still do not have, the perception of feeling my personal identity. I appear to myself as the place where something is going on, but there is no 'I', no 'me'.

Claude Lévi-Strauss (*Myth and Meaning*)

Part 1

Chapter One

BARAWA LIES BETWEEN the Bagbe and Seli rivers—a succession of grass-covered plateaux drifting into the haze of the distant Loma Mountains. Granite inselbergs stud the horizon, their vast surfaces pitted by centuries of rain. Paths of iron-red laterite weave through the landscape, connecting hamlets whose conical thatched roofs are all that appear above the tall elephant grass. Log bridges are thrown down over rusty streams. . . .

THE ANTHROPOLOGIST stopped writing and looked up from his desk—littered with dog-eared papers and yellowing documents: the accretions of years of fieldwork in West Africa. He stared out the window at a flock of birds against the evening sky—a flung seine net it seemed, or a handful of grain broadcast into the wind.

He did not know how to go on. At first it had seemed so clear. Wearied by years of academic writing in which the lives and identities of actual Kuranko people had disappeared under a welter of interpretative ideas about totemism, witchcraft, sacrifice, divination, initiation, and narrative, he had at last given himself a task that might be totally authentic—to enter freely and imaginatively into the lives of those whose names were by now as familiar to him as the names of his own forebears, to write from within their consciousness of history, to bridge with metaphor the gap between aspects of his own experience and theirs. For it was his hope that anthropology might move away from a yearning for essences, causes, and determinate meanings to an open-ended quest for connections and juxtapositions—striking common chords, finding common ground, disclosing common historical horizons without the pretence of arriving at any necessary truth.

He leafed through his notes again. How was he to bring to life these figures, whose very existence was so often reduced to a name, a single detail, an event, or a mere linking role in a chain that stretched back . . . ?

He remembered the Kuranko adage—*soron i le ko yolke*, "one's birth is a link in a chain." And then, *soron i le ko yagbayile*, "one's birth is like the rope tied to the platform from which birds are scared away from the growing grain." All the tributary strands are knotted together; to move one was to move all. Perhaps, he thought, the answer would be to allow the unity of the subject to dissolve into the unity of a place, to see Barawa as a kind of genealogy in which he, too, figured.

THE MARAH have ruled Barawa for more than 350 years. In the past they offered sacrifices for the protection of the country at the foot of Senekonke, "gold mountain." To this day people speak of hearing snatches of xylophone music borne on the wind, the calling of praise-singers, and the creaking of stone doors as the mountain presages the death of a ruler.

According to the genealogists it was Yamisa who first settled the country, descending from the forested foothills of the Loma, where his elder brother Borsingbi had made his home. It is said that Yamisa declared, *"M'bara wa"* ("I am going to my own place"); thereafter the country became known as Barawa.

HIS AUDACITY surprised him. In effect he was casting himself in the role of a Kuranko bard—seizing upon the story others had told about their world in order to tell a story that had meaning for the present—an endless narrative availing itself of a finite number of elements. But at the same time, he remembered the urging of Kuranko friends that he chronicle the events that had recently brought Barawa back onto the political scene—a struggle for identity and autonomy that went back long before the advent of colonial rule.

More confident now, he saw that his book would be a kind of allegory of cultures in contact, a meditation upon knowledge and power, in which his own story would be analogous to others. It would show how people—their lives contingent upon history and changed by adventitious encounters—nevertheless shape their several destinies. And its key image would be of birds because, though we are all prefigured by our social and historical origins, no two of us, the Kuranko say, ever trace the same path across the sky.

There then occurred to him the story of Marin Tamba, tenth ruler of Barawa, who in the mid-eighteenth century was visited by a Fula teacher, Karakome Alfa Ibrahim, who endeavored to convert him to Islam.

The anthropologist had recorded the spare details of this incident, and his Kuranko field assistant had once shown him a document bequeathed by his father that also referred to the event. But to amplify it he would have to have recourse to experiences of his own, in particular with the hadjis who had badgered him for days during his last visit to Barawa, trying to convert him to Islam.

THE ZEALOUS MUSLIM came before Marin Tamba, who was seated on the porch of his house, out of the sun, and surrounded by councilors and praise-singers. Karakome Alfa Ibrahim stood in the courtyard, on the bare earth. His eyes watered. The gowned men whom he addressed regarded him stolidly, impassively, and when the speaker relayed the Muslim's words to the pagan ruler there was little hint of the one emotion upon which the proselytizer had hoped to play—fear.

"Allah created the seven decks of the sky and the seven layers of the earth! But he did not create fetishes or magical medicines. Nor did Allah ordain that men offer sacrifices to such things or consult them about human destiny. There are no pillars holding up the decks of the sky. The words of Allah hold up the sky! It is the truth of the words of Allah and of his prophet Muhammad that sustains the sky and earth. You can build a house on a lie, but you cannot roof it or support its walls with a lie. You must destroy all your fetishes and magical medicines!"

The Kuranko ruler listened patiently. "We have heard all this before," he said. "But we are *sunike* here, we are agnostic."

"Have you then heard how Allah built the two houses of heaven and hell, and how those who deny the words of Allah will go to hell? Do you know how a man enters heaven? The price of heaven is fasting, sacrifice, prayer, hospitality, truthfulness, and almsgiving. Consider, for instance, a child that loses its father at a tender age. You must pity the child and take care of it. You . . ."

5

"Such *is* the custom among us," the ruler interrupted. "An orphan child is raised by its father's brother."

The Muslim, annoyed by this pagan obduracy and by the heat, hurried on with his catalogue of works. "You must give to the needy. Whoever does this will go to heaven. And there are other good works: you go on a hadj, you build a mosque, you sacrifice a cow to Allah, you undergo circumcision. All these things are the price of heaven!"

Several of the Barawa elders were yawning. Others stared at the Muslim. Some got up and walked away with practiced disdain, twitching the sleeves of their gowns up over their shoulders.

"And the fetishes we use, you say they are the price of hell?" asked Marin Tamba.

"If you believe only in those things, yes, Allah will send you to hell."

A shadow passed across Marin Tamba's face. "And being sunike will we go to hell?"

"Ah!" expostulated the Fula, "it will be an eternal imprisonment and everlasting solitude. Angels will torment and punish you with rods of iron. You will wear gowns of fire, and scalding water will melt your skin. There will be no respite from pain. . . ." He paused, and cast a snide, almost pitying glance at the ruler. "Do you believe this?"

"I do not know."

"Then do you believe that when you die your life will leave your body?"

"Yes."

A knot of Marin Tamba's councilors murmured their own understanding.

"Where does it go then?" the Fula challenged.

"I do not know."

"Do people dream of kinsmen who have died?"

"They do. Even I have dreamt at times of my father, Mamburu, and of my grandfather, Tilkolo Yira."

"This shows that their lives exist somewhere! You cannot dream of things that don't exist."

"This may be so, but we uphold the words and deeds of our forebears, and they were not Muslims."

The Fula, judging his advantage, now shuffled closer to the porch, and wiped the sweat from his eyes with his thumb. With lowered voice he prepared to triumph over this infidel, whose face betrayed growing anxiety.

6

"Did your forebears make themselves or were they made by someone? If the rain does not fall the rice will not grow. You can plant the rice, but you cannot make the rain. The rain comes from Allah!"

"There are certain people who have the gift of making the rain come and go," Marin Tamba replied.

"It is Allah's doing, not theirs! They lie if they say they make the rain. It is Allah who makes them what they are."

Who can say what moved Marin Tamba to embrace Islam? The grim images of hell? The tedium of the Fula's argument? A need to appease the Fula proselytizers, who had recently formed a military alliance with the Yalunka of Sulima to the north, and whose invasive presence might have been felt in the allusions to hell and rain? Whatever the reason, the Barawa ruler finally told the itinerant Muslim that he was happy to accept Islam, and thereby acquired the nickname Sewa, meaning happy.

His happiness was short-lived.

The elders protested that they were Marah. "Is it not true that our very name means to command and subjugate? Is it not true that our praise-word is *nomor*, person of force? And is it not said that a person could be older than a Marah, but that it is under a cotton tree planted by the Marah that he was raised?"

The praise-singers took up the refrain. They sang of Lord Yilkanani, who commanded the world from where the wind comes from to where the wind goes. They sang of the two horns upon his head, and of his wealth and progeny. They sang of Saramba, who came down from Mande and apportioned the conquered lands among his sons and allies. "Allah made the world," they sang, "but the Marah made our customs and they own the law."

Through the music, Marin Tamba heard his ancestors speaking and glimpsed the shimmering plains and devastated towns they had made their own. Stirred by the xylophones and exhortations, he renounced Islam.

That same dry season, Barawa was invaded from the north.

WHEN NEWS REACHED Marin Tamba that war had entered his country, he turned to his elders and said, "Take my body too." Then he went into his house and plunged his war sword into his belly.

On the day that Allah finally took Marin Tamba captive, the skies of Barawa were empty of birds.

The Fulas and their Sulima allies were defeated not long afterward on the Sankaran by Konde Braima. In Barawa, Marin Tamba was succeeded by his eldest brother, Morowa, who ordered the reconstruction of the country and built up a warrior force capable of withstanding any invasion. Magical medicines marked the corners of the chiefdom, and when Morowa left the country to attend festivals or funerals in other chiefdoms, a pale-skinned virgin girl would be sacrificed for the safety of the country and be buried at the boundary, her mouth stuffed with gold and her head covered in a gold-encrusted calabash. Fula cattle herders, mindful of past defeats, avoided Barawa, and rumors abounded of Marah who turned into leopards and attacked the livestock of strangers.

Morowa died in the last decade of the eighteenth century and was succeeded by his younger brother, Balansama, who continued to reinforce the boundaries of the country. The renown of his warriors led neighboring rulers to seek Balansama's protection, and under Balansama's rule trade routes were opened up between Barawa and the Sankaran to the northeast. Camwood and cloth were exchanged for salt from the Atlantic coast.

It was at this time that the first reports were received in Barawa of the *tubabu*, the white men, who had come out of the sea and were thin because they ate nothing but fish. Mandingo traders told of a place called Saralon on the edge of the great salt water where the tubabu lived. The tubabu owned immense houses filled with cloth and beads, and they were in possession of a book which, unlike the Qur'an, contained the secrets of wealth.

Sudan

Region of our disdain,
whose quiet men have injury
and pillaged caravans in their gaze;
I came here
to obtain no silver, no provisions
for my journey back,
but to look into the eyes
of men who no longer own the earth
of women who abandon the black tents
at dusk
and descend
to draw water for any stranger.

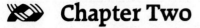 **Chapter Two**

IN 1819, ALEXANDER GORDON LAING arrived in Sierra Leone to join his regiment, the York Light Infantry. He was twenty-four and had recently been promoted to lieutenant.

The colony of Freetown was thirty years old and its population was around five thousand. In the bush-covered hills of the peninsular, villages called Leicester, Regent, Granville Town, Wilberforce, Gloucester, Leopold, Charlotte, Bathurst, York, Wellington, and Waterloo had been founded for liberated slaves. To many Europeans the colony was a "pestiferous charnel house," and to most of the repatriated Africans it was at best a dubious homeland.

Laing had been a schoolmaster in Newcastle before enlisting in the army. The shambles of Freetown disturbed him. He complained to his superiors of finding a European teacher lying drunk in the street, of local women brazenly offering their children for sale, and of insolent former slaves who did nothing all day but loiter about the palm-wine stalls in cocked hats and mountebank coats. Fatigued by fever and the fear of fever, his superiors found such moral concern tedious. Laing turned more and more to his lifelong ambition to explore the interior of Africa. More than anything, he wanted to be the first European to find the source and termination of the Niger.

Beyond the mountains that had given Sierra Leone its name lay an unmapped hinterland. Vast plains of mangrove, mudstone, oil palm, and scrub vanished into a haze of dust or mist. All that the British knew about the interior had been pieced together from talks with Temne chiefs and reports by Mandingo traders who occasionally descended to the coast.

Despite such a paucity of detailed information, it seemed there could be commercial advantage in making contact with rulers in the interior. Late in 1822, Major General Sir Charles MacCarthy, crown governor of the colony, decided to send a mission to Kambia and the Mandingo country "to ascertain the state of the country, the disposition of the inhabitants to trade and industry; and to know their sentiments and conduct as to the abolition of the Slave Trade." Laing, who had been agitating to be sent on such an expedition, was chosen to lead it.

He traveled northeast under bruised skies, along the right bank of the Rokel through Temne districts.

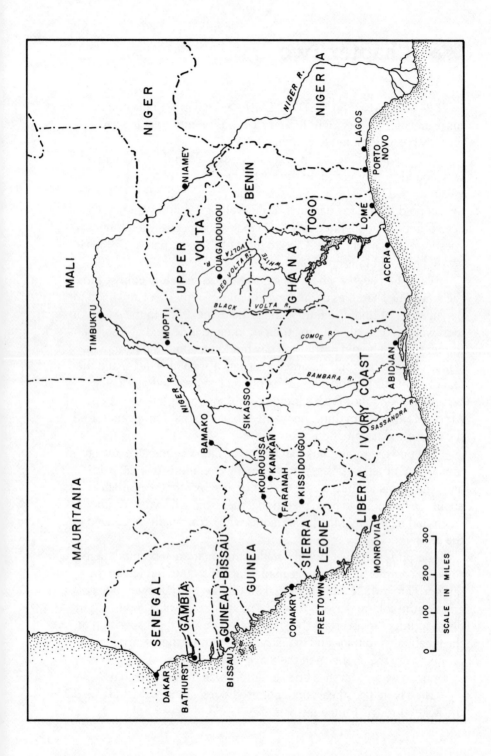

Around the Tenene hills beyond Mabum the landscape became more rugged and forested, and where the Rokel became the Seli, Laing entered Kuranko country. At Kulufa he was welcomed as the first white man ever to set foot in Kuranko. Salt was vital to them, the town chief explained, giving his blessing to Laing's plan "to open up a good road to the sea."

At Simera the chief echoed this view. "If a path is open, then there is trust; when two people pass to and fro along the same path, then there is friendship."

"Trade is a great boon between nations," Laing agreed, imagining caravans of rice, camwood, and gum-copal reaching the markets of Sara-lon.

But the going was not all easy. Laing grew impatient with the rig-marole of interpreted speeches. He became irritated when chiefs urged him to stay and live with him, "to get fat on the meat of cows and quench his thirst with draughts of milk." In the gloom of a mud-walled house with rafters festooned with sooty cobwebs, he was haunted by the fear of oblivion. At first light he rose cold and cramped from his camp bed and surveyed the mist-swathed bush with an air of bewilder-ment and despondency. Kuranko men clustered around makeshift fires in the courtyards and greeted one another with the litany of phrases Laing already knew by rote. He joined them for the warmth of their fire, and on one occasion allowed himself to experiment with a native toothbrush—a frayed piece of lophira stick. Its bitter aftertaste was a reminder of his impeded destiny.

In his journal, however, he gave vent to only one frustration—the delays and difficulties in hiring carriers. At Kania he threatened to set fire to half his goods unless the chief ordered porters to carry them to Sandia. His impatience amused his hosts. The town chief explained at length that a state of war existed between Kania and the towns across the Seli: it would be dangerous for the white man to set off before a truce had been agreed. It was the chief's onus to keep his white stranger from harm. And anyway, many of the young men were away at the war or preoccupied with farm work. It would take time to organize the number of bearers the tubabu demanded. Laing's interpreter, Tamba, added that it was, moreover, customary in Kuranko for a guest to spend some time enjoying the hospitality of a town, and it would be unseemly to make off within a day of arriving at a place.

That night the *luiye* fires sent showers of sparks into the darkness and threw fluttering shadows on walls daubed with white mud. Groups of women hovered at the edge of the firelight, the decorative weals on their breasts shining like smears of water. *Jelibas* sang of the white man who had come to their town, of the household of coins he owned, of the bolts of cloth, the beads and finery such as had never been seen in Kuranko. "Do business with the thin salt-water men," the praise-singers exhorted, condemning husbands who did not want to see their wives dressed in fine cloth and rulers who did not want the white man's coins. Laing told Tamba to sing, in turn, of Sierra Leone, where there were houses a mile in length filled with money, and such an abundance of cloth and salt that it would easily carpet a whole town. "But," finished Tamba, "if you wish some of the rich white men to come into your country, you must not trouble this one. Whoever wants to see a snake's tail should not strike the snake on the head."

When Laing reached Kamato he met emissaries from Sulima who guided him across the tawny plains of plum grass and acacias to their capital, Falaba, in the north. Here Laing learned that he was only three days' march from the source of the Niger, and he petitioned the Sulima ruler to allow him to go there.

Unfortunately, the enmities of the 1750s had not been forgotten. After the Fula and Sulima invasions, Barawa had recovered its might and strengthened its alliances with other Kuranko chiefdoms to the east. It was through these enemy chiefdoms that Laing would have to travel on his way to the upper Niger. The Falaba ruler was determined to obstruct Laing's plans.

"How will you cross the large rivers without a canoe?" he asked.

"I suppose I must swim across them on gourds," Laing replied.

"*Allahu Akbar!* There are swamps on the way into which you will sink. How will you pass over them?"

"I will fell trees and lay them across the mire, and so walk over them. Indeed sir, I assure you that neither river nor swamp will deter me, if you are only kind enough to grant me leave to go."

"*Alhumdulillah,*" exclaimed the chief, shaking his head. "Then go!"

But Laing had not reckoned with augury. A day after his departure from Falaba a messenger caught up with him and relayed a dream of the Falaba ruler's in which the ruler had found himself in a dense forest. On the same night, the chief had dreamt of a vast swamp where, in its black mud, the face of the moon was shriveled like an old orange. Convinced of some conspiracy, the ruler ordered Laing's immediate return.

From the summit of a hill not far from Falaba, Laing thought he made out the blurred range from which the Niger issued. His instruments indicated that the river's source was sixteen hundred feet above sea level (it is actually twenty-eight hundred), which settled him in his belief that the Niger did not flow north toward Lake Chad but east, ultimately to the Atlantic.

(But he was never to find the source, which lies in a sparsely inhabited region of Kuranko country, hidden among a pile of moss-covered boulders in a ravine. Water trickles from sandy hollows and forms a small stream, which local people say is the home of a *djinn*.)

As he retraced his steps south across tablelands of elephant grass and contorted lophira, Laing took with him only a handful of wild beliefs about the stream: that anyone trying to leap over it would be instantly swallowed up by it, that it is a fountain of gold, that anyone trying to take water from it would have the vessel wrenched from his hand by an invisible power.

On reentering Kuranko country, Laing decided to make diplomatic contact with the Barawa ruler, Balansama, who commanded the principal trade routes to the east. Four days after sending word to Kulakonke, the Barawa capital, Laing met Balansama in Kamato.

The Barawa chief arrived with three hundred armed men, as many women, and an equipage of drummers, xylophonists, flautists, trumpeters with elephant-tusk horns, lutanists, and praise-singers. The warriors wore burnt-umber gowns covered with sachets of magical medicine. At a shout from their commanders they drew their swords from tasseled leather sheathes and, brandishing them and short bows, broke into dance. The ground shook from the stamped rhythm of their feet. The air filled with red dust, and the columns of men intoned in deep unison.

Laing noticed that three of the drummers were decked out in brand-new uniforms of the Fourth West Indian Regiment and the Royal Africa Corps. He surmised that the outfits had been sold by pensioners of the regiments and had found their way upcountry with other merchandise.

In the midst of the throng moved Balansama, seemingly oblivious to the din and clatter. Laing remarked about the goiter on the ruler's neck, and the rhetorical overtures, whose form Laing now knew so well, were quickly done with. Balansama presented Laing with an earring of gold filigree to give to Governor MacCarthy as a token of the Barawa people's desire for friendship with his people. To demonstrate his willingness to trade, Balansama at once dispatched some of his entourage to return to Kulakonke and declare the road open to commerce so that Sankaran and Kuranko gold, cloth, and ivory might descend to the white men by the sea. To seal the alliance, he ordered his brother, his son, and one of the Kamato chiefs to accompany Laing to the coast. Afterward he proposed that everyone dance.

To the sound of tinkling hawk's bells Laing found himself stabbing his elbows into the air and lurching about in the dust in embarrassed mimicry of the Kuranko men.

❧ Chapter Three

THE SUCCESS of Laing's trade mission to Falaba did nothing to assuage his longing to find the source of the Niger. Back in Freetown he was plagued by the memory of his abortive journey, and was determined to complete Mungo Park's work by discovering the main course of the river and, above all, its termination.

Laing's undisguised ambition annoyed his brother officers, and his habit of writing poetry made him the butt of their sarcastic sallies. "The lieutenant is beset by a habit characteristic of all expatriot Scots, of romanticizing everywhere north of where they actually are," remarked a captain of the infantry.

"Let us dare hope," replied his companion, "that he will be sent to this war that has broken out in the Gold Coast."

Promoted to command a native company in the Royal African Colonial Corps, Laing saw twelve months' service in the Ashanti campaign of 1823 and was commended in the field for his skill and bravery. "Surely now," he wrote in his diary when dispatched to London to report on the state of the campaign, "my experience will entitle me to some advancement and qualify me for further expeditions."

In England he petitioned his commander in chief, H.R.H. the Duke of York, for promotion. No preliminary notice was given to his commanding officer, Major General Turner, who was not to forget this impropriety. The promotion was refused, but Laing got Lord Bathurst, H.M. Secretary of State at the Colonial Office, to persuade the Duke of York to grant him additional leave. Again Laing left his C.O. uninformed.

When Laing finally did receive his promotion to major he found to his dismay that Turner had been appointed successor to Governor

MacCarthy in Sierra Leone. In a letter to Lord Bathurst dated April 9, 1825, Turner expressed his contempt for Laing. "His military exploits are worse than his poetry. . . . I humbly beg your Lordship, in the name of the Regiment, that he may be removed from it—and that we not be subject to the mortification of his calling us Brother Officers."

A few months later Laing was given command of an expedition "for scientific researches in the interior of Africa." His assignment was to follow the ancient Roman trade route from Tripoli to Timbuktu, locate the Niger, and follow it to its end.

THE PORT OF TRIPOLI was surrounded by irrigated fields of corn, barley, and watermelons. Date, fig, olive, and mulberry trees dotted the outlying plain. Beyond them the embrasured walls of old forts and the domes and minarets of mosques crowded the seaward promontory. Within the city decaying walls enclosed squalid courtyards and labyrinthine streets. The shadows of consular flags fell on shuttered windows.

Laing lodged with Colonel Hanmer Warrington, the British consul general, whose magnificent private villa, The Garden, lay two miles from the city in the oasis of Menchia. The dilapidated consulate bore such a contrast to The Garden that local gossip never tired of conjecturing how the plump Englishman, whose diplomatic blunders so often earned rebukes from Whitehall, could afford to maintain himself in such luxury. The truth was that Warrington had married an illegitimate daughter of the prince regent, Jeanne-Eliza Price, and it was to this connection that he owed his munificence.

At the time of Laing's arrival in Tripoli, English influence was low and French influence high along the Barbary coast. Warrington resented the French consul, Baron Rousseau, and scoffed at his intimacy with the Moorish ruler (the bashaw) and his scholarly devotion to Arabic.

Laing, however, regarded these as good reasons for meeting Rousseau, and he managed to do so without Warrington's knowledge.

Sitting in the French consul's study, Laing sipped Turkish coffee and ate apricots and grapes from a silver platter while the baron expounded his views:

"Timbuktu has become for us what the enchanted city of Iram Dhat al- 'Imad was for the ancient Arabs. The sultan Hadramawt built a pleasure city to rival the deity, and we French and you English, to rival each other, have built in our imaginations a similar city. But do you not agree that it may be a chimera which will evaporate as soon as the many obstacles that block its access have been surmounted?"

15

"With respect, Sir, I do not," Laing replied. "My compatriot, Mungo Park, received reports of great splendor and wealth, and it is said that the king has a great treasure of minted coins and gold ingots."

"The ingots weigh more with every telling. Al-Bakri, al-Idrisi, Ibn Khaldun, and finally al-Hasan ibn Muhammad al-Wazzan al-Zayyati, who you will know as Leo Africanus . . . they have all described this gold and it grows bigger as the centuries pass. There is a mystery to Timbuktu, to be sure, but the mystery may be like the fountain of youth."

Suspicious of the baron's skepticism, Laing began to share the English consul's blighted opinion of Rousseau. In any event, when Warrington embarked on a clumsy plan to humiliate his rival, Laing did not demur about his part in it. For some time the French consul's son, Timoleon, had been courting Emma, the delicate and sentimental daughter of the English consul. Now Warrington encouraged her to entertain the major and show him the city.

The young couple strolled through streets filled with stalls of dried fruit, gum, carob, watermelons, ostrich feathers, senna, madder root, barilla, and saffron. On Laing's urging, Emma took him to see the Roman triumphal arch, erected in A.D. 164, near the sea gate. It now enclosed a storehouse.

"There are some Roman ruins near The Garden too," she explained. "Father is a fossicker in his leisure time and has unearthed pieces of glass from Roman sepulchral urns."

In the evenings they sat in the garden. The air was fragrant with jasmine and violets. Laing spoke of the white desert to the south and of elusive fame. As the light faded they went indoors for supper, and afterward played vingt-et-un. When the first copies of his book (an account of his travels in Sierra Leone in 1822) arrived from England, Laing inscribed one for Emma, "with deep affection."

The consul had not intended this convenient friendship to develop into a romantic infatuation. Watching Laing and Emma trot out their Arab horses through the wrought-iron gates of The Garden, he would turn with exasperation to his bureau, racking his brains for some way of dissuading his daughter from her growing attachment. Every morning he would accost her on the verandah with some new argument.

"I am aware that Major Laing is a very gentlemanly, honorable, and good man. But my dear Emma, I must insist that this attachment is reckless. The major is about to embark on a journey whose dangers must be perfectly apparent. Under these circumstances how can you consider an engagement? And have you taken into account the opinion, the feelings, of your poor mother?"

"My attachment," Emma responded, "was fostered and approved by you, Father. And as for Major Laing's expedition, it is for us both a seal upon our love and an affirmation of our steadfastness that we should be wed before he leaves."

Aghast at her resolution, the consul relented: six weeks after their first meeting Laing and Emma were married in a civil ceremony performed by Warrington himself. But the consul reserved the final say in the matter. On the afternoon of the wedding he wrote to Lord Bathurst outlining the terms that his son-in-law had sworn to abide by:

After a Voluminous correspondence, I found my wishes, exertions, Entreaties, and displeasure, quite futile & of no avail, & under all circumstances, both for the Public good, as well as their Mutual happiness, I was obliged to consent to Perform the Ceremony, under the most Sacred & most Solemn Obligation that they are not to cohabit till the Marriage is duly performed by a Clergyman of the established Church of England, and as my honor is so much involved, that I shall take due care they never be one second from under the observation of myself or Mrs. Warrington.

Two days later Laing set off into the Sahara. He faced two thousand miles of desert and the ambiguous renown of reaching a city founded on hearsay and dreams. Plundered by Tuareg raiders, cheated by caravaners, exhausted by the heat, and oppressed by illness and malfunctioning equipment, Laing remembered a virgin bride sitting delicately among the geraniums of a cool, white villa, and the sea glimpsed through palms. Each night he diligently recorded the day's events in his journal or dutifully drafted a letter to Warrington summarizing his slow progress.

Warrington read Laing's unpredictable letters warily, for he still supposed that the explorer's heart might turn his head and rashly bring him back to Emma. Selecting those of Laing's letters that Emma might peruse, the consul justified to himself that romantic passion could still jeopardize the expedition on which British prestige in Tripoli so much depended. Emma was distressed that Laing's messages to her were so brief and formal. She at once commissioned a family friend, Josef Gomez Herrador, the Spanish consul general, to paint her portrait in miniature to send to Laing.

By the time the portrait arrived at Ghadames, the heat had stopped Laing's chronometers and evaporated the ether in his hygroscopes. In the spurious shade of his tent the explorer contemplated the pallid cameo of Emma. It was the first time he had felt any misgivings about his venture. He promptly wrote to Warrington urging the consul to let him know if Emma was in poor health.

Tell me, has Mr Herrador, or has he not, made a faithful likeness?—If he has, my Emma is ill, is melancholy, is unhappy—her sunken eyes, her pale cheeks, and colourless lips haunt my imagination, and adieu to resolution—Was I within a day's march of Tombuctoo, & to hear My Emma was ill—I wou'd turn about, and retrace my steps to Tripoli.

When he had finished the letter he placed the cameo in his tunic pocket with great tenderness, then strode out to attend to the fractious camels. That night he strolled to the edge of the oasis and saw a comet crossing the sky toward the southwest. He took it as a sign that his wife's illness had passed, and he imagined the star marking the source of the Niger.

Emma's sentimentality embraced augury too, and when she was awakened months later to a storm wind off the sea lashing the palms outside the open windows she was convinced her husband was dead. She threw herself into her father's arms and made him swear that he truly wished to see his son-in-law return safely. Warrington saw that the servants fastened a slamming louvre, then assured his daughter that such storms were common at that time of year. "Yet we experience no more calamities than usual."

As for Laing, he lay bunched in the sand at Wadi Ahnet, left for dead by a band of Tuaregs from the Ahaggar Mountains who had joined the caravan unasked some days before; no one had wished to invite trouble by ordering them to leave. One night they had cut the tent ropes and plunged their swords into the collapsed canvas around Laing until he ceased to move; they murdered whoever had not escaped into the darkness, and plundered the stores.

For months Laing was barely able to travel or write. He had received ten saber cuts to the head, a musket bullet in the hip, both legs had been badly injured, and his hands had been mangled as he tried to fend off the swords and free himself from the tent. It was five months before Emma's interpretation of the storm was corroborated. One morning in November she chanced to see a letter from Laing dated July 1 lying open on her father's bureau. It was suddenly clear that her father had been keeping her in ignorance of much of what Laing wrote in his letters. Although the consul was embarrassed, he chided his daughter for tampering with official matters.

18

"But much of the letter is addressed to me," she protested.

"That is so, that is so. But when such news as this contains is so out-of-date when it reaches us, I thought it best to save you from the suffering it would surely cause."

Emma flung herself from the room, and when that evening Warrington brought her the letter containing Laing's reticent account of the attack at Wadi Ahnet, she took it from him without a word and sat in the darkness of the verandah for hours before she read it.

When she put it down, she felt as if a stone were lodged against her ribs. The consul found her staring at the stars.

"Emma, you must come inside. You are unwell."

Only when her father placed his arm around her shoulder was she able to speak. "Can any man endure such suffering without losing his reason?"

"I cannot tell," replied the consul, "but of one thing I am certain. Your Major Laing is no ordinary man."

That night Emma did not sleep. Between bouts of sobbing she wrote a letter to her husband, to be included with other messages being taken by caravan to Ghadames the next day. "Oh my beloved dearest Laing," she wrote,

alas, alas what have you been exposed to, what danger, what suffering, to have saved you one pang I would with joy have shed every drop of blood that warms this heart—Had I been with you in that fearful moment my arms which would have encircled you might for some time have shielded you from the swords of those Daemons—and at last we might have fallen, pierced by the same weapon, our souls might have taken their flight together to that land sorrow can never come to—My beloved Laing sorrow has laid a heavy hand on your Emma's head & so it has on yours—Alas Laing how cruel, how sad, has been our fate—Are we destined to endure more misery, or will a kind providence at length pity our unhappiness and restore us to each other—Will you my own idolised husband return to your Emma's kind arms, will you come & repose on her faithful bosom—Will you restore happiness to her torn heart—

Warrington had not told Emma that Laing had announced his intention of returning to Tripoli from Timbuktu rather than continuing down the Niger. Nor had he allowed her to see a note from Laing, marked "Very Private," which had been enclosed with the July letter. In the note Laing asked: "Will you still consider it necessary to keep me to the promise which you have from me *in writing?* (and which wou'd be sacred was it merely verbal) or will you absolve me from it?"

The consul did not regard correspondence as a suitable place to discuss such a delicate matter, and so left Laing's question unanswered.

THE SURVIVORS of the attack at Wadi Ahnet spent three months recuperating in the camp of a friendly Arab chief before yellow fever broke out in the camp and Laing's last European companions succumbed and died.

Against the advice of the Arab chief, Laing pushed on to Timbuktu, arriving there on August 13, 1826. The city, which had become for Europeans a symbol of splendor and wealth, turned out to be an arid warren of mud-brick dwellings in a desert of smudged lilac sand. The roofs were flat, and decayed beams jutted from eaves and squat turrets. Laing was met by an air of appalling desertion everywhere. The city was disputed territory and many of its Songhai inhabitants had fled when war broke out between the Tuareg and Fulani. The leader of the Fulani regarded Christians as children of Satan, and had vowed to prevent Laing's entry into Timbuktu.

Laing delayed in the city for two days, studying fragments of Arabic manuscripts in a vain endeavor to know how Timbuktu's power and wealth had vanished and where it had gone. He felt sick in his stomach as he remembered Baron Rousseau's opinion of the place. Yet he could not believe that his suffering had brought him to a mirage. When he quit the city for Ségou in the west, bypassing the Niger because its banks were occupied by the Fulani, he told himself that time would reveal the wealth he had missed.

In a letter to Warrington he referred to another consolation:

I sometimes give the river a left-handed blessing, when I think it is the cause of my separation from my Emma; at other times I am more charitable towards it, when I consider that had it not been for the Niger, I might never have been blessed with a sight of the dear object, which I prize more than life—

Laing was with Bungola, an African servant whom he had freed, and an Arab boy. They had walked thirty miles from Timbuktu when four horsemen rode up. Their leader was Muhammad ben Abayd, a fanatical sheikh of the Berabich tribe who controled the route as far as Arawan. Laing had already sought and obtained his permission in Timbuktu to go that way.

The sheikh and his men dismounted by an *atil* tree. Bungola looked at Laing in terror. The carriers bolted.

"Follow them!" Laing yelled to Bungola.

The sheikh's men approached, casting their eyes over the boxes and papers and instruments the carriers had thrown down. Laing addressed the sheikh by his more familiar name, Ahmadu Labeida, and asked what had brought him thither.

Labeida launched into a tirade against Laing's faith, and demanded that he embrace Islam. Laing refused with an obstinacy that enraged the sheikh. Labeida's men pinioned the explorer's arms and Labeida drew his sword. At the instant the blade plunged toward his heart, Laing remembered a cobbled Edinburgh street in the rain and the black claws of a gothic arch.

The Arab boy, who had interpreted Laing's final defiant words, had fallen onto his knees whimpering. Labeida ordered him killed.

They severed the explorer's head, then broke open the boxes. The sheikh made a souvenir of Emma's portrait. Laing's papers were burned for fear they possessed magical properties. It was September 24, 1826.

IT WAS NOT until almost two years later—in August 1828, when Bungola arrived back in Tripoli—that Laing's death was confirmed. Emma's grief was greater for reading Laing's last letter, in which he excused himself from writing to her personally despite her being upper-most in his thoughts. Laing's parents piously ignored her, and War-rington was too obsessed with the political implications of the ill-fated expedition to pay much heed to his daughter's distress.

The consul had become convinced that his son-in-law's death was the result of a French plot. He even believed that the explorer's journals were in the hands of Baron Rousseau. The ensuing accusations and counteraccusations caused an international scandal, and the French con-sul was forced to return to France to defend his good name. Tripoli passed once more into the hands of the Turks. Warrington took his pen-sion and retired to Patras to live with his eldest daughter and her hus-band, who was consul there.

Three years after Laing's death, in April 1829, Emma married again according to her father's wishes. Warrington himself again performed the ceremony. Her new husband was the British vice-consul in Benghazi. But the frail girl whom the explorer had imagined waiting for him in the cool, white arbor of The Garden died of consumption at Pisa less than six months after her wedding. Since Laing's death she had suf-fered from insomnia and a dread of summer storms. Her father duly reported to Bathurst on the circumstances that had brought his "adored daughter to an untimely Grave."

Thus has that Monster of Iniquity the Baron Rousseau sacrificed two Vic-tims to His Diabolical Intrigue—for to my last, shall I conscientiously believe He was concerned in that sad History.

In the same year that Emma died, a twenty-year-old poet won the chancellor's medal at Trinity College, Cambridge, for a poem entitled "Timbuctoo." His name was Alfred Tennyson. In the poem he asks if the rumor of the city of "argent streets imaging the soft inversion of tremulous domes" might not be a dream "as frail as those of ancient Time." He answered:

> . . . the time is well-nigh come
> When I must render up this glorious home
> to keen discovery: soon yon brilliant towers
> Shall darken with the waving of her wand;
> Darken, and shrink and shiver into huts,
> Black specks amid a waste of dreary sand,
> Low-built, mud-wall'd, Barbarian settlements.
> How chang'd from this fair City!

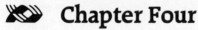 ## Chapter Four

VULTURES WHEELED slowly in the sky and gunshots echoed against the granite face of Senekonke. Through the grasslands men with their cutlasses held hilt-down hurried toward the Barawa capital.

In Kulakonke an orator was addressing a young man.

"Dambati Bolo," he declared solemnly, "I have something to tell you, something you have not heard before in all your life and will never hear again. Your father, Balansama, is dead."

In fact Balansama had died and been buried two days before. The orator's announcement simply marked the beginning of ceremonies, attended by rulers from other chiefdoms, in honor of the late chief.

Young warriors poured into the town firing guns and cutting the air with their swords. In the great courtyard the xylophonists cried, "This year a great cotton tree has fallen, oh, a golden cotton tree has fallen this year, oh, a cotton tree that reached the sky has fallen. . . ."

The women chimed in, "Where shall we find such support and shade again? . . ."

Girls, some covered with ashes and carrying bundles of faggots on their heads, ran distractedly through the town lanes; others cast about with nets or broken calabashes for fish and rice. The roof of the chief's house had been toppled to the ground during the night, and a melee of

Barawa Succession (from the mid-eighteenth century)

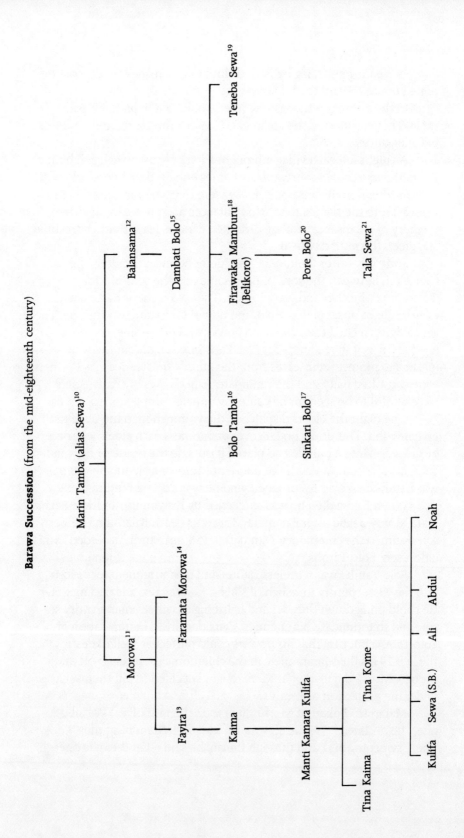

dancers wearing pelts, leg bells, and cloth masks rushed wildly past the ruined house toward the far end of the town.

In the afternoon the visiting rulers spoke out in praise of Balansama. They recollected the greatness of Marin Tamba and remembered old allegiances.

As night fell each villager brought a log or leafy branch and built a fire in the late chief's courtyard. As flames engulfed the wood, old pots and clothing from Balansama's house were thrown onto the pyre. Salt was cast into the flames to sanctify alliances and purge the chiefdom's memory of Balansama's failings. Masked dancers leapt through the blue and green fire until daybreak.

Forty days after the funeral the succession was decided. The choice fell between the sons of Balansama and the sons of Morowa (Balansama's brother and predecessor). The two factions had existed even while Balansama was alive, and now their rivalry was intense. The genealogists recited their claims to power, and praise-singers emboldened them as if in readiness for war. Each side sought out medicine-masters to protect themselves from the other's sinister designs. Diviners were consulted daily, and the candidates killed cows in sacrifice and were careful to be seen in the company of pale-complexioned virgins.

One night the elders dispatched the young men to the bush to gather wood. This done, under cover of darkness each elder tied some of the wood into a bundle and placed it outside the house of the candidate he preferred. At dawn the house of Morowa's eldest son, Fayira, was half-hidden by piles of wood, and he was declared chief.

When Fayira died he was succeeded by his younger brother, Faramata Morowa, and after Faramata Morowa's death Balansama's eldest son assumed the chieftaincy. Dambati Bolo was in turn succeeded by his eldest son, Bolo Tamba.

Bolo Tamba was a tireless fighter and made frequent incursions into the Kissi country in search of slaves. He was also a feared magician. He could bring down thunder and lightning at will, even in the dry season, and so intimidate his enemies. Outsiders lived in trepidation of Bolo Tamba but saw that his powers could protect as well as destroy. In the late 1950s the Marah rulers in the chiefdoms to the east—Neya, Mongo, Morfindugu—met at Kamaron and decided to put themselves under the protection of Barawa.

Maran Lai Bokari of Morfindugu took the initiative. "We are all one," he declared. "We are all sons of one ruler: Mansa Saramba." Then, sweeping his hand through the air, he said, "Let there be one man to keep scavenging birds away from our rice. Let Bolo Tamba take our countries into his heart so that we can all live without fear."

Bolo Tamba was mindful that their common enemies were on the Sankaran, east of Morfindugu. "If I am to safeguard our lands and livelihood, then it is only proper that one of you should keep vigil on the bird-scaring platform. Let that man be Maran Lai Bokari."

But Bolo Tamba disliked being under constant threat of invasion and decided to go to the Sankaran to negotiate with the warlords there. It was agreed that the Kuranko and Sankaran peoples would not threaten one another; together the rulers ate consecrated rice flour to seal their pact. Afterward, as Bolo Tamba prepared to return home, news reached him that Barawa had been invaded by the Kono from the southwest.

According to tradition the SaNieni Kuranko, whose chiefdom abuts Barawa in the southwest, are said to have abetted the invasion. The SaNieni would later protest, however, that their ruler at the time, Yelimusu Keli Koroma, had come under attack from the Limba in the west: when their capital, Yifin, fell to the Limba, a corridor was opened up through which the Kono could invade Barawa.

Coming from Yifin and Funumba under Sinkerifa, the Kono warriors entered Barawa at Gbendikoro and sacked the town. The defenseless country was rapidly overrun and thirty-four of its forty-three towns were plundered and burned. Refugees from Barawa fled eastward into Morfindugu, where Bolo Tamba rejoined them. With him they traveled to the northwest boundary of Kuranko country and settled in the Wara Wara hills.

Under the rounded granite escarpments of the hills the Barawa exiles built their new settlements: Dakunaia, Bankolia, and Mamudia. But it was not always easy to find farmland without encroaching on Limba land.

One day Aisetta Karifa went into the hills to cut thatching grass for his house and was driven off by irate Limbas. Bolo Tamba decided that force was the answer and his warriors successfully claimed the area as their own. There they built their main town, calling it Albitaiya, which means "under the protection of Allah."

✖✖ Chapter 5

A FEW YEARS AFTER the Kono's desolation of Barawa, a young Englishman arrived in Sierra Leone, determined, as he put it, "to open up a new region, and to have a red line of my own upon the map." He was traveling under the auspices of the Royal Geographical Society and had been given generous funding by a fellow of the Society and merchant on the Gold Coast, Andrew Swanzy.

It was 1868. Winwood Reade was thirty. In the previous ten years he had published three novels, a history of the Druids, and an account of a journey to Gabon. The novels had been slated by literary critics for the tediousness of their dialogue, the shallowness of their characters, and the insolent didacticism of their tone. It was said that Reade was less interested in the craft of fiction than in emulating his famous Uncle Charles, whose adventure novel, *The Cloister and the Hearth*, had been published in 1861.

In that year Winwood Reade had gone to Gabon. Darwin's *Origin of Species* had appeared in 1859 and a popular misconception had arisen that Darwin claimed man to be descended from apes. Showmen paraded stuffed apes and monkeys in European cities to capitalize on this outrageous view. In London a Frenchman named Paul de Chaillu exhibited stuffed Gabon gorillas. He was denounced as a charlatan. But Winwood Reade, who had read natural science for a while at Magdalen Hall, Oxford, was impressed by the Frenchman's grotesque and decayed specimens. Raising money on his inheritance, he boarded the SS *Armenian* in December 1862, bound for Africa, where he hoped to study gorillas in the wild.

In Fernando Po, Reade stayed in the house of H.M.'s consul, Richard Burton. Burton was away, climbing in the Cameroon mountains, whose vague outline could sometimes be glimpsed across the strait. To while away the time Reade cleaned and catalogued the books in Burton's library. Turning pages eaten by cockroaches and white ants, the boards cracked by the harmattan and marbled with mildew, Reade found the musty volumes a painful reminder of the fate of all print.

Nevertheless, he assiduously kept a journal in Gabon, and although he found no gorillas, felt he had the beginnings of a successful book. Late in 1863 he returned to Fernando Po on his way back to London. Burton was again absent, but Reade befriended a Scots doctor in whose company he passed the evenings.

Their conversation would begin with the pouring of two tumblers of brandy. The doctor would then direct his mulatto servant-girl to dust the hooded cane chairs on the verandah before the two men sat down.

"Well then, Mr. Reade. How did you spend the day?"

"I went looking for Lander's grave."

"And did you find it?"

"No sir, no one can even recall his burial. But then, great travelers are creatures of their day and can reap but little posthumous renown. Their destiny is to be curious rather than creative."

If Reade's pontifical manner had not also amused, the doctor might have been repelled. As it was, the young man's absurd self-seriousness gave the doctor ample opportunity to bait his traps.

"And what is your own destiny, Mr. Reade?"

Reade added some water to his cognac. "I hope to contribute to a scientific understanding of Africa. In Gabon, for example, I made several observations on malaria that I intend to publish."

The doctor suppressed a smile and urged his companion to elaborate.

"I am convinced," Reade went on, "that malaria is contained in rain. One may thus estimate the amount of malaria by the amount of moisture. The commencement of the rainy season, when the rain lies on the ground in puddles and putrefies, and the commencement of the dry season, when the sun exhales noxious vapors from the soil, are the two most unhealthy periods of the year."

"The natives also assert that the rain is pernicious if it falls on the naked skin," the doctor essayed.

Reade nodded and returned to the matter of poisonous atmospheres. "If the noxious vapors that float over swamps are inhaled they may be later communicated to others. The native's breath is thus a proximate cause of infection."

The doctor poured two more brandies. "I take the view that a brandy ahead of the fever is as good a remedy as sulphate of quinine." Leaning forward, he handed Reade his drink, then crushed a cockroach underfoot on the burnished boards of the verandah.

"I prefer to rely on my robust health," Reade answered, observing the squashed cockroach. "Have you not noticed that the Negroes, born and bred in these malarial regions, lose their bodily constitutions and become prematurely senile? I am inclined to believe that their black hue answers to the livid color among us, that it is the color of disease."

"And what is your judgment on the moral and intellectual capacities of the Negro, Mr. Reade?"

Mr. Reade was happy to dilate: "In certain physical characteristics the Negro approaches the ape. The brain, for example, has retreated to the back of the head, the skull is extremely thick. . . . Indeed, the Negro breaks sticks across his skull where an Englishman would use his knee. The virile member is also much larger than is found in Europeans . . . excepting in those who are idiotic, of course. And you may have observed that the great toe is separated from the others by a wide space, as in apes."

"But surely that is because their feet have never been confined and distorted by footwear?"

"In some respects," Reade continued, "I grant you, the Negro is more like a child than an ape. The simplicity of cerebral convolutions, the marked curve of the spinal column, and the flattened nose, for instance. In other respects he presents the characteristics of old age. I mean the general lack of enthusiasm and the love of repose, the flatness of the cornea and feebleness of muscles."

"You do seem well assured of your facts, Mr. Reade."

"They are not merely my facts, sir. It has been generally proven by microscopes and analyses that the typical Negro is something between a child, a dotard, and a beast. Who am I to struggle against these sacred facts of science?"

In 1864, Winwood Reade published a hastily written narrative of his travels. Although filled with "sacred facts of science," its tendentious tone and lack of heroic grandeur bored its Victorian readers. Depressed by the failure of his book, Reade might have imagined the opening sentences of his uncle's best-seller as describing his fate:

Not a day passes over the earth, but men and women of no note do great deeds, speak great words, and suffer noble sorrows. Of these obscure heroes, philosophers, and martyrs, the greater part will never be known till that hour, when many that are great shall be small, and the small great: but of others the world's knowledge may be said to sleep: their lives and characters lie hidden from nations in the annals that record them.

WHEN HE ARRIVED in Sierra Leone, Winwood Reade had three years' medical training behind him. Since the publication of *Savage Africa* four years before, he had vowed to take no more short cuts to fame and to begin no new ventures without careful planning.

He rented a cottage in Regent in the hills above Freetown. It was the end of the rains. Ink-colored clouds slipped back from the bush. Indigo lizards with bright orange necks peered and skittered across mildewed concrete, and at dusk bats flittered upward from the direction of the sea, mewing and squealing.

Reade was oppressed by Freetown, its rutted streets sown with Bermuda grass, the stench of its drains, the cryptic exuberance of Krio marketwomen who plied their daily trade in thread, ribbons, fishhooks, nails, and madras cottons, and at night sat in the high windows of frame houses overlooking the harbor. He cut his official visits to the minimum, preferring the humid wilderness of the hills to the hubbub of the city. He wrote in the mornings, and spent the afternoons putting Latin names to the curious lacquered shrubs—black, deep purple, and mottled lime—that filled his garden.

It was not until December that an idea for the Swanzy Expedition presented itself to him. During a visit to the government interpreter, he chanced upon a copy of Laing's *Travels in the Timannee, Kooranko, and Soolima Countries.* That night he read it straight through and at once resolved to travel to the source of the Niger. The years of inertia and mediocrity were over. He would fulfill Laing's ambition and connect his own name forever with the Niger. At the same time he would study firsthand, customs that might throw new light on the history of religion.

Reade left Freetown in January 1869. The Geographical Society had lent him a sextant and artificial horizon to make precise measurements at the Niger source, but Reade regarded the instruments as an encumbrance and left them behind. As for finding his way north, he placed every confidence in the accuracy of Laing's map. But Laing's map was not accurate, and Reade drifted westward into Limba country where belligerent faces watched him pass. But the young adventurer saw no reason why a perfect stranger should not walk uninvited through chiefdoms and villages as long as he made gifts of tobacco and red worsted from time to time.

In late January he reached Kabala on the edge of Kuranko country. There Bolo Tamba received Reade's dubious gifts and offered his safe lodging in return.

Since being driven from Barawa, Bolo Tamba had formed an alliance with Sulima, and his warriors under their war leader Korgeyi had been called to Falaba several times to help repulse the Fulas. Korgeyi also raided the Kissi in the east for slaves.

Now he led his warriors in a dance to celebrate the white man's visit. Brandishing their swords and firing muskets, the men filled the courtyard with a mimicry of battle.

As the sun fell in the sky the war leader left off dancing and strode up to Reade, who was sitting with Bolo Tamba. Korgeyi towered over them, his chest heaving, perspiration streaming down his face.

"Korgeyi is named after the salt water from whence you came," Bolo Tamba said, addressing Reade through his interpreter.

"I don't understand," Reade said.

Korgeyi boomed an answer. "My nickname is 'salt water' because none of my enemies would dare eat me for fear of vomiting me up again."

READE'S HOUSE was within Bolo Tamba's own courtyard, a large circular space completely enclosed by thatched conical houses. In the morning, as women swept the yards or spread unhusked rice on mats to dry, the older men lounged in raffia hammocks under the eaves of the verandahs and eyed the white man with interest.

"Do his gifts represent *all* that the white men make?" asked one.

"His tobacco leaf is inferior to ours and his cloth too thin for our use," said another, referring to the cheap Manchester baft that Reade had given to Bolo Tamba.

"Why has he come here?"

"He spoke yesterday of journeying to a great river in the east."

"Why should he travel so far from his own country merely to find a river?"

"Fish!" suggested one.

The men laughed softly as the speaker went on. "I have heard that the white men have an insatiable appetite for fish. They catch them in the salt water."

"A pity then that he does not bring us salt," said the man who had begun the conversation, "then we would no longer need to exchange slaves to get it."

Reade set up his folding table and chair in the shade of an orange tree in the middle of the courtyard. Inquisitive children shuffled around him as he began to write. From the verandahs the old men heard him call out to his Mandingo servant and, when the servant came running, ask him how to say "go away" in Kuranko. Reade's attempts to pronounce the words drew instant gales of laughter from the children. The men in the hammocks smiled wryly to themselves. They watched the white man abandon his table and stride off toward the hills, followed by a train of children.

He succeeded in throwing them off only by walking quickly into the dense grass, away from the pathway. Once hidden, he found a boulder to sit on, and there he wrote, looking up from time to time at the stone flank of the tor.

In the evening Bolo Tamba invited the stranger to eat with him. Using Reade's morose interpreter the ruler tried to find out the purpose of the white men's journey. The effort proved futile. The white man seemed bent on no other goal but getting to Falaba, and was disappointed that no one could tell him anything about the large river that lay in the direction of the sunrise. Bolo Tamba organized carriers for Reade's bales and boxes, and sent him on to Falaba with his blessing. In due course he might hear of the stranger's motive for going there.

The dry grasslands were being fired. From the ridges smoke poured up into the sky, and elephant-grass canes crackled and exploded. Filigree of ash covered the paths. On the charred plains only crumpled and blackened lophira trees survived.

Reade was exhilarated by his progress. He even found himself revising his views of Africans: "Experience has taught me," he wrote, "that they are sometimes very *trying*. But I must not be impatient and ill-tempered; they are only grown-up children after all."

ON REACHING FALABA, Reade asked if he might stay in the capital for a while. The Yalunka ruler, who had never before seen a white man, assured the visitor that he would receive hospitality and protection. Reade had hardly finished arranging his boxes and furniture when gifts arrived from the chief: kola nuts, two chickens, and a large pannier of husked rice. He sent his servant, Abdulai, to thank the chief. His own supplies were almost finished and he wanted to keep his trade goods for the final stretch of the journey.

Reade soon learned that Sewa's rule did not extend as far as the Niger. The ruler stressed the particular dangers of a town called Dantillia, a two days' journey to the southeast, and warned of the possibility that the Fulas might assault Falaba. Mindful of Laing's tribulations forty-five years earlier, Reade decided to bide his time—until a propitious moment arrived to announce his plans.

Sankaran caravans of gold, ivory, and hides—the revenue of which was Sulima's main source of wealth—passed through the town almost daily. Laden donkeys and scores of bearers would wind in dusty files through the great pallisades of cotton trees. Reade talked to the caravaners, who told him that the Joliba, or "great river," which Europeans called the Niger, was a three days' march to the east, and the impatient Englishman heard all the same fabulous stories of the source that Laing had heard in his time.

In his journal, which he now wrote in the solitude of his house, Reade anticipated his goal.

I shall associate my name for ever with its course, and earn a place in the history of Africa, for I shall strike it higher by at least a hundred miles than any other European. The Niger is only fifty miles off: let me reach it, and I have my reputation!

Five weeks passed; Reade informed Sewa of his intentions, only to be rebuffed.

"Fulas beseige us, enemies live in that direction, the country is unsafe. I cannot let you go. Stay here. Accept my hospitality. Learn our language. Marry!"

The explorer lapsed into melancholy. He would stroll aimlessly around the town, molested by children. Or he would watch the young men building pallisades. Occasionally he tried to persuade his taciturn and homesick interpreter to ask the old men questions about the dusty fetishes that hung over the door lintels. But he could not bring himself to record even the little he learned. Mostly he lay on the clay bed in his house, scratching notes in his battered journal. Not even the trial and execution of a Fula spy roused him from his torpor.

All has been in vain. I have done nothing. I have merely reached a point where another traveler has been. I am close to the Niger, and yet I might as well be a thousand miles away.

Am I never to succeed? For ten years I have been writing and writing, and fiasco has followed fiasco; that is my own fault; I have only to curse my own incapacity. But here I have done all that a man could do. I selected my route with prudence; I have followed it up with resolution; I have patiently submitted to tedious delays and vexatious degradations—yet all is in vain. It seems that this passion for glory by which I am tormented is an evil spirit devouring my life. Had I not been ambitious I might have been happy; but what am I now? A man who has mistaken his vocation. A man who has climbed in public and has fallen, and who must go through life with the stigma of failure upon him. Even if I write a good book, people will always be able to say, "Yes he did *that* well enough; but he broke down in Africa, you know." And then I shall have to answer such questions as these: "Why did you not go on to the Niger when you were so close? Well, *I* would not have given up. Don't you think that Baker or Livingstone would have managed to get on somehow or other?"

At night he dreamt of cathedrals and colleges, of empty halls and bewildering corridors. He found himself walking through a colonnade, looking for a room where he was to register his name. Waking at first light, he wrapped a blanket around him to keep out the cold and damp and heard the raucous crowing of cocks across the town. The memory of the dream disturbed him. He told Abdulai, his Mandingo interpreter, what he had dreamt.

"You, too, want to go home," answered Abdulai.

When Ahmadu brought him his rice, Reade seized the plate and threw it on the ground. A scrawny chicken started pecking at the white grains. "What have I done to deserve such degradation!" Reade cried.

Ahmadu slunk away without a word. Abdulai later commended his silence. "To speak would be to put a hen in a hammock," he said. "Leave him."

Reade again approached Sewa for permission to leave Falaba. Again he was rebuffed. Out in the grasslands the repetitive cooing of a bird was like an echoing humiliation. *Sulukuku, sulukuku, sulukuku, sulukuku.* At dusk he lay exhausted on his clay couch listening to the panting and slurring of drums. Laughter and chatter rose and fell around him, and he came to believe that he was the Yalunka ruler's prisoner.

April arrived. He fell sick. His servants urged him to return to Freetown and forget the great river. They brought him oily red concoctions for his dysentery. He crawled from the house on his hands and knees, whimpering and moaning. The servants looked on. He cursed them. Squatting over a fly-ridden hole in the yard, waves of nausea and cramp overcame him. He cried out. He could not eat, and the water tasted of smoke and dry leaves.

He prepared to die. He penned a rambling letter to an imaginary mistress, declaring his fidelity, assuring her of his tenacity of purpose. Outside, a group of women were pounding rice and improvising a song.

> The winds blew, the rain fell down;
> famished and weary the white man came
> and sat under our tree.
> He has no mother to give him milk
> no wives to pound his rice,
> Oh let us pity the little white man,
> no mother has he. . . .

Sewa came to see him. The chief stooped under the lintel and peered at Reade with concern and perplexity. There were several empty chlorodyne bottles on the dirt floor.

"You suffer." Sewa said.

"I suffer because you have detained me in this place and thwarted me," the white man retorted.

It was some time before Abdulai was able to interpret his master's words.

"Ah!" the chief exclaimed, "you have malice in your heart against me. I see it in your sky-blue eyes. That is why you are ill. Do you see that fetish on the wall behind you? That is the spirit which protects me from your malevolent designs!"

Reade was too weak to protest. When the chief had gone he tried to get Ahmadu to take down the fetish, but Ahmadu was unwilling to touch it. The small device of knotted cord and grass was beyond Reade's own grasp. He stared at it in silence. He heard the tinkling of a bell.

"What is that?" he asked, thinking he might be delirious.

"The chief has been to a diviner." Ahmadu replied. "The bell and the white cloth are a sacrifice to speed your recovery."

Despite further bouts of malarial fever and enervation, Reade gradually got well. He learned that during his illness the Fulas had beseiged the town. But they had not persisted in their attack. Sewa explained that the road to the south was safe and that the white man was free to return whence he came.

Chigoes had burrowed into the soles of his feet and their eggs were beginning to hatch. Ahmadu dolefully dug out the larvae and dressed the ulcers that covered Reade's feet. Scarcely able to walk, Reade had to be carried in a hammock most of the way back to Freetown. He arrived in May with the first rains.

From a Bath chair in his Regent cottage, Reade remembered Laing's troubles in Falaba and berated the colonial secretary, who had expressed the opinion that the young man consider his experience a salutary lesson and exercise more caution in the future.

"But don't you see, Sir, that had Major Laing found everything easy he would have left nothing in this country for me, his successor! My failure is eating into my soul. I would not care for captivity or sickness if I had only done something! I will go at it again; I will not leave Africa til I have written my name somewhere on the map."

The colonial secretary turned his gaze at Reade's bandaged feet and formally forbade him to leave Freetown until he was completely well. Reade was undeterred. Within a month he again set off for Falaba. He traveled light, intending, as he put it, "to live off the land."

In Falaba, Sewa greeted him with gifts of rice and red kola. Reade took them as a sign that the ruler regretted his past obstructiveness, and when Sewa told him he was at liberty to travel to the great river whenever he wished, Reade misinterpreted the statement as a private triumph. In fact, military campaigns had been called off with the onset of the rains, and for the first time in half a year the land was safe for travel.

When Reade had gone, Sewa said to his elders: "To go in error once would make most men wiser; to repeat the error is either sheer stupidity or an inborn flaw of character."

After a day's march Reade reached Gberia Timbako, where Laing had been forced to turn back as a result of Sewa's grandfather's dream of swamps and forests. The following evening he arrived in Dantillia. The old chief, who was nearly blind, expressed his pleasure at seeing a white man before he died. Reade was interested in what the old man then revealed.

"Sewa usurped the rule of Sulima," he said. "By rights it belongs to our house."

"So that is why Sewa detained me in Falaba," Reade thought, "to prevent me from hearing about this discreditable affair."

In the morning, the chief gave Reade a calabash of rice and some baked cassava. As the white man and his small train of servants disappeared into the grassland, the chief muttered to himself, "May he go with Allah's protection. If a cow has no tail then only Allah can keep the flies from bothering it."

Read passed through a landscape of locust trees. Their crimson flowers were falling to the ground, and their feathery canopies gave the travelers shade. Two mornings after leaving Dantillia he reached the Joliba.

Elephant grass cut his hands as he thrust his way to the river's edge. He sat down and watched the turpid water slipping by under a somber sky. An immense sadness took hold of him. By finding the river, he had escaped the opprobrium of failure, yet it gave him no confirmation of success: two hundred years of muddy water and an endless expanse of grass and oil palms killed every thought of having reached a goal.

As three canoes crossed the river toward him, he asked his guide, "Who are they?"

"Sankaran," the guide answered. "You will need their permission to go further."

While waiting for them, Reade opened his journal. Light rain spattered the page as he wrote: "I feel all unstrung; it seems to me as if I am in a dream."

The Sankaran men drew up their canoes onto the greasy bank. Abdulai stepped forward to greet them. He asked how far away they were from the source of the Joliba.

The Sankaran men answered in snatches. They were distracted by the white man, who sat further up the bank scratching at a kind of white leaf with a stick.

"That country is not good," Abdulai explained. "There are slave hunters there; all the towns are spoiled; it is dangerous for us too much."

Reade patiently extracted more information. The river near the source was called the Tembiko. It was two days' distant. The source belonged to a Kuranko clan, the Koroma, who killed a black cow there every year and threw the head into the river as a sacrifice to a djinn. If the offering was accepted, the djinn brought the cow back to life; its head would reappear downstream, ears pricked up and eyes open.

Reade had heard these stories before. What was new to him were the Sankaran men's reports of gold in the Bouré country far to the east. "Even if the gold does not exist," Reade thought, "I could aim to reach Bamako, Mungo Park's highest point on the Niger, and so unite Laing's discoveries with those of Park. This surely would win me a celebrated place in the history of African exploration." Forgetting about the source, he turned eastward.

The Niger widened. He crossed the Sankaran region and hastened on through unmapped lands, intoxicated by every vista.

"This is mine; here no European has been; it is Reade's land! That hill, that river, that lake, I can call them what I please!"

In September he reached Bamako. The gold proved to be illusory, but he reckoned he had done enough to guarantee his reputation.

BACK IN ENGLAND he presented an account of his travels to a meeting of the Royal Geographical Society. He was taken to task for his lack of firsthand observations and exact measurements, and reminded of the great value that the Society set upon the discovery of the source of the Niger and the calculation of its height above sea level. Mere descriptions of places, culled from African informants, were thought to be worthless.

"Your lack of scientific data is regrettable," the president told him, "and your romantic inclination and impetuosity not entirely suited to the business of exploration. But there is much to discover, and you have made a courageous beginning."

Winwood Reade was not interested in this small consolation. So ill-treated did he feel, he could not bring himself to write up an account of his African journey. Shunning society, he gave all his time to writing an encyclopaedic denunciation of the established church. The book, *The Martyrdom of Man*, appeared in 1872 and was immediately slated by the press.

He began to imagine the friendship of a refined and intellectual woman, and to dream of the patient understanding, esteem, and pure pleasure that such a woman might give an unjustly maligned man. He composed letters to his imaginary mistress, addressing her as Margaret and assuring her that he desired only her devotion and regard. Gradually the letters became an account of his travels in Africa.

Before *The African Sketch-Book* was published he left England for the Gold Coast on a commission from the *Times* to cover the Ashanti uprising. At Kumasi the British commander was obliged to reprimand the journalist. "Your brief is to report the campaign, not fight in it, Mr. Reade. If your vengeful hatred of the Ashanti is so great as to prevent you from carrying out your proper commission, it would be better for us all if you returned home."

Back in England he was beset by heart and liver ailments and struggled to complete a novel about the persecution of those who speak out against Christian dogma. Entitled *The Outcast*, it was, like all his novels, a flop.

It was *Martyrdom* that made Reade's name. Although never favorably reviewed and never advertised, fifteen thousand copies had sold between his death in 1875 and 1909, and in 1940 it went into its twenty-fourth edition.

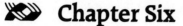 **Chapter Six**

DURING THE 1870s, Samori, a Mandinka from the Konia country, organized a personal following of armed horsemen known as Sofas and conquered a wide area of the upper Niger. He declared a jihad against the pagan Yalunka and Kuranko.

In 1884 the Sofas attacked Falaba. The horsemen were thrown into confusion by the narrow paths and dense thorn scrub around the stockaded town and suffered heavy casualties from Yalunka bowmen and musketeers stationed behind high fences and log ramparts.

The attackers decided to beseige the town. Food supplies soon ran out and wells dried up; people ate rats and licked the dew from the yam leaves to try to slake their thirst. Sewa's advisers urged him to call for a truce; it would at least give them time to summon Bolo Tamba's warriors to their aid. But Sewa knew that the Kuranko were themselves under attack and that Korgeyi had been killed.

At last the ruler—whom fifteen years earlier an ailing white man, impatient for a glimpse of a distant river, had blamed for all his miseries—ordered that all the remaining gunpowder be stacked in his house. Rather than submit to capture he and his wives blew themselves up.

After the fall of Falaba, Bolo Tamba and his allies vainly sought to defend the eastern approaches to Kuranko, but his warriors were powerless against the turbaned invaders whose caparisoned horses gave them unmatchable mobility and placed them beyond the reach of swords.

Korgeyi's successor as leader of the Barawa warriors was Manti Kumara Kulifa. His given name was Yira but he had earned the nickname Kulifa ("leopard slayer") as a boy. In the year of his initiation he had been on his way to pay his respects to kinsmen at Bandankoro in the foothills of the Loma. It was just after daybreak. Mist still covered the forest. He was crossing a granite-studded clearing—an old farm site—when without warning a leopard sprang from a huge boulder beside the path and bore him to the ground, gashing his forehead and cheek. He struggled to unsheathe his sword. Mouth and eyes filling with blood, he had a blurred vision of the great cat slithering across the ground then wheeling about, snarling in readiness for the kill. Its eyes were like sunlight on river water.

A numbing silence seemed to have seized the forest. Kulifa no longer felt a part of his own body. The leopard crouched with its fore-paws tensed against the earth, fangs bared and hind quarters drawn up. It thrust its head forward. Suddenly the boy heard the pulsating trill of insects again, and the breath began to come back into his aching chest. He shook the blood from his eyes, gripped the hilt of his sword, and waited for the leopard to spring. At that moment the animal seemed to relax. Still crouching, it licked its lips and edged backward. With a single fluid movement, it turned and lunged off into the forest.

Kulifa was convinced he had seen an apparition, but its scrape marks on the laterite were clearly visible and he could still smell the stale, warm odor of its pelt. When he reached home five days later he told his father what had happened, only to be told in turn that the leopard had been a lineage enemy in animal form. "Your scars will never cease to remind you of what men will do or conspire to do to achieve power. If you had not been protected by the magical medicines I gave you, the leopard's claws would have held you and its jaws crushed your skull. But who knows . . . it may have been as much your bravery that saved you."

Uncertainty about his courage made him seek every opportunity to prove he possessed it. During his circumcision he insouciantly snatched the cap from the circumciser's head to show his indifference to pain. After his initiation he joined the hunters' association and made solitary forays into the bush at night to pit his courage against his trepidation, daring the wilderness to visit its full terror upon him. He was known to journey alone to the haunts of leopards (not to kill them—for the leopard was his clan totem—but to smother the last suspicions of his fear) and became known as Kulifa; moreover, it was rumored that he wrestled with leopards and could even change into one.

Years later, when the Sofas raided Kuranko, there was no one believed to be more fitting to lead the campaign against them than the leopard slayer, Manti Kamara Kulifa.

It was the privilege of a principal warrior to be able to take his wives with him on his campaigns. Kulifa took his first wife, Kumba (who hailed from the Sankaran country), and left his younger wives, Sirasie and Tina, to look after the children.

Moving constantly from one strange place to another under threat of attack, Kumba yearned for home and asked her husband if she might go back to her parents while the war lasted. Manti Kamara Kulifa refused to let her go. One evening, on the pretext of collecting firewood in the bush, she ran away. Her husband set out after her the next day, despite warnings from his men on the dangers of penetrating Sofa-held country.

When he reached Kumba's village her parents implored him to leave their daughter in their care. But his pride would not allow it. He said he would wait three days; this would be time enough for them to remind Kumba of her duty to remain with her husband.

At midnight on the third day, alarmed by hearsay reports of Sofa spies, he went into the forest beyond the village to reimmunize himself against swords and sorcery. Under the feeble light of a waning moon he sprinkled herbs and gunpowder in two calabashes of water, then stripped naked and sat between them. The water began to stir and simmer and, without his aid, stream across his body from one vessel to the other.

He was never to know that a Sofa spy had overheard Kumba gossiping about him that afternoon and had bribed her to confide the secret place and time that Manti Kamara Kulifa was without his sword and war gown. Before the magical immunization could take effect, he was seized by the Sofas.

He was taken to Worekoro the following day, and then, wrists bound and legs shackled, he was led out of the town to an outcrop of granite surrounded by bones. The Sofa leader remarked on the deep scars on Kulifa's face and assumed they had been left by a Sofa's sword.

A light rain was falling across bright sunshine. Kulifa recalled with bemusement how his father used to tell him that in such weather the leopard spotted her cubs. The Sofa leader ordered Kulifa's head shaved lest his hair was imbued with the power to deflect swordblades.

As the swords were lifted to kill him Kulifa's last thoughts were of his youngest son, Tina Kome, born after a dream of leopards.

Manti Kamara Kulifa's youngest widow, Tina, was inherited by his younger brother, Sewa. Tina had two sons, the youngest of whom was two years old when Kulifa was killed. Tina Kome grew up hearing the story of his father's betrayal by his first wife. His "younger father," whom he addressed as Fa Sewa, had lost another brother besides Kulifa in the campaigns against the Sofas and nursed two grievances all his life: that the white men had supplied the Sofas with arms, and that women were more ruinous than war. "A man may conquer most deceit," he reflected bitterly, "but he will never conquer the deceit of women." Years later, even though three wives would desert him, Tina Kome vowed never to pursue an errant wife and warned his sons to divine well the character of a woman before marrying her.

THE SANKARAN and Kuranko countries were devastated by the Sofa invasions. Courtyards overgrown with grass and combretum, and burned houses, their rafters strung with the nests of palm birds, marked the sites of towns. Piles of bones marked chiefdom and village boundaries alike. Villagers who had survived the war now lived deep in the bush far from recognizable paths in makeshift houses of palm fronds. They ate wild yams and fruits, and camouflaged small gardens of rice and cassava around the swamps.

Over this wasted region British and French diplomats wrangled, seeking treaties with Samori while negotiating their own spheres of control. When the Sofa wars finally ended, the two European governments ordered a joint commission to plot the course of the upper Niger and its tributaries and thereby "mark out on the ground" the boundary between their domains. An agreement signed in Paris on January 21, 1895, had already determined on paper the line of partition. The line ran right through the heart of Kuranko.

In 1896 the Barawa people were still living in towns around Kabala. Bolo Tamba had died, and had been succeeded by his son, Sinkari Bolo. Reports had spread for years that the Sofas had formed an alliance with the white men. Another rumor was that the Sofas had been defeated. But few people dared travel to the country they had fled forty years earlier.

It was only because he was preparing for his initiation that Tina let her eldest son, Tina Kaima, go to Barawa to visit the site of the town where his father had been raised. Once she had told him he could go, she could hardly prevent Tina Kome from going with him. The boys were to pass through Barawa to SaNieni and stay there awhile with their mother's people: her marriage to Manti Kamara Kulifa had been arranged as a seal upon the friendship between the Koroma and Marah ruling houses after the Kono war against Barawa. She knew that her sons would be in good hands and that their grandmother would be overjoyed to see them for the first time.

For the journey the boys wore buff-colored country-cloth tunics. Their hair was plaited, and around their necks hung leather pouches containing protective charms. Each carried a raffia bag, and Fa Sewa had given them swords. Yet, for all these precautions, they did not enter the ruined towns but skirted them, looking carefully for the paths and landmarks Fa Sewa had told them about.

Only when they forded the Seli River into Barawa did they feel secure. Although the country was deserted except for yelping monkeys and cacophonous birds, they could imagine it filled with warriors and the music of xylophones. At night in the firelight at the edge of a noise-less stream they recollected stories that the old men had told them—about Kulakonke, Firawa, Yamisaia, and Sanyala, the abandoned towns. In the cool evenings they lay under locust trees identifying inselbergs and hills, whose names Fa Sewa had made them memorize. The wizened black pods of the locust trees were like charred tongues.

ONE MORNING, before the mists had lifted from the valleys, they decided to catch birds. They mixed sap from a rubber vine with the juice of a wild lime, and chewed the stuff until it was gummy. Then they pressed grass seeds into the gum and stuck it onto a branch, hoping birds would get their feet caught in the tacky gum when they came to eat the seed. The boys made cages from pithy raffia stems, jointed with quills.

They had just finished caging two birds when they heard voices. They looked at each other, hearts pounding. The dank atmosphere of the mist gave way to a sensation of pulsing heat. Dreadful tales of the Sofas raced through their minds. Quickly they drew back into the shelter of the raffia palms and grass to watch as a file of more than a hundred bearers, headed by several white men in pith helmets and boots, moved across the black swampy lowland. The white men were clearly not Sofas, though one of them carried a rifle. Without a glance to left or right, speaking a strange sibilant language interrupted by hoarse shouts, they pressed on. One of the white men was carried in a hammock, and as the boys watched he prodded the leading bearer with a knobbly polished stave then leaned over the side and vomited a greeny liquid onto the mud. Behind the hammock walked a black boy trundling a small wheel at the end of the stick.

When the long file had passed, the boys came out of hiding. They decided to get to their mother's people's place as quickly as possible. Tina Kaima took his bird with him, but Tina Kome released his and threw the cage into the swamp.

THE EUROPEAN COMMISSIONERS and their train of policemen, army engineers, local escorts, interpreters, servants, hammock boys, and carriers, circled Barawa and passed on south of the Loma Mountains as far as Kurubonla. They rested there awhile among granite thimbles and palisades that had withstood Sofa attacks, dispensing Manchester cotton, fancy smoking caps, penny mirrors, Florida water, tobacco leaves, salt,

beads, and threepenny pieces in return for having a track cut in the
direction of the Tembiko.

From mid-January to early March they duly surveyed, measured,
and described the source of the Niger using plane tables, meridian and
circummeridian observations of the stars, trigonometrical plotting, and
lunar distances, cursing the watershed for its impenetrability. They
found a bottle with a note in it from a Captain Brouet, who had been
there the previous year. As with all sacred sites, photographs of it failed
to come out.

Thus, in the same year that the British proclaimed a protectorate
and divided Kuranko country by an international boundary, the source
of the Niger was finally fixed by men whose names have all but been
forgotten.

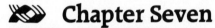 **Chapter Seven**

WHEN THE BROTHERS reached their mother's hometown they excitedly related what they had seen, only to be told that it was old news.
The white men had passed through Alkalia and Kilela the previous
afternoon.

"But setting eyes on you is better than seeing any tubabu!"
declared their grandmother as she pressed their heads against her
breast. Then she bade them sit away from her so she could look at
them properly. The boys sat on the clay bench that encircled the room,
feeling awkward under her admiring gaze. From time to time she
fetched a deep sigh. "Ah, Bokari! Eh, Kaima!" and lapsed back into rev-
ery.

Their mother's brother, Karifa, appeared in the doorway. "Well,
you have come. Have you eaten?"

The old woman clapped her hand across her mouth. "Ah, I have
forgotten!"

She called in the direction of the backyard, "Aissa, bring rice. And
catch that red hen. And heat some water!" At that moment, she noticed
the crowd of children clamoring around the back door, trying to get a
glimpse of the visitors. "Go on now! All of you!" she cried. "And Aissa!
Bring me that length of country cloth from my room, and some kola."

When the young girl came with the things, the old woman broke the kola and gave each boy half. She gave Kaima the cloth. "Let this be for your gown," she said, "when you leave the initiation house."

The boys were famished. For four days they had been living on rice flour, locust-seed cakes, and peppered meat, apart from a handful of *sonson* grubs they had roasted over their fire in Barawa.

"How is our sister?" asked their uncle.

"Well."

"How is your father?"

"He is there, Uncle."

"And your people?"

"They are all well."

"How is Chief Sinkari Bolo?"

"Well."

"How is Kabala?"

"Nothing amiss there, Uncle."

"How was your journey?"

"Nothing untoward happened," said Kaima.

"Except for the white men," said Tina Kome.

"Except for the white men," repeated his uncle. "We must amuse you while you are with us," he added.

The old woman sighed rapturously. "Ah, Bokari! Eh, Kaima! You are both the very image of your father, both of you. Look at their eyes, Karifa. Look now. It was not for nothing that their father was called leopard slayer. To think that they came all the way here alone!"

They slept in their Uncle Karifa's house, their mats side by side near the hearth in the central room. Tina Kaima dreamt that he was given a leaf parcel of seven ripe pepper seeds: tokens of a challenge to a wrestling bout. His younger brother dreamt of the bird he had set free in Barawa.

NEXT DAY Kaima's premonition was confirmed when some local boys invited him to wrestle.

The wrestling ground was a hard, dusty clearing half-shaded by an enormous mango tree. An excited and unruly crowd pressed forward with the "leader of the young men" ordering them to stand back and shouting for silence.

Kaima's opponent began crawling on his knees and elbows across the open space. When he reached Kaima he stood up and examined him with a mixture of scorn and uncertainty. Kaima waited tensely for the challenge. Suddenly it came. The local boy made to grab Kaima's testicles. Kaima countered the move and seized the boy's wrist, but his opponent quickly brought up his left hand and clouted Kaima across the forehead. Kaima was dazed and his eyes smarted. Sensing a reluctance to fight, the local boy stepped back, his lips trembling. He spat vehemently into the dust. "Come and clean up your brother's shit!"

Tina Kome saw his brother's eyes darken. Kaima took a pace forward and ground the spittle underfoot. He took off his tunic and tossed it to his brother. "He has taken up the challenge," someone yelled.

Kaima fought tenaciously against an opponent who was heavier, more aggressive, and more skilled. And lost.

As he drifted away from the wrestling ground, caked with red dust and sweat, his younger brother tried to console him.

"You had him off balance. You would have thrown him easily, but he grabbed your hair. He shouldn't have done that. It's against the rules. . . ."

Kaima said said nothing.

"There was no defeat," their uncle said. "Strength begins with self-mastery, not mastery of others."

"There was no shame in the loss," Kaima murmured, bruised by the memory of his defeat.

In the days that followed, the boys spent most of their time helping their uncle with his work: making new elephant-grass fences for the yard, mending the crumbling edge of the front porch, cutting and toting grass to repair the thatch. Sometimes Karifa took the boys out to his new farm site to help cut and clear the undergrowth in preparation for burning. The farm was an hour's walk from town, and as they filed through the bush Karifa amused his nephews with anecdotes.

A yellow-mantled whydah flew across the clearing, and Karifa launched into a tale, explaining that the bird's yellow back was the stigma it carried for once stealing okra from an old woman's garden and lying when the woman asked all the birds in turn who had eaten her crop.

Coming upon a column of soldier ants on the path, Karifa bent down, threw back the sleeves of his gown, and asked them how the war was faring.

Tina Kome knew what was expected of him. "Why are you talking to the ants, Uncle?" he asked.

"Aha!" began Karifa, a smile breaking across his face. "There was once a great chief, you see, called Muluku Sulaiman. Every living thing was under his command. But the termites were insubordinate! Muluku

Sulaiman therefore sent the soldier ants to bring them into line. But then he died. He died sitting on his throne. One day the termites came and devoured the throne: *wunya, wunya, wunya.* The dead ruler fell to the ground, whum! But to this day the soldier ants have not learned that their master is dead. They still go off to war. That is why you can ask them how the war is faring and where they are going to fight next. And if you get close enough you can hear them talking over their campaigns!"

Tina Kome laughed. Kaima feigned indifference and walked on ahead.

"Are such tales beneath the dignity of men?" Karifa cried.

"I do not know, Uncle, not yet being a man," the boy retorted.

"Then be a child and enjoy childhood while it lasts! The sweetest sauce does not stay on the rice for long."

Karifa rambled on to Tina Kome about his boyhood. "I and my age-mates, we used to steal corn and hens, and meet up in a hideaway in the bush and feast on all the food we'd pilfered. There was nothing we dared not do."

In the evening Tina Kome relayed his uncle's anecdotes to his grandmother.

She shook her head. "Eh! It was just like that with him all right. And now he's too fond of telling stories. I often wonder where he finds the energy for work."

Karifa glanced at the boys. "Stories are like music; they make the work easier. Isn't that so boys? Besides, when was this house without a full granary?"

On moonlit nights Karifa always had an audience of children on the verandah. He would lie in his hammock teaching them riddles or regaling them with stories until they had all nodded off to sleep.

Tina Kome had wanted to ask his uncle about something that had been on his mind ever since coming to the town. One night he asked outright.

"Where do the white men come from, Uncle?"

Karifa was silent for a while. He sat up in his hammock and tugged his snuff pouch free from the pocket of his gown.

"I will tell you about that," he began, sniffing the powder from his palm. "Long ago there were only four people in the world. They were black. Two men and two women. One night, one of the men had a dream. The dream told him that he should go to a certain small lake not very far from where he lived. He was to go to the lake, very early in the morning on a particular day, and bathe there. The man told the others about the dream, but they refused to believe it. They said, 'Why should anyone go and bathe in a cold lake early in the morning?'

"On the appointed day, the man and his wife went to that lake very early in the morning. They jumped into the water. When they came out they found that they were changed. Every part of their bodies was different. They went back to their village.

"When the other man and his wife saw them they ran away in fear. The man said, 'Don't be afraid, we are the people who live here with you.' The others came out of hiding and asked how they had become so changed. The man and his wife told them exactly what they had done. Then the others decided that they would do the same. They ran to the lake. But by the time they reached it, the sun had evaporated the water and only a few small pools remained. So they put the palms of their hands in the pools and paddled in them. Then they scooped up some of the water and rinsed their mouths with it.

"That is why the inside of our mouths, the palms of our hands, and the soles of our feet are different from the rest of our bodies. We are the descendants of that man and his wife. The white men are the descendants of the man who had the dream, and his wife."

Some of the children giggled and shuffled about. Tina Kome, crammed into the darkest corner of the verandah, sat spellbound.

"It happened thus?" asked one incredulous boy.

"Exactly so," said Karifa.

An old man emerged from the darkness of the courtyard and hobbled toward the house.

"Wait for me," he cried, "I can tell you about this white-man business."

The children pushed themselves back to make room for him. Several of the smaller children had dozed off and they now whined and murmured as they were shoved against the rough clay wall. The old man grasped a verandah post and lowered himself down. "Let *me* tell you about the tubabu," he said.

"There were once two brothers. One was the ancestor of the blacks, the other was the ancestor of the tubabu. The ancestor of the tubabu was the older brother.

"One day Allah came up to the ancestor of the blacks. He had some gold in one hand and a covered calabash in the other. He said to the younger brother, 'Choose one of these things.' The ancestor of the blacks took the gold. The ancestor of the whites got the covered calabash. Inside it was the book of knowledge. From that time forth, the white men did not have to work. Everything comes to them and works for them. They have food in abundance and never go hungry, and they own things that could not have been made in this world."

Karifa pointed out that the book of knowledge was different from the *kitabu* Qur'an.

"Can we ever get that knowledge?" Tina Kome asked.

The old man half turned and looked at him quizzically. "The white men live by themselves in a far country and do not share what they know or what they own."

In the days that followed, it was decided that Kaima should return to Kabala. The moon was almost full and the initiations were due to begin. Tina Kome would stay on until the end of the dry season and help his uncle with the farm work.

An itinerant Mandingo goldsmith was traveling north and agreed to have Kaima accompany him. On the morning of his departure, Tina Kome and his uncle went with him as far as the river. Squirrels darted and loped ahead of them, and once they disturbed a troop of red patas monkeys, which withdrew into the elephant grass and stared haughtily at them from a safe distance. At the river they all shook hands and said goodbye. Kaima's last gesture was to snatch the cap off his uncle's head. He splashed across the river and disappeared into the trees beyond the river, with Karifa calling mock threats after him and laughing.

Chapter Eight

IN 1904 THE BRITISH established their administrative headquarters at Kabala and appointed G. H. Warren district commissioner. Tina Kome was twenty.

The Barawa exiles watched the barracks being built. In the cool evenings, as the sun plunged into the Wara Wara hills, the constables paraded and drilled. Cattle egrets, which all day had picked their way between the feet of unperturbed cattle, suddenly took to the air and winged in formation toward the darkening inselberg. The town was covered in a haze of smoke from cooking fires, and on gloomy verandahs men addressed the east with their prayers.

Fa Sewa, wandering home after a day in his tobacco garden, drew his stoical conclusions about the newcomers. "Yesterday and today are not the same. Yet, whatever sun shines, that is the sun in which you have to dry yourself."

Sinkari Bolo was dead, and had been succeeded by one of Bolo Tamba's younger brothers, Firawaka Mamburu. He was known everywhere as Belikoro, "mighty elder." Belikoro had inherited the power to command the thunder and call down lightning. He would seldom attend one of District Commissioner Warren's meetings without first destroying a cow or splitting open a tree to impress the assembled chiefs. It was rumored, however, that white men were immune to such powers and that Warren, whom everyone called Warensi, was not even impressed by them. Belikoro also liked to enter Kabala with an entourage of jelibas playing his favorite refrains on their xylophones and extolling the virtues of his forebears.

Under the jackfruit, mango, and flamboyant trees at the foot of the hill where he had built his bungalow, the district commissioner presided over endless inquiries in an attempt to unravel the history of the peoples living in and around Kabala.

Tina Kaima and Tina Kome took little interest in the constables. They farmed together near Belikoroia and traveled the five miles to Kabala only to sell a little rice after harvest and buy soap, matches, palm oil, and kerosene.

Late in the dry season of 1906 their only sister, Tina Dondon, married a man from Sengbe and went to live in Koinadugu Town. No one expected the marriage to last. The husband was an old man, indifferent to women and partial to palm wine. Before the rains were over that same year, Tina Dondon left her husband and ran away with her lover.

The old man's sons came to Kabala and brought a lawsuit against Tina Dondon's brothers for refund of the bridewealth.

For two days the receipts were laboriously recalled and counted. Tina Kaima and Tina Kome watched the pile of stones growing as the court accountant recorded all the things the husband's family had given to their family on this or that occasion: the mats, salt, palm oil, kola, soap, and rice during Tina Dondon's initiation, the five days' hoeing done for their mother-in-law, the *lapa* and head-ties given to their mother-in-law, the necklaces and trinkets given to the new bride, the lengths of country cloth and bunches of tobacco given to their father-in-law, Fa Sewa. . . .

The brothers pleaded for time to make the repayment. But the husband's people were against such lenience. "It is the custom to make the refund on the same day as the accounting," they declared. "We never wanted this divorce. It creates bad feeling all round. Your sister always seemed happy. But what is done is done. We cannot change it."

Tina Kaima and Tina Kome sought help from friends and distant kin, but the main rice crop had not yet been harvested and they found themselves unable to amass even half the amount needed. They considered going to fetch their sister from Lengekoro, where she had fled with her lover, and demand that she return to her husband. But Fa Sewa reminded them of their father's misadventures and advised them to admit defeat rather than lay themselves open to further humiliation.

Thus their in-laws descended on Belikoroia like scavenging birds. First they blundered about the courtyard berating the brothers. Then they thronged into the house and brought out everything they could lay their hands on: hoes, machetes, boxes of clothing, sandles, hearth-stones, mats, baskets, rice, pots, mortars and pestles, and even a bunch of unripe bananas were piled up outside. While the women chased hens around the yard, trapping them against the fence, the men entered the gutted house and hoed up the clay floor, hacked at the walls with their machetes, tore the thatch from the roof, and made up bundles of poles to carry away. Fa Sewa was in his garden and was spared the spectacle, but Tina saw it all, and wailed and lamented as if it were a person being torn apart before her eyes. Her eldest son made no attempt to calm her. But he pulled off his gown and threw it to the ground for the crowd to claim. Tina Kome was suddenly reminded of the time in SaNieni when his brother took up the challenge to wrestle, and lost. He took off his gown too and threw it down beside his brother's.

That evening, when the scavengers had gone, the brothers were left with nothing but the trousers they were wearing. Their mother had only one lapa.

They lodged with Fa Sewa and gratefully accepted friends' invitations to meals, donning frayed gowns that Fa Sewa found for them, and chewing bitter kola to assuage their hunger. In the ensuing months they worked from daylight to dark on their neighbors' farms, repaying kindnesses and earning the right to call on help to make farms of their own. Their mother wore herself out pounding rice for neighbors in return for a small pannier of grain, some groundnuts, and red peppers. Her three hearthstones, made of the clay from an anthill, had been taken, but she refused to replace them; for cooking she made do with a hearth of river stones and a chipped country pot.

Toward the end of the dry season Belikoro was visited by a British officer of the West African Frontier Force and was asked if he would persuade some of his young men to enlist. Tina Kome was eager to see something of the white men's world. He said to Fa Sewa, "If I join the army I will be able to provide for you and my mother, but you must tell me what I must do."

"The world has already passed through three ages," Fa Sewa answered cryptically. "We are now in the age of the white men. The age that follows will be the age of death. But I cannot see far into the future. You should consult a diviner."

Tina Kome handed his kola to Kumba-the-Red and told the diviner that he was going to join the white men's army. "Will it go well for me? What obstacles lie in my path?"

Kumba-the-Red took the kola nuts and mingled them with his river pebbles. Then he laid out Tina Kome's destiny on the mat. "There is prosperity ahead of you," he said, looking steadily at the pattern of the stones. "But you must offer a sacrifice of rice flour to your late father."

Tina Kome did as he was bidden. Then, with thirty-five other young men, he set off for Freetown. His mother stood on the roadside with the other women. She held her head high but tears ran down her cheeks and her lips trembled. She remembered the grief of her husband's death, the destruction of her sons' house, and the brine of tears on another day when she stood at the edge of a path, her wrists bound with soft cotton cord, as Tina Kome went into the bush to be initiated.

The young men marched off in rough columns, and Fa Sewa, whom Tina Kome would never see again, reflected on the changes that had engulfed their lives. Turning to Tina Kaima he remarked dismally, "Your little brother has courage sure enough. He has thrown his life to the winds and become a child of the white men."

Tina Kome was enlisted in Freetown in April under the name Bokari Kabala so that the military authorities would always be able to trace his provenance.

IN KABALA, District Commissioner Warren went on trying to unscramble the history of settlement in the area. A certain Karamorgo Yafode, having lost out in a contest for chieftaincy in Banko in Guinea, had come to Kabala and asked if he could settle there. The local chiefs refused to accommodate the stranger and took the matter to Warren. The district commissioner made up his mind that there were too many chiefs vying for authority, and he looked for a pretext to assert his own and, if possible, relocate some of the people.

He made a tour of his district and visited the almost-deserted country of Barawa. The Kuranko would always remember Warensi for the cases of champagne he required them to lug around the country, and the tent he preferred to a house.

Upon his return to Kabala, Warren assembled the chiefs and asked them whose country lay between the two rivers.

Belikoro nodded his intention to speak. "The Marah own that country," he said.

"*Nomor!*" echoed a praise-singer. "The first, first, first ancestor of the Marah: Yilkanani. From Yilkanani: Saramba. Saramba said: 'Borsingbi and Yamisa, you go to Woli and Barawa.' We are all children of Mansa Saramba, but Barawa is the seed of the whole country!"

"Barawa was the home of my elder brother Bolo Tamba before the wars," Belikoro explained.

"Nomor!" the praise-singer cried. Then he named all the Barawa rulers from Yamisa to Belikoro.

Warren questioned Belikoro in the hope of finding out why he was living near Kabala and not in Barawa. In reply Belikoro's praise-singer artfully played up Barawa's occasional altercations with the Limba and made it appear that the Barawa people had won, through conquest, the right to settle around Kabala. Nothing was said of the Kono invasions that had actually brought about their expulsion from Barawa.

Warren dug his pen into the inkwell and scrawled notes in his minute book. Still poised in that gesture, he told his court interpreter to point out to the Kuranko chief that Barawa was a rich country, with an abundance of palm-oil trees and game animals.

"D.C. Warensi himself shot an elephant there!" the translator concluded, putting a polite intepretation on Warren's lamentable wounding of an elephant cow near Senekonke.

Warren directed Belikoro to take his people back to Barawa or forfeit the country to some other chief. Belikoro saw no point in argument; several of his elders were already agitating to return to Barawa now that the British had pacified the country.

"We will go back at the beginning of the next farm season," he announced.

As for Karamorgo Yafode, the Muslim stranger, Warren ordered that he be granted the right to settle in Sengbe. He took his followers to a clearing by the Kinfa stream, buried a parcel of suras, planted an orange tree, and named the new settlement Dar-es-Salaam.

Belikoro gave the drum of chieftaincy to his daughter Sayo, and then gave her in marriage to Fode Yala Koroma, the town chief of Kabala. Tina Kaima returned to Barawa with Belikoro. Some of the people founded hamlets en route; some went to already-established towns, such as Kemor Homoro's town, Barawa Komoia. Others rebuilt towns whose original sites had long since been reclaimed by the forests and whose names had become legendary.

Tina Kaima's grandfather and namesake had founded the town of Kurekoro when returning exhausted from a border skirmish. The warriors had been famished and thirsty, and had rested in the shade of a *kure* tree. They had eaten ripe fruit and drunk cool water from a nearby stream, and when they were replenished Kaima had declared that they would come there to farm and build a town called Kurekoro, "under the kure tree." Tina Kaima remembered the year of his initiation, the sonson grubs he and his brother had roasted by the streamside, and the kure fruit fallen from the same tree that had once nourished their grandfather. But he decided that one could not rebuild a memory. Joining others of the ruling lineage, he gave his energies to creating a new town. The town was sited where two streams flowed into a third. Surrounded by water on three sides and overlooked by steep hills, it was named Firawa, "forest place," after one of the old towns.

 Chapter Nine

WHEN WAR BROKE OUT in Europe, the Sierra Leone Battalion of the West African Frontier Force was made ready to embark for the German colony of Neu Kamerun.

During his seven years in the army Tina Kome taught himself to read and write; now he was shocked by stories in the Freetown newspapers of German atrocities in Belgian towns. The wars he had heard about as a boy paled by comparison. As reports began to circulate of babies impaled on bayonets, women raped and disfigured, and men castrated, he wondered at his childhood terror of the Sofas. There were not even words in Kuranko for these European barbarities. Was it really possible that such a war could be waged?

"Yes, it is all true, horribly, horribly true," an English noncommissioned officer assured them. They should get ready to do their bit in their own part of the world and rid a neighboring country of German tyranny, just as the British soldiers were doing in France. "In Cameroon your African brothers live in slavery. The Germans impose harsh levies, and when the people resist, their villages are burnt, the women raped, and the men hanged."

Many of the troops grew alarmed at the prospect of fighting Germans, but their officers quietened their fears, telling them that the Germans would be hiding behind Cameroon conscripts. "You will overwhelm them easily. You are better equipped and better trained. Besides, they are fighting only because they fear German reprisals against their families. And we have God on our side!" Many of the English officers were secretly uneasy at the thought of African troops witnessing whites fighting whites.

The sea stank of dead fish and engine oil. Cramped in the ill-ventilated hold of the troopship *Elmina*, Tina Kome chewed limes and red peppers to suppress seasickness. The rusted plates thudded and reverberated, and ropes holding gun carriages and ammunition boxes strained against the pitch and yaw of the ship. At night he lay awake in the sticky heat, hearing a furnace door slam or the clanking of ash buckets. Pale globe lamps picked out rivets along the beams, and cockroaches, fattened on oil refuse that clotted in every crevice, scurried over the men's half-naked bodies and gnawed at soles and fingers. From time to time someone would wake shouting and try to escape his fetid prison, only to be fetched back into reality and the shadows by the irascible muttering of his companions.

After a naval bombardment, Duala was taken on September 27, 1914. The Sierra Leone troops, shaken from the rough sea voyage and the deafening barrage of naval guns, disembarked and joined up with Gambian, Nigerian, Gold Coast, and Senegalese contingents. Tina Kome watched black smoke belching from a smoldering warehouse near the quay. A white flag hung from an improvised mast over the customhouse. In the deserted town a pungent odor of mangrove forests, salt water, and cordite mingled with the acrid fumes of burning rubber.

In their overcrowded billets the men's khaki uniforms were saturated with sweat. Leather belts and webbing became covered with mold overnight. A taste of mildew permeated the food. Some of the English N.C.O.s became irritable and one was heard complaining about the smell of Negroes, cursing his bad luck in not being with his comrades in France. It was rumored later that he had been transferred to the Nigerian regiment.

They drilled and waited. As he stamped his bare feet on the red earth or threw the heavy rifle butt across his shoulder, Tina Kome hardened himself against needless emotion. He thought of his forebears who had always been fighters; now it was his turn to show his mettle.

One Sunday there was a mandatory church parade. Some of the men thought this meant they were going into action, and they broke open cartridges and ate the gunpowder to give themselves courage. The British commanding officer explained that prayer was the only proper moral preparation for battle and ordered latrine duty as punishment. Tina Kome surreptitiously drank water in which his father's war sword had been dipped. The dark-green bottle of sour liquid had been Fa Sewa's last gift to him. Knowing how the English liked to taunt Africans about their "jujus," he tried to keep his observances to himself. His companions mistook his reticence for pride, and ribbed him for having become a white man. "Rather rule yourself than let another rule you," Tina Kome responded. A friend retorted, "And he who keeps to himself will in the end bury himself."

The Sierra Leoneans' first engagement was at Yabissa, north of Duala on the Wuri River. Mist clung to the forested shores of the tidal river as the troops trudged in a thin column toward the town. Suddenly a maxim gun opened up from a concealed emplacement of logs and boulders, raking the path and slashing at the elephant grass. It was the troops' first time under fire. Carriers panicked, dropped their loads, and rushed for cover. Tina Kome's legs went weak. He concentrated all his attention on moving, but it was as though he were blinded, stifled, benumbed. The blood pounded in his head. His ears rang. He felt nauseous with the effort of trying to move, trying to control his reaction to the gunfire and his fear. He staggered into the trees, tripping over a wounded carrier who lay in the grass clutching at his knee and staring incredulously at the blood that oozed through his fingers.

A British colour sergeant was regrouping men under an embankment in the trees and preparing an attack on the German position. But a runner arrived with orders that the advance column should retire to the river. With the falling tide, the gunboats and transports were aground and vulnerable; the Sierra Leoneans were to dig trenches and set barbed-wire entanglements in case of a counteroffensive. A second assault on Yabissa was planned for the morning.

That night, huddled in a stony trench, Tina Kome strained his ears to identify the sounds of the darkness: the trilling of cicadas, the distant barking of monkeys, snatches of laughter from the riverside as the Nigerians struggled with a hymn ("What a friend we have in Jeesus . . ."), and from the British bivouacs a melancholy mouth organ echoing the tune. From time to time the moon appeared through the mist and lit up the sluggish river, and toward dawn a British colonel came along the line chatting to the men about the day's engagement.

After Yabissa was taken the troops pushed on, northward, from Kribi to Mbo to Mbureku, marching barefoot through abandoned banana, cocoa, rubber, and oil-palm plantations, and slogging along mountain trails turned into quagmires by the rains. A foul atmosphere of dysentery and fever pervaded the miserable camps. Rations were scanty. Supplies were held up for weeks by washouts on the forest roads. Carriers fell down exhausted, their feet ulcerated by chigoes, their spirits broken by the dead silence of the endless rain forests. But despite sickness and heavy casualties, discipline did not flag, and the British, who had begun the campaign loathing the thought of commanding African troops in battle, praised the men for their fortitude and bravery.

In June 1915 the Sierra Leoneans were withdrawn to Duala. Tina Kome was assigned to garrison duty outside a hotel where several German families had been confined. Already the war had changed his attitudes. He remembered a dead German soldier near Woia, stiffened against a rock, his bloated face greenish black like a rotten mango, his nostrils and lips simmering with flies. The ruptured corpse stank like any other. Now he watched the Germans in white drill trousers strolling in the hotel courtyard with their tallow-skinned wives, and felt almost supercilious toward them. But their children, playing with makeshift hoops in the shadows of the coconut palms, entranced him. They flitted like small birds behind the wrought-iron colonnade and against the ornate balustrading of the vast building. In the sound of their laughter he momentarily recalled his own childhood. But it seemed part of another person's life, and his memories of the years before his enlistment were vague and alien.

The second campaign began. After a series of desperate skimishes the Germans fell back to the town of Yaounde in the south. In January 1916, they retreated from Yaounde and took refuge in the Spanish enclave of Rio Muni. While British and French diplomats busied themselves with the process of partitioning African territory, the Sierra Leonean troops embarked for home.

The ship was less crowded than it was on the outward voyage and many of the troops slept on deck under canvas awnings. The sea was calm.

One afternoon Tina Kome found a swallow that had strayed off course and fallen exhausted onto the deck of the ship. He resuscitated it by feeding it droplets of water with the blade of his army knife. By evening the bird had revived and flown away in the direction of land.

A group of wounded Senegalese soldiers regarded the incident with scorn.

"You are a fool if you think you are returning from war," one said. "The war is ahead of you."

When Tina Kome asked the soldier what he meant, he was told about the recruitment methods of the French in Senegal, methods no less violent than those of the Germans in Cameroon. The Senegalese went on to complain vehemently about their forced participation in the European war. "Thousands of Senegalese conscripts go to their deaths on the Western front in a war that is none of our business. And here, in Africa, we are fighting black men like ourselves so that another lot of white men can oppress them, can force them to serve in their wars and work on their plantations."

Tina Kome was staggered by the bitterness of the soldier's remarks. He said nothing. But some of the Sierra Leoneans voiced their disagreement. They pointed out that they were not conscripts, and praised the British officers who had endured with them the privations of the war.

The Senegalese soldier screwed up his face. "Pah!" he spat. "You cannot accept that you have suffered for nothing. But you will see. Now they have trained and armed you they will come to fear you. Then you will see how they repay your loyalty!"

In Freetown, Tina Kome put this episode out of his mind, and as soon as he got leave made his way to Kabala and on to Barawa.

He was surrounded by praise-singers and the music of xylophones. He heard his name joined to the names of great warriors. He could hardly move for the press of bodies around him. Children who had never before heard of him clamored around, were shooed away by elders, returned, leapt about, clapped their hands, fell silent with awe, then resumed their excited activity. Belikoro danced, and Tina Kome danced with him. Women clapped and beamed as the drummers lifted the tempo and beads of sweat stood out on the old chief's brow. No one could remember when Belikoro had last given himself to such exertion. The courtyard filled with dust and shrieks of laughter, and the pulsing drums and tinkling xylophones continued into the dusk after Tina Kome had left the chief's courtyard and gone to his brother's house to eat.

The two men sat on the edge of the porch, eating in silence. With deft fingers they dipped into the same calabash, forming balls of rice and cassava-leaf sauce to slip into their mouths. They did not once lift their faces to one another.

When they had finished eating they rinsed their hands in water from an army mess tin. Tina Kome passed his tobacco pouch to his elder brother. They lit their pipes, still without saying a word. The sun, crimson and blurred, dropped into the hill through a haze of dust and smoke.

"You have come home," Tina Kaima said at last.

"One day I will come home," Tina Kome said, "but not now. The world is bigger than we were told it was. I want to get the measure of it."

"Han!" Kaima exclaimed. "I have married two wives and they are harder to control than we were ever told it would be. You are welcome to your far-off places. For myself, there is hardship enough in my own house!"

"Do you remember," Tina Kome mused, "how Fa Sewa used to tell us that a squirrel could say it was the only one in its hole but never that it was the only one in the whole field?"

"Yati," Kaima said, "I understand."

Several young men were clustering around the porch. They fired questions at the returned hero. "How many men did you kill? Did you kill a white man? What sort of weapons did you use? We have heard of guns that fire hundreds of bullets without needing to be reloaded. Is it true? How can that be? Heh! the white men are ingenious. Isn't that so?"

Tina Kaima saw his brother's annoyance, and told the young men to go away and let their uncle rest. "Come back in the morning," he told them. Then he turned to Tina Kome and reflected, "They will be wanting to join the army now instead of getting initiated."

Tina Kome felt awkward that so much attention had been centered on him. He wanted to defer to his elder brother, and asked him about the circumstances of their mother's death two years before, and about Fa Sewa, who had died the same year. Then he pressed Kaima to tell him about the chieftaincy, about the extent to which the British were meddling with customary law, about the system of taxation, and about Belikoro's relations with Kabala.

"It takes three days to reach Kabala," Kaima said, "and the constables never come here." He stared into the darkness. Beyond the elephant-grass fence at the edge of the courtyard a fire had been lit, and sparks flew up into the smudged indigo of the night sky. The drumming had begun again. The dancing would go on all night.

Tina Kome invited his brother to refill his pipe. "The time will come," he said, "when the chieftaincy will return to our line, just as it was in Morowa's day. But in the future a ruler will have to know what the tubabu knows, and his children will have to go to school in order to get that knowledge."

"We may get back the chieftaincy, but lose our children's respect," Kaima said.

Two days after his return to Firawa, Tina Kome offered a sacrifice of two cows and of rice flour and kola. Kaima announced and led the sacrifice, calling the heads of all the lineages in the town to attend.

First the rice flour and kola were consecrated. The men squatted around the calabashes, their right hands stretched out over them. As a genealogist called the names of their ancestors—Manti Kamara Yira known as Kulifa, Kaima, Manse Faramata Morowa, Manse Fa Yira, Manse Morowa—Tina Kome pondered the wilderness of time and the countless lives linked by that rope of names. *"Amina,"* the men murmured in unison as each name was recited. The genealogist asked the named ancestors to pass on the sacrifice to the unnamed. Tina Kome felt as if the names were a river coursing through him. He half closed his eyes and glimpsed uplands of dun-colored grass waving to and fro in the wind. He sensed the momentum of the sea.

Tina Kaima gave out portions of the consecrated rice flour: some to the leader of the young men, some to the lineage heads, some to the mistress of the young women, some to the Muslim who would slaughter the cows. The xylophonists also received their share. They plunged into their playing and singing with even greater zeal. "A man is best known in his own place," they cried. "A man is best recognized in his home."

As soon as the cows had been consecrated, the young men fell on them. The first cow was pinned to the ground and its throat cut. The Muslim officiant turned away, wiping the blade of his sword. The cow's eyes swiveled and bulged, and blood pumped from the severed artery, forming a black stain on the earth. The second cow was slaughtered. Banana fronds were laid out and the butchering began. A head was given to Belikoro and, on Tina Kaima's advice, the heart and liver of the first cow were presented to the Balansamaia house. The rump went to their lineage sisters, the neck to their sisters' sons, the hooves to the genealogists. Every family in the village received a share of the meat. Then, for good fortune during the farm season, some of the older men told their sons to collect handfuls of the blood-soaked earth to mix with the seed rice at sowing. Tina Kome looked up from where the coils of purple entrails had been heaped. Five vultures wheeled over-head, but one had come down and perched on the thatched topknot of Tina Kaima's house. The ancestors had accepted the sacrifice.

When Tina Kome returned to Freetown it was rumored that Sierra Leone troops were about to be sent to join other units of the West African Frontier Front in East Africa. But they were suddenly ordered to Nigeria. A French outpost at Zinder in Niger had been attacked by the Tuaregs under the urging of Sanusi chiefs from Tripolitania. The Sanusi were calling for a jihad in Niger and Nigeria, and the British believed that German advisers were encouraging the rebellion. The Nigerian regiment was in East Africa, so four companies of Sierra Leonean troops were dispatched to back up the French force.

The Tuareg uprising was put down without the Sierra Leoneans' being called upon, but during their months in Nigeria they were not entirely inactive. An emir of Zaria, echoing a tradition of spirited resistance to British rule, refused to pay taxes. The Sierra Leoneans were ordered to take the emir into custody and bring him to Lokoja.

The episode provoked heated discussions among the Sierra Leoneans, many of whom recalled the hut-tax wars in their own country and the violence with which the British had put down Mende and Temne uprisings. Because Kuranko chiefdoms had not at first been subject to the hut-tax laws, Tina Kome had no personal grievances to air. But he listened to his comrades' reports of the aftermath of the Mende uprising, of chiefs sentenced to flogging and hard labor, of villages plundered and burned, and felt deep misgivings. He remembered a gibbet and a row of ruined houses along an eroded embankment in Cameroon and found himself again forced to consider what kind of rule justified the scores of dead soldiers and carriers whose bodies, pummeled and sponged by the rain, had lain for weeks in rutted forest tracks in a foreign land.

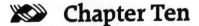 # Chapter Ten

AFTER DEMOBILIZATION Tina Kome went home to Barawa, accompanied by an army friend, Manga Sori Mansaray. Before heading north the two men spent a few days at Mapema, Manga Sori's hometown. Manga Sori had asked his father if his infant sister, Aisetta, could be betrothed to Tina Kome, and after long discussions it had been agreed. The family was Muslim and not altogether happy about a marriage with an infidel. But no one doubted the strength of the friendship between Manga Sori and Tina Kome, and the marriage was seen as an affirmation of that bond, of the "straightness of the path between them." So Tina Kome tied four kola nuts in a leaf parcel and presented them to his friend's father, then tied the red thread of betrothal around the little girl's wrist.

It was in a buoyant mood that Tina Kome returned to the north. He took the journey slowly, accepting invitations from town chiefs or the headmen of wayside hamlets to stay a night or two. Manga Sori remarked on the tremendous popularity his friend enjoyed everywhere he went. It was not just the prestige of a returned serviceman, nor was it merely a matter of people's curiosity to hear about the war. Tina Kome seemed to be regarded as a kind of sage, and villagers would ask him to intervene in local disputes, or give his advice on how they should proceed with cases in the Native Administration courts that the British had established in the region. One of Tina Kome's interventions became legendary.

He had stayed overnight in a hamlet not far from Koinadugu Town. In the early hours of the morning, while it was still dark, he was awakened by the sounds of a fierce altercation nearby. A man was belaboring his wife for her flagrant infidelity, and as far as Tina Kome could make out, the wife's lover was also at the scene, pleading a feeble pretext for his presence in the woman's room at that hour of the night. As Tina Kome listened the man's voice reached the point of hysteria, and the woman's cries of protest collapsed into a pitiful and drawn-out ululation. Then silence fell. Tina Kome was about to go back to sleep when the flimsy, mud-daubed door of his room was wrenched open, and the town chief appeared, imploring him to come quickly. He donned his gown and crossed the courtyard. The air was cold and damp and a film of mist covered the dark-blue corridor of bush beyond the houses.

The town chief was holding a hurricane lamp over the prone body of a young man. Tina Kome approached and saw that the man was clutching at his ear and whimpering like a kicked dog. Then he noticed that blood was streaming from between the man's clenched fingers.

"The old man cut his ear off," the town chief said. "He is still in the house . . . over there . . . his wife too!"

By now everyone in the hamlet was awake and cautiously assembling around the groaning lover. "It's old man Kande," one man observed. "He's been threatening to do this for a long time."

"He was provoked," another man said. "This young man taunted Kande, saying he was impotent, that his tinder was wet."

After much conjecture the town chief decided that the old man would have to be fetched from the house and disarmed. But no one was willing to penetrate the dark curtain between the courtyard and the silent house. The town chief turned to Tina Kome. "You are a soldier, my friend. Will you bring him out?"

As Tina Kome strode toward the house a soft murmur went up from the small crowd. The first wan streaks of light were breaking in the eastern sky. Birds whistled in the bush and a rooster crowed. The lover continued to whimper and groan, clutching the bloody gap where his ear had been torn off.

As he entered the house Tina Kome was assailed by the dry odor of wood smoke. It reminded him of the war. The old man was cringing against the far wall, and held a machete. "Leave me alone! I will kill you!" he cried. Then, "Who are you?"

Outside no one could hear what the soldier was saying, but the old man cried out hoarsely, "Who are you? Is he dead?"

Two figures soon emerged from the house. Tina Kome had a machete in his hand and was gently gripping the old man's shoulder. The woman fled through the backyard and ran wailing into the mist of the river road.

As the sun rose languidly over bands of hoary mist, the villagers bandaged the young man's ear and calmed the cuckolded husband with assurances that his action had been provoked and that he would not be held entirely culpable. "It is your wife who must bear the blame," they said, and looked into the mist. As they went on exchanging clichés about the untrustworthiness of women, Tina Kome remembered Fa Sewa's misogyny and wondered if he would fare any better in his marriages.

The town chief was alarmed that the district commissioner in

Kabala would hear about the affair and send police to the village. Tina Kome told him not to worry. The town chief wrung the soldier's hand. "You were brave to accost him. Yes, brave. Only a soldier would have had the courage."

Tina Kome shrugged off the chief's remarks. "No problems will come of this," he said, "so long as you make sure that the woman is driven from the hamlet back to her own people. And the young man must go too. Do you understand? Do you agree?"

Later he was chagrined at the thought that he had given advice without a moot of the elders and with no understanding of the background to the affair. But Manga Sori, though he had slept through most of the fracas, was loud in praise of his friend's courage and alacrity. "You have the natural gifts of a ruler. Besides, everyone said that the woman was to blame. Do you hear me?"

Tina Kome heard, and assented to the tidy view his friend proffered. He even tried to make light of the episode. "If the young man had heeded the old man's threats he might well have kept his ear!"

"Exactly so," returned Manga Sori, "*si ban to 1 sa*, life soon ends for those who do not listen."

Firawa had changed little. A few new houses stood on the western edge, the bush around the town was sparser, and the mango trees in the Woldugu courtyard had grown taller and bushier. Some men of the Muslim Sise clan had been forced to hive off and found a hamlet a few miles away, where they kept a small herd of cows. Belikoro had adamantly maintained that cows meant Fulas and Fulas meant Islam, and Islam had brought more trouble in the past than all the praise-singers of Kuranko put together! Moreover, the cow dung spattered in the town streets was dirty, so the cattle owners had been obliged "to cut their mouths off" from their natal settlement.

When Tina Kome heard of this he felt embarrassed for his friend, who was a Muslim. "Manse Belikoro is chauvinistic because his head is full of the past," he explained.

Manga Sori brushed the matter aside. "Your cattle owners at least have a livelihood. What of those who have none?"

Tina Kome knew that his friend was alluding to the hundreds of men who had been demobilized in Freetown and had decided to stay on in the city. For them, farming had become degrading work and they saw less indignity in the poverty of Freetown than in the isolation of the bush.

At the beginning of the farm season the two friends joined Tina

Kaima's work cooperative, hoeing and sowing on the cleared slopes above the Konkon stream. In the evenings the men relaxed and talked quietly on the porch of Kaima's house. Later, as the sun melted away into the western hills, Manga Sori went out into the courtyard and offered his prayers to the east, standing beside the frayed raffia prayer mat that he had carried with him throughout the war.

Tina Kome watched his friend, and envied his asylum of faith, the easy encapsulation of the world in a few fixed phrases. Yet he could not reconcile Islam with the traditions to which he was heir, and he liked to regard his return to Barawa as a return to those traditions. Already he harbored the thought of contesting the chieftaincy when Belikoro died. Glancing toward his brother who was lying back in his hammock, hands clasped behind his head, he also envied his self-containment, though not his indifference to the future. He mused upon something that had happened that evening while they were eating. Some rice had fallen on the ground. Tina Kome had thrown a handful of gravel at the palm birds that had swooped down to eat the grain. "Eh!" Kaima had exclaimed, "why bother with the birds?"

"Better the hens get the rice than the palm birds," Tina Kome had answered, "We can eat the hens but not the wild birds!"

Manga Sori finished his prayers and rolled up his prayer mat. Tina Kaima rubbed some tobacco leaves in his palms and carefully filled the tin that his brother had brought him from Freetown. Tina Kome peered out into the darkness. The indigo sky was littered with stars and smudged by the milky way. He saw a falling star. He was about to say what he had seen when Manga Sori, who had also seen the star fall, said, "Well, someone's life has gone out somewhere in the world."

✖ Chapter Eleven

TINA KOME'S RETURN to Barawa lasted seven years. It lasted until the British, with their penchant for trying to solve administrative problems by redrawing boundaries, decreed that the chiefdoms of Barawa and Nieni be amalgamated and the paramountcy given to the Nieni chief at Yifin. It lasted until Belikoro died in 1925 and Tina Kome saw the futility of gaining power in such a diminished province. It lasted as long as he thought he could settle down to farming and endure the isolation of the rains. It lasted as long as he kept alive the illusion that he could accomplish in his own lifetime something that in his heart he had always known could be done only by his sons.

He had ended the war as a company sergeant major and had no difficulty in being taken on as a sergeant major in the Court Messenger Force. His first posting was Panguma in the south of the country. He delivered summonses, accompanied arrogant clerks to outlying villages to collect taxes, and marched rueful thieves to court. By day he wore the starched khaki uniform of a policeman. But every evening he laid aside the broad leather belt with its huge buckle bearing the anchor and oil-palm insignia, and donned his indigo gown and the embroidered *bambedon* cap of the Marah, the shape of which imitated the mouth of a crocodile. He set up a folding chair in the courtyard, smoked his pipe, and listened to the gossip and complaints of his neighbors. Even in the south he acquired a reputation for sagacity. "He has salt in his head," people pronounced. "He has understanding."

Aisetta was sixteen when she came to live with Tina Kome in 1929. She was tall and carried herself with authority and self-assurance. Manga Sori often came to visit them. He pressed pennies into the tiny palm of Kulifa, Tina Kome's first-born, and laughed outright at the quizzical expression on the infant's face. "Will this one wrestle leopards like his grandfather, or fight Germans like his father?"

"Since he is my first-born he is most likely to grow up fighting *me*," Tina Kome mused.

"He certainly *looks* like you!" Manga Sori said.

Not long after the birth of his daughter, Ai, Tina Kome was transferred to Sefadu in Kono, and a few years later to Moyamba in the southern province. Here the children started school.

As he padded down the dusty and potholed main street carrying a sealed O.H.M.G.S. envelope—the contents of which he was, as usual, kept in ignorance of even though the English assistant district officer insisted its importance was "of the utmost"—he passed the government school where the children were chanting arithmetic tables. He measured the opportunities his children would enjoy against his own lot, and so curbed his nostalgia for Barawa and his resentment of the whites at whose beck and call he crossed and recrossed Moyamba in the heat of the day.

He sensed in his second son a special destiny, and named him Sewa Bockari. The child's first food was kola and spice, which Manga Sori chewed and spat into its mouth, so imbuing it with his virtue. Manga Sori voiced his own thought about Sewa's destiny:

65

"Birth is like the many-stranded rope we spread over our fields to keep the birds away. Your strand, my friend, and his are one."

Tina Kome named his next two sons Ali and Abdul in celebration of Islam, which he at last embraced on the urging of his friend as a consolation to Aisetta and a compensation for his own lost country.

It was in Bonthe in 1942, a region of estuarial inlets and mangrove forests oppressed by humidity and the stench of the sea, that news reached him of the death of Tina Kaima. Tina Kome decided that it was time to go home for good. He was near retiring age anyway, and entitled to a government pension of two pounds a month. His last-born son, Noah Bockari, was a babe in arms, and Tina Kome decided that the older children should stay on in Moyamba to finish their schooling while Abdul and Noah, with their mother, returned with him to Barawa.

Tina Kaima was buried at the edge of the Woldugu courtyard in Firawa. At the head of the grave Tina Kome planted a coconut seedling that he had brought from the south. "We were separated by the sea," he said, "and now the salt of tears has brought us back together. When I die, let me be buried beside my brother and a coconut palm planted on my grave as well."

After the burial Tina Kome went to Pore Bolo, the chief, and announced his intention of clearing the old site of Kurekoro and going to live there. "The town was built by our grandfather Kaima, and we will rebuild it in the name of our elder brother."

A few of the older men cautioned him against disturbing the spirits of the dead. "They were more disturbed in life," Tina Kome said bitterly. Then he looked away, waiting for the chief to make his reply.

Pore Bolo was a reluctant ruler, appointed at the behest of the English when the Barawa elders had been unable to decide between more eager candidates for Teneba Sewa's succession. The chief's diffidence also betrayed a preference for palm wine over palaver.

"Yes, go," he declared at last, "there is plenty of farmland in that area and you will do well there." Years before, his father, Teneba Sewa, had made Tina Kaima court speaker as a concession to the Morowaia house, but Pore Bolo did not relish the thought of Sergeant Major Bockari Kabala sitting beside him.

The new Kurekoro did not last long. The men who built it were motivated only by loyalty to Tina Kome; at heart they were despondent about life in the remote hamlet beseiged by dark forests. It became clear to Tina Kome that he could not hold them, that the force of friendships forged in Firawa would sooner or later lead them to cut off and go back to the main town. He was divided between his self-esteem and his duty to the others, and was reluctant to visit Firawa, where people were already wise to his dilemma.

Then Pore Bolo died suddenly, and Tina Kome moved back to Firawa to contest the chieftaincy. As with a house fallen into ruin, so with Barawa: he would repair its walls and cut new thatch for its roofs.

He considered his years in the army, his service in the Court Messenger Force, his wide knowledge of Sierra Leone, his literacy, and above all, his genealogy. Everything counted in his favor.

Abdul and Noah watched their father lay out yellowish papers and six tarnished medals on the worn mud surface of the porch. "This is the 1914 Star, this is the British War Medal, this is the Victory Medal, this is a Long Service and Good Conduct Medal, this is a Jubilee Medal, and this is a Coronation Medal from King George." He made the boys pronounce the English names. They laughed at their own awkwardness with the words.

When Tina Kome went to Makeni to submit his letter of candidacy to the commissioner of the northern province, Abdul and Noah accompanied him as far as the Konkon stream. Years afterward, Noah would guess his first memory to be of his father, dressed in a new gown, waving to them from the other side of the stream before vanishing into a labyrinth of elephant grass. And he would remember how a confetti of yellow butterflies filled the sunlit spaces in the trees along the stream.

Tina Koma's bid for the Barawa chieftaincy failed. He contemplated the irony of the situation. In the army he had often been ribbed for mixing with the English noncommissioned officers: "*miliju farinya lek good sol poke*" ("mildewed cassava pap is palatable if you have good salted pork to go with it"). Now it was the English who held against him his literacy and familiarity with the colonial administration. They preferred men they could manipulate.

Many of the disappointed Morowaia men drew solace from a report from Kulanko. A clan sister had confessed before dying that she was a witch. She alleged that the Morowaia house had conspired against Pore Bolo and killed him through sorcery. She had taken her revenge. She had set the English against Tina Kome by changing herself into an elephant and attacking some English hunters at the edge of the Bagbe Forest. Then she had gone by night to Firawa in the shape of an owl and sought to kill Tina Kome's sons. But the house had been ringed

67

with protective fire that had driven her back and left scorch marks on her skin. She had sickened and died, covered in welts from the searing fetishes around Tina Kome's house.

Aisetta observed in her husband a mood of resignation, which she would have liked to explain away as part of his growing old. But she had heard village gossip that their twin daughters had malevolent powers and, in retaliation for some slight, had robbed their father of his self-possession on the day he went to see the English about the chieftaincy. Thus his taciturnity and irascibility worried her.

She shuddered at ideas that passed through her mind, and forced herself to concentrate on combing Dondon's hair.

"Ouch!" the girl cried, as her mother tugged the comb through a knotted braid.

"Then be still," Aisetta said sharply.

On the front porch Abdul and Noah were playfully swinging their father in his hammock until they, too, were castigated. "Leave it!" he snapped.

That night Aisetta again overheard Tina Kome reprimanding the boys, this time for using Mandingo words in their conversation. "You must speak correct Kuranko, only the pure language!" he shouted. Aisetta remembered when he used to laugh at his sons' use of borrowed words and their mimicry of the dialects of neighboring chiefdoms.

Chapter Twelve

WHENEVER HE TRAVELED outside Barawa, Tina Kome took Noah along with him. He would hoist up the bleary-eyed child to the shoulders of Yeli Pore, his xylophonist, and set forth in the misty darkness of the sleeping town on a jaunt to Kabala or another distant place.

Aisetta seldom saw her son, but she was keenly aware of the reason for her husband's attachment to his last-born child. Once when she had quietly suggested that he indulged Noah too much, he had replied, "I will be dead by the time my first grandchild is born, so let Noah be my grandson."

Lodged in a strange house, Noah would lie awake listening to the raised voices of men arguing out their grievances. Then the voices would fade, giving way to the drone of Yeli Pore's four-stringed harp and his entranced songs of the lords of Mande, of wars and migrations that had swept like wild fires across the grasslands of the Sudan. The child would drift to sleep and perhaps wake once to the noise of rain far away or to his father's gown, pungent with indigo, rough against his face.

Sitting on Yeli Pore's shoulders Noah scanned the landscape for signs of animals. Tina Kome moved ahead, glancing back from time to time to call out, "Heh, Noah, your horse has a fine saddle but slow feet!" or simply to mutter "Elephants" and point to a blunt depression in the path. He never passed Senekonke without waving his arm in that direction and telling Noah once more how the great stone doors on the mountain slammed and boomed when a man of their lineage was about to die. "Even the jelibas are up there," he would add wryly, "playing their xylophones for pennies!" A smile would spread across Yeli Pore's face. Such raillery was supposed to be *his* stock in trade.

They always stopped at the same places to eat or rest. If they left Firawa at night they would pick their way through the ghostly forest, the lantern's halo showing up bosses of rock and roots along the path. At Barawa Komoia they would build a fire from old thatch and twigs and wait to greet the town chief at first light. Beyond the Keronki stream there was a boulder-studded hill where they would retire from the heat of the day in the shade of locust trees, with Tina Kome handing out the cassava cakes and slices of sweet potato that Aisetta had prepared for their journey.

When they reached Yirafilaia late in the day, Noah would run down to the river for a swim. While his father took a nap in the village, Noah played with the local boys, diving from a steep bank and floating downstream, pretending to be crocodiles. Dead leaves lay like fish in the amber shallows. The boys pounced on them, yelling and laughing. Later they spread themselves out on the warm sand. Downriver they heard the murmur of rapids, and the vast canopy of the forest stirred and then hushed as if it were alive.

For Noah the best time of year was when the men banded together to clear and burn their farm sites. One season in particular he would never forget.

They arrived about mid-morning at a stretch of bush along the Yilbe stream where some of the men had already begun making their farms. Trees had been felled, and a sunken mattress of wilted foliage lay on the hillside ready to be burned. Around the clearing stood the unfelled forest, its ribs exposed, lianas streaming down through the gloom like strips of biltong.

The men pushed on up the slope, hacking at the fallen foliage with their machetes. They reached a grove of immense cotton trees whose flanged roots were webbed with smooth gray hollows. Tina Kome had brought the foodstuffs to be sacrificed: rice, corn, cassava, kola, groundnuts, bananas, and sesame. He set down the basket at the bole of the biggest tree. Noah stood a little way off, watching the soaring cumulus clouds high above the crown of the tree. He felt giddy.

The men squatted around the sacrifice as the *karamorgo* addressed the djinn of the forest, begging them to accept the offering of food and leave the farmers in peace. Some of the men remembered the last time they had farmed in the vicinity. A djinn had jolted one man's elbow as he was hoeing and the man had gashed his foot with the blade of the hoe. Another man was forced to abandon his farmhouse after his family had been terrorized night after night by a djinn grunting in the adjacent darkness.

In the afternoon they set fire to the felled bush. Dry leaves crackled and exploded, and showers of sparks scurried skyward. As the sheet of flame reached up the slope the sky seemed to melt. In Firawa that evening Noah made out the distant pall of smoke over his father's farm. The air smelled of ash.

During the days that followed, Noah, Abdul, and several of their older lineage brothers worked on the farm, stacking unburned logs at the edge of the clearing. Noah would occasionally glance up at the cotton trees on the ridge and wonder if the djinn had taken the food. He dared not go to find out and was ashamed to ask his brothers to take him.

The skies filled with clouds. At night thunder rolled across the mountains and flashes of lightning quivered and lit up the horizon. It was time to sow.

The hoers formed a long line across the clearing. As drummers and flautists played, they began to move forward, measuring their hoeing to the beat of the music. The hoes were lifted and held for a moment before they fell, clutching the dark-red earth. With deep resonant voices the young men sang in unison. In the intervals of their song a few of them twirled the handles of their hoes or passed the hoes from hand to hand. The drummers tilted their heads and smiled as they kept up an unbroken momentum.

"You aren't working hard enough!" a man panted at the drummers.

"And your hoe makes a dull music!" one of the drummers yelled back.

By early afternoon most of the farm had been covered. Tina Kome subsequently declared that the remaining strip should be hoed as a contest. He placed a haunch of venison on a tree stump and called for challengers.

Sira Braima Sise stepped forward. "Give it to me; it's as good as mine!" He was more than six-and-a-half-feet tall, sinewy of build, and a tireless worker.

"Where is a Marah to meet him?" Tina Kome shouted.

"Let Noah take a hoe!" someone joked.

Tina Kome joined in the play. He thrust the long-handled hoe into his son's hands. "Hoe for the venison!" he urged.

The boy looked up at his father in bewilderment, but at that moment his lineage brother Yandi took the hoe from him. "I'll take up the challenge," he said.

Two men scraped lines on the ground, marking out ten equal sections. Tina Kome told the drummers to play and waved for the hoers to begin.

As soon as each man finished a section he would leap over to the next, working his way uphill. "Hoe deeply!" yelled the onlookers. "The whole section, the whole section, Marah!" they cried. "Sira Braima, you are falling behind!"

But there was no real question about who would win. Sira Braima gained the top of the slope and looked back at his rival toiling away on his second-to-last section. Yandi looked up. "Forgive me . . . friend . . . for presuming to . . . challenge you. . . ." he said, struggling to get his breath back.

Sira Braima flung aside his hoe and laughed. "That's all right," he said, "we'll share the meat tonight at my place."

When they returned to Firawa that evening Yandi staggered along under the weight of the hoes that he had to carry back to town as his price for losing the contest. Noah tried to help by grabbing hold of a protruding handle. "Leave it!" Yandi said sharply. Then, changing his tone, he added, "Next time, we will win."

The following day they sowed. Noah trailed after his father, who with unfaltering steps moved across the hillside, broadcasting the grain.

With wide sweeps of his arm he sent the seed scything downward to the earth. The women moved behind him with small hoes, gently covering the seed with a scraping of soil.

Tina Kome announced that they would live on the farm that year. Although he did not speak of it, he had decided that Noah should go to Kabala to live so that he could attend school. This would be their last chance in a long time to be together.

Through the desolate months of the rains they remained on the farm. At night Noah heard what he thought were the footsteps of djinn outside the farmhouse. Above the sound of the rain he heard monkeys yelping, and the repeated wailing caw of a night bird. Abdul swore that he had actually seen a djinn. One day he led his younger brother across the swamp and pointed out the place where it had appeared. All Noah could see was a clump of moss on a rotting stump, and was annoyed that the djinn should be invisible to him. But then, everyone said that djinn feared people and avoided contact with them. Aisetta warned the boys never to have anything to do with such unpredictable beings.

"There was a man," she said, "who lived in the forest."

Her voice grew hushed. In the darkness beyond the house the rain fell steadily.

"This man had lived in the forest for a long, long time. He had met a djinn there who provided him with everything he wanted. In return the man had promised to give the djinn a human being."

Tina Kome recognized the fable and interrupted his wife. "In this world, never promise to do something that you know you cannot do. If someone asks you for something and you know that you cannot give it, you must never say you can." Aisetta ignored the interruption and went on:

Now, because that djinn had provided this man with everything he wanted, the man had promised to give the djinn a human being.

There came a time, however, when the man realized that he would not be able to keep his promise. But there was a small boy who lived nearby, as close as we are to Fa Yira's farm. This boy was very clever, cleverer than many adults! The man made up his mind to go and catch this little boy and give him to the djinn.

He went with a lump of meat. He thought he'd be able to seize the boy when the boy came to take the meat. But he did not realize how clever that little boy was.

Noah's eyes were wide with awe as he listened to his mother.

The little boy was with some adults, so the man decided to remain at the edge of the farm and call the boy from there. He hid himself in the trees and began to call the little boy, singing this song: "Child little child, *kundu munu ya, ya kundu munu*, come and take your meat, *kundu munu ya, ya kundu munu.*"

The child sang back: "Put it on the ground over there, *kundu munu ya, ya kundu munu.*"

The man replied: "The ground will make it dirty."

"My mother will clean it for me."

"The water will spoil the taste of the meat."

"My mother will put salt on it."

"The salt will make you go bald."

"There is a medicine for baldness."

"Little boy, you have the gift of the gab."

"But sir, I have no special gifts; I am doing what is natural for me to do."

"So this is the nature of a child."

The man went on like this for a long time, trying to entice the little boy away from the adults and toward the edge of the farm. He did everything in his power to catch the little boy, but to no avail. Finally he decided to go away.

No sooner had he returned to his own place than the djinn came and demanded his due. The man was unable to fulfill his promise. The djinn felled him with his cudgel and the man died.

That is why you must never say that you can do things that you cannot do. If you make promises you cannot keep, you will end up like that man.

For days afterward, Noah's head was filled with thoughts of djinn. He found himself singing the refrain, *"kundu munu ya, ya kundu munu,"* and implored Abdul to tell him what djinn looked like. Abdul would only say that djinn were djinn.

"Are the white men djinn?" asked Noah.

"Yes, of course. They are great wizards too. They make vehicles that bounce along the roads at great speed. They make machines that fly in the sky like birds, and others that cross the salt water filled with hundreds of people. Father has told me."

As harvest approached, the boys kept vigil on a platform high over the farm to frighten away scavenging birds with their slingshots. Tina Kome worked at making repairs to the low fence around the farm to keep out cane grass and animals. He was finding it hard to tell Noah that he would soon be sent away to school. He delayed until after harvest.

The skies were cloudless. Golden sheaves of rice lay heaped on a circular stack outside the farmhouse.

Aisetta spent much of the day threshing grain and spreading it out on mats to dry in the sun. Dark crimson fire-finches darted about under the tattered palm-frond eaves of the house, or fluttered across the hardened patch of earth that had been her cooking yard for half a year. Seeing the birds, some of which harbored the spirits of children who had died in infancy, she reflected on her own fortune in having never lost a child.

Tina Kome sat apart, entangled in long strips of cane that he was weaving into a rotund granary basket. The twins toddled toward him. Dondon fell down and was about to dissolve in tears when her father smiled at her and urged her to get up. She walked a few more paces, and fell against his leg. Then he lifted her up and placed her in the basket. She tumbled about happily while her sister tried to force her tiny body through the strands of cane.

When the family returned to Firawa for the dry season, Tina Kome finally found his pretext for going to Kabala.

"I'll sell enough rice to buy kerosene," he said to Aisetta. "Noah can come with me."

Noah remembered the journey for its haste. His father made none of his usual prolonged visits, and Yeli Pore did not accompany them. They reached Kabala in three days.

As they neared the town, the Wara Wara hills loomed over the acacias and thornbush. The vast granite sides of the inselberg had been weathered into long fissures like claw marks, and blackened as if by fire.

Tina Kome recalled other partings he had endured and promises he had made to no one but himself. Along the last stretch of path he urged his son to bear up. "The world is a place of hardship. But what counts is how you face that hardship."

When they passed the school building in the main street, Tina Kome told Noah how in the old days they had gone into the bush for their schooling. "Now we go to the white man's school," he explained.

"Will I go to school, father?" Noah asked.

Tina Kome told him that this was the very reason for their visit to Kabala. To his surprise, his son showed no alarm at the prospect of starting school. The boy's only doubt was that he would not undergo initiation with his age-mates at Firawa. But Tina Kome assured him that he would, in due course, be initiated with his friends.

"And will I learn to farm at the white man's school?" Noah asked.

His father laughed and said nothing.

Noah was enthralled by the town. While his father went to the mosque Noah sat outside one of the Syrian stores and watched the trucks bowling up the road in a turmoil of dust. They lurched to a standstill by the market, radiators hissing, as a horde of shouting travelers spilled from the running boards and wrenched suitcases and bundles from the overladen roof racks. In the shade of the verandahs, Fula tailors treadled away at their sewing machines, busily running up seams and deftly folding pieces of embroidered cloth under the rapid needles. From the mosque came the drone and babble of men's voices in prayer.

It had been arranged that Noah would live with his father's lineage son-in-law.

Tina Kome bid his son goodbye. *"Ma sogoma yo. Ma si ma nyorgoye,"* he said, and once again urged him to take heart. Then he pressed a penknife into Noah's hand. It was the knife he called his "Cameroon knife"; he had acquired it in the army thirty years before.

Noah took it, more in bafflement than in gratitude. Then his father was gone.

Noah joined the other children at the back of the house. Small oil lamps flickered in the yard, casting huge shadows across the battered sheets of corrugated iron that separated the house from the hubbub of the market. Down the street, cries and shouts signaled the beginning of an altercation, and nearby some children were drumming on discarded tins. Noah was confused by the noise, and by the coming and going of strangers. Everyone spoke Krio, a language he did not understand. But he felt sure they were all talking about him.

His half-sister came and stood over him. She listed all the chores that he would be expected to do every morning before going off to school: filling two buckets from the well, splitting firewood, doing his own laundry. . . .

The girl smirked. "Your father is not around to pet you now," she said, and ran off laughing into the darkness.

✖◆ Chapter Thirteen

HOW NOAH CAME to be pledged to a Mende trader and lost in the south for several years is something about which one may never know the complete truth. Twenty years after it happened, Noah could remember very little about the circumstances of his departure from Kabala. One day a lineage brother turned up and told him to accompany a friend and help drive his cattle to the south. He thus embarked upon a seemingly endless journey down boulder-strewn roads between brakes of flourishing grass, driving a herd of reluctant cows before him. His taciturn companion, whose name was Kemo, gave him corn and curdled milk to eat. He watched women in the fields, hoeing up mounds of lumpy black earth. He saw children his own age splashing and laughing in river pools below the girder bridges they crossed. The air was fragrant with the perfumes of flowers after rain, but in the towns the streets were quagmires that stank of cow piss and dung.

In the south, at a town called Bamatuk, Kemo took leave of Noah, telling him that he was to remain there and work for Mammy Kasan.

Noah saw money change hands. This accomplished, an enormous woman, whose brow was creased with an expression of intense disapproval or worry, gathered her flowing blue robe about her and led him to the outhouse where he would sleep.

The main house seemed like a mansion to Noah. The walls of its central room were covered with framed photographs of men in army uniforms and women in vast white gowns and towering headkerchiefs. Padlocked doors led to rooms he was not allowed to enter. All the windows in the house were barred against thieves, and it was Noah's job to see that the shutters were securely bolted every night. Along the front porch of the house ran an ornate concrete balustrade, painted bright yellow. At one end of the porch was Mammy Kasan's shop. Its ceiling was hung with lengths of baft, hanks of rope, metal buckets, and kerosene lanterns. Its shelves were filled with packets of Tate and Lyle sugar, boxes of Bryant and May matches, bars of soap, bottles of pills, and enamelware. On the worn counter were piles of onions and arrays of okra and red peppers.

Mammy Kasan sat behind the counter frowning at the street. Hardly an hour passed without her summoning Noah, whose name had become Kekura, to do some chore for her.

"Ke-kura, Ke-kura, Ke-kura," she would call monotonously. Then more stridently, "Kekura!"

Noah would come running from the back of the house, his hands dripping with soapsuds.

"Kekura, do the ironing now," she commanded.

He would leave off doing the laundry and heat up the heavy iron by filling it with coals from the fire. Then he would struggle with one

76

of Mammy Kasan's voluminous gowns on a rickety table that creaked ominously as the huge iron was edged along a fold of the cloth. No sooner had he begun to make some headway when he would hear again, slowly and regularly at first, "Ke-kura, Ke-kura, Ke-kura." So he would scoot round the side of the house dodging the rain puddles under the eaves, and hear the voice raised into an angry summons. "Kekura, come now. Kekura!" He would arrive, breathless, at the bottom of the steps and be told, "Kekura, you still smell of Kemo Sise's cows."

Noah quickly learned that Mammy Kasan made such remarks when she wanted to give herself time to remember what it was she had wanted him to do. When the chore came back to mind she would indolently lift and extend her right arm and with her left hand hitch the billowing sleeve of her gown up onto her shoulder. "Kekura, fetch firewood," she would say. Or simply, "Bring water." Noah would lower the bucket into the well, and as it hit the water he would see his silhouette jolt and shatter, and a blue half-circle of sky turn into a muddy potholed road.

He found solace in the company of Denka, Mammy Kasan's husband. Denka had been blinded by a spitting cobra a few months after he had joined the army in 1939. Gossip circulated that Denka's mind was a bit touched as well.

The blind man, feeling his way along the scarred plaster wall of the house to the back steps, often came into the yard when Noah was working there and would launch forth in a display of parade-ground drill. Noah would have to push basins aside and kick firewood out of the way lest the blind soldier trip over them.

Denka marched up and down, shouting orders to himself. "Lep rite, lep rite, lep rite, lep. Riiiii wheel. Lep rite, lep rite, lep. Squaaad halt!"

He would spring to attention facing the mango tree, his hand quivering at his forehead in salute.

Noah would say, "I am over here," and Denka, nonplussed, would wheel toward the voice and repeat his salute.

The boy flinched as his blind companion stumbled over outcrops of pitted rock or waded into a puddle scattering the ducks. But Denka was tireless. "Give me the pestel" he would order, and taking it from Noah he would shoulder and present arms while the boy dodged the flailing pole.

At first Noah was unsettled by Denka's ghosted-over eyes. They reminded him of the spectral gaze of the people in the parlor photo gallery and of the locked rooms he thought to be occupied by the spirits of the framed figures. But familiarity soon allayed his fears, and lying awake at night on his mat in the outhouse he would be lulled by the sound of Denka's flute warbling and trilling above the rain—until Mammy Kasan's voice broke the spell, calling "Ke-kura, Ke-kura, Kekura! Come now."

From time to time Mammy Kasan went on what she called an "errand" to another town. Denka said she went to collect debts. Noah went as Denka's guide, each holding an end of a long pole, the boy steering his blind companion down the narrow bush paths while Mammy Kasan bustled ahead, her gown catching the breeze and billowing out like a sail.

One morning at Sirabo, Mammy Kasan sent Noah off to buy some bananas.

As he sauntered along a row of stalls in the market he was startled to hear snatches of Kuranko. Looking around, he spotted three men, one of whom wore an indigo gown like his father's. He sidled up to the men and greeted them cautiously.

"Eh, *m'bonnu!*" one of the men exclaimed to the others, "the boy speaks Kuranko."

"What is your name?" asked another.

"They call me Kekura."

"Kekura!" said the first man, surprised. "And where do you hail from, 'new fellow'?"

"From Kabala."

"Kabala! Eh, *m'bo*, you are a long way from home."

"We are also from Kabala," said the second man.

Noah fumbled in his pocket for the knife his father had given him.

"My father gave me this when he sent me away to school," Noah said.

The first man took the knife and turned it over in his hand. "He sent you to school, here? In Sirabo?"

"No, in Kabala."

"Hun!"

"It's a fine knife," said the second man.

The first man made to go. "*Awa,*" he said, "*mi nala;* we will see you later."

Noah felt a lump in his throat as he watched the Kuranko men disappear into the crowded market. He hung around until late afternoon in the hope that they would return, but dreading Mammy Kasan's ire he finally gave up his vigil.

NOW, NOAH'S ELDEST SISTER Ai was married to Alhadji Momodu Salloh who lived at Bonthe in the southern province. On a trip to Bantai chiefdom to buy rice she chanced to meet the Kuranko men whom Noah had talked to at Sirabo.

Tina Kome had written to Ai about Noah's disappearance, and when the travelers mentioned the small Kuranko boy with an army knife Ai was certain that it must be her little brother. Although puzzled by the child's nondescript name, she immediately took a truck to Sirabo, where the market people told her about Mammy Kasan and her houseboy. Ai came on foot to Bambatuk the next day.

The town was on an island in a tidal river lined with mangrove swamps and muddy shell banks. The only way across to the island was by ferry, a wooden raft given buoyancy by empty oil drums, which the ferryman winched across the river by means of a cable attached to trees on either bank. After asking directions from the ferryman, Ai proceeded to Mammy Kasan's house.

Mammy Kasan was ensconced behind the counter of her shop. Ai greeted her and asked casually if she was the trader who had a small Kuranko boy called Kekura working for her.

Mammy Kasan's frown deepened. "Kekura is there," she said, tugging at the sleeve of her gown.

"I am sure that Kekura is my brother," said Ai. "The last we heard of him, he was in the care of a certain Kemo Sise, a cattle trader."

Mammy Kasan said nothing.

"May I see the boy?" Ai asked.

Mammy Kasan simply repeated, "He is there."

Ai walked into the house, calling "Noah, Noah, are you there?"

Denka, sitting in a gloomy corner of the parlor, muttered, as if to himself, "There is nobody here called Noah."

Ai asked if he knew of a boy called Kekura.

Denka at once sprang to his feet. "Att-en-shun," he shouted. Then, tilting his head as if to listen for some reply, he called, "Kekura, Kekura, come here."

At first Noah hardly recognized his sister in the dim light, but Ai led him to the back door to get out of Denka's hearing. Noah, seeing her face clearly, could not suppress his joy.

"Calm, calm, keep calm," Ai whispered. "You must pretend you do not know me. Just wait. I'll come back this evening."

Ai returned to Mammy Kasan and asked if Noah could go back to Bonthe with her. "Perhaps only for a short while," she added, noticing Mammy Kasan's deepening frown.

The trader's blunt refusal convinced Ai that further pleading would be a waste of breath.

"Even if you were the boy's mother, which you are not," Mammy Kasan pontificated, "I would not let him go with you. He is pledged to me, and Kemo Sise has gone to Liberia."

"Then may I spend the night here?" Ai asked. "I'll go on my way in the morning."

Mammy Kasan gave her gruff assent. "Kekura!" she shouted, "bring food!"

That night Ai stole down to the outhouse and explained to Noah that he was to run away in the morning. She carefully outlined her plan, making him repeat what he was to do and impressing upon him the need to keep calm until they had made their escape. It was well after midnight when she returned to her own room.

The day dawned bringing high cirrus clouds like rubbed tobacco, and a sea breeze. Ai thanked Mammy Kasan for her hospitality and asked if she might come and visit her brother again. She said goodbye to Noah, and walked away quickly, down the path to the ferry landing.

Noah waited for Mammy Kasan to go into her shop.

He approached her with his heart thudding. His mouth was filled with the stale, musty taste of dried fish.

"I am leaving to cut firewood," he said weakly.

He was wearing two pairs of trousers and two shirts, and was fearful that Mammy Kasan would notice. But she was preoccupied counting out pills from a brown bottle into the palm of her hand.

Noah raced through the coconut grove and on through the scrub and grass, taking a roundabout route to the ferry landing. Ai had dashed the ferryman a pound note and told him to wait for Noah. He grinned as he watched the boy squelching clumsily across the mud flats, then stumble breathlessly down the landing stage.

"My sister . . ." Noah began.

"Come on Kekura," the ferryman laughed, "let's go."

As the ferry slid slowly out into the stream, Noah looked back anxiously at the path to Bambatuk. He half expected Mammy Kasan to appear, with her gown billowing about her, to order them back.

"You were lucky," the ferryman said, straining at the rusty winch. "If your sister had chosen to cross in the evening time, the river would have been down and *you* would have been stranded."

Noah watched the blurred shadow of the raft in the olive water. Mangrove pods drifted in the stream, and yellow butterflies caught by the river wind flapped and flurried near the surface.

The ferry bumped against the landing. Ai seized Noah by the arm and hastened him away from the river.

They skirted the first village they came to, using a grove of mango trees to keep themselves out of sight of the houses. But they were close enough to hear the murmur of voices and the thud of pestles, and they feared that some kind of alarm would be shouted at any moment.

Clear of the village, they regained the path and walked on through the heat of the day. The air was heavy with humidity and Noah's ears throbbed. He complained that his legs were numb and his throat dry, but Ai insisted they continue without a stop. All night they walked, picking their way down the moonless path through a wilderness of mangrove forest. Occasionally they disturbed a nightjar resting in the warm dust of the path, and it would fly up clumsily and break the cloying silence with its churring cry.

At noon the following day they reached a town where Ai had friends.

That night Noah woke from a dream in which Denka was fumbling in the darkness for his flute. It was the first time he had thought of the blind man since the morning he had left Bambatuk. "I must whittle him another flute if he cannot find that one," he thought. Then weariness enclosed him and he fell back to sleep.

Two days later they reached Bonthe, where everyone fussed over Noah and pressed him to recount his adventures. Ai had scarcely seen her brother in the eight years since Tina Kome had left Moyamba, and as Noah spoke of his vicissitudes she responded with reproachful signs and exclamations of incredulity.

"Han!" she cried, as Noah listed the chores he had had to perform for Mammy Kasan. "Han, that woman made you work so?"

Ai knew that Noah was pining to rejoin his father, but she was unsure how to arrange for him to go home. Days passed, until one day a friend of the family, who worked in the colonial administration, dropped by to announce that he had been transferred to Port Loko. On hearing of Ai's predicament, Mr. Banya said he would be only too pleased to take Noah north as far as he was going.

With great trepidation, Noah passed into the charge of another stranger. Yet by the time Mr. Banya put him on a truck at Makeni bound for Kabala, the boy's anxieties had vanished.

The vehicle jerked and swayed over the rutted road. Noah was jammed into a corner among sacks of rice, bundles of rank-smelling tobacco, and creels of trussed and frightened hens. He tried to make sense of a story a young man was telling.

"I won't name the town. I won't name the lover. I'm not even going to name the cuckolded postmaster in that town whose name I won't mention," he prattled, knowing full well that most of his fellow passengers knew of whom he was speaking.

"But friends, there was no man to equal that postmaster for jealousy. He wouldn't let his wife out of his sight for a moment: poor woman, she couldn't visit her parents, she couldn't even go to the market without having him tagging along like a famished dog.

"Well, it came to such a pass that her husband's jealousy made her sick. Lovesick you might say, for a certain young man, who shall also be nameless. . . ." The storyteller winked and lowered his voice. "She got diarrhea . . . really . . . bad . . . diarrhea!"

Men guffawed and women giggled as he continued: "Her diarrhea was so bad that she had to spend much of the day in the lavatory behind her house. A good deal of the night too! But luckily it was a very well-built lavatory, that postmaster's lavatory. In fact it was a very comfortable lavatory."

Everyone chortled.

"In fact," went on the storyteller, "you would not have thought the seat of that lavatory was made of wood, it was so comfortable."

"And did the woman get well?" someone joked.

"Yes," a woman answered, "but she contracted another sickness not long afterward."

The raconteur fell silent, and someone began another anecdote.

Noah huddled further into the corner, trying to escape the elbows of the woman beside him. Amid laughter and shouts and the occasional squawking of a hen he drifted off to sleep.

It was past midnight when the truck pulled up outside the Kabala post office. Its headlights surprised some strollers along the road who half turned, trying to penetrate the glare and identify the vehicle.

Barely visible were the letters *D E S T I N Y* painted on the front of the cab in the form of a garlanded trellis.

Noah clambered down from the truck and vanished into the darkness, determined to avoid his relatives in Kabala and get home to his father.

He arrived in Firawa several days later, footsore and alone. His father clasped him in his arms and fought back tears. Aisetta's joyful crying brought neighbors running. Yeli Fore put all his heart into his xylophone, and the thrilling, melodic phrases took such a hold of Tina Kome that he shouted to the whole town to come and celebrate his son's homecoming.

That afternoon, when the excitement had died down, Tina Kome sacrificed a cow in gratitude to Allah, and vowed that his son would never again leave his side.

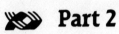 **Part 2**

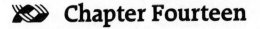 # Chapter Fourteen

FROM THE PORCH of his house Momodu Kande watched the white man picking his way down the rain-eroded street. Momodu thought: "It is not yet noon, but the white man has already made three trips to the market and will probably make a fourth."

The white man stumbled over a rut, and onions tumbled from his folded arms. A pariah dog sniffed at one of the fallen onions, then backed away as the man bent down to retrieve it.

Momodu hailed him. "Heh!"

The white man squinted into the sun and pointed at himself as if to ask, "Are you talking to me?"

"Yes, you," Momodu called. "Come here."

The white man approached the porch and set down his provisions. More onions escaped from the crumpled scrap of newspaper in which he had tried to wrap them.

"Sit down here by me," Momodu said, patting the cushionless chair beside him.

The white man took Momodu's extended hand and shook it weakly as if he were being careful not to touch the several rings of filigree and purled gold on Momodu's fingers. He sat down on the hard chair.

"What have you come to Kabala for?" Momodu asked.

"To learn Kuranko," the white man replied, half-truthfully.

Kuranko Territory

Momodu studied the pallid and bewildered face of the stranger.

"I am Mandingo," he said quietly, "but I speak Kuranko. Kuranko, Susu, Fula, Temne, Krio . . ."

Momodu paused again and looked steadily at the white man. *"I toge kama?"* he asked abruptly.

"I don't speak any yet."

"I toge kama? What—is—your—name?"

"Michael Jackson."

"Malaika?"

"No, Michael."

"Malaika. That means angel."

"No, *Michael.*"

"Yes," Momodu said calmly. "Only, we say Malaika. It's Arabic. It means angel. So, your name is Michael? *I toge le* Michael, *yo?*"

"Yes."

"And you have come to Kabala to learn Kuranko?"

"Yes."

"I kusan Krio kan fo la?"

A look of confusion passed over Michael's face.

"Do you speak Krio?"

"No."

"I bonne mi? Where do you come from?"

Michael found himself reacting to Momodu's interrogation with half-truths and evasions. "From England," he said.

"Ah," Momodu breathed, as if something had been confirmed.

The street was deserted now except for a lone pariah dog that drifted panting up the hill in the stony glare of the sun. People were sprawled asleep on mats and chairs in the shade of porches.

"Well," Michael said, "I must be getting back to the guest house. My wife will be waiting."

He edged forward on the chair, and his shirt, damp with sweat, clung to his back.

Momodu clasped him by the shoulder and stopped him from standing up. "I may be able to help you," he said.

I would be happy to . . ." Michael began, unsure of what he really wanted to say.

"There is a young school teacher . . . Mr. Marah. He is Kuranko. I could arrange for you to meet him. He could teach you Kuranko. You couldn't find a better man."

"Fine," Michael said, only half listening to Momodu. He was trying to wrap up the onions again.

"*I wa ta, in ni i la muse kondon,*" Momodu said, as Michael prepared to go. "If you're going, give your wife my greetings."

"Yes, yes I will."

"Say '*n'sa a l ke,*' I will greet her," Momodu urged as Michael moved out into the glare of the open street. "You must speak Kuranko now, only Kuranko. *N si tere yan, yo!* I will meet you here later, all right?"

Indeed they did meet later, when Michael made the predicted fourth trip to the market, this time for bananas and oranges.

"*Tana ma tele,*" Momodu called.

"Ta-na ma telly," Michael essayed.

"Good, good. That is good. *I la musi, e nyo?* Is your wife there?"

"Yes," Michael replied, rather nonplussed.

"Then you should say, '*tana wo sa nyo,*'" Momodu instructed, pressing him to sit down. "There is no hurry," he said. "Why are you in a hurry?"

Momodu began to explain how his son, who had been in America, was due home sometime that month. "But," said Momodu gravely, "until he reaches Kabala, I am unable to pay school fees for my youngest boy. It's embarrassing for me to have to tell you all this, but I can see you are a sympathetic chap. I worked for the British for many years. Did I tell you that? No, I didn't, did I? Yes, for fifteen years . . . as an interpreter. But times are hard for us now. You understand? Very hard. Without school fees my boy won't be able to continue his education. And I don't have to tell an Englishman about the value of an education, do I? So I'm asking you . . . I can see you are a sympathetic person . . . I'm asking you to help lift this burden from my mind. A gentleman's agreement, you understand . . . just between the two of us . . . a small loan to help pay my boy's school fees. Forty leones. A loan mind you! Just until my son comes back from America."

Michael was sure he was being conned, but he drew out his wallet, peeled off twenty red Le.2 notes, and handed them to Momodu.

Momodu was rather taken aback. He looked at Michael suspiciously, as if trying to fathom whether the young man was gullible or generous.

"*Ko baraka baraka,*" he said in a congratulatory tone, and pumped Michael's hand. "Come back here this evening and we will go together to Mr. Marah's house."

At dusk they made their way along the path behind the police barracks, Momodu urging Michael to repeat after him a Kuranko phrase of greeting. "Mr. Marah will be impressed if you greet him in Kuranko. Now, say '*in wura.*'"

"In woora."

"*In wura, in wura,*" Momodu corrected, as he walked ahead hitting at the air with his cane.

To their right was an open field, recently burned over. Along the left side of the lane were six houses, the first of which was a faded sienna color. Its sagging corrugated iron roof was streaked with rust.

A small girl was drawing water from a well in front of the house, hauling up a battered kerosene tin with a frayed rope. In the light of the setting sun her skin glowed like dark honey.

Momodu levered himself up onto the porch with his cane. The effort left him breathless. "Noah . . . Noah," he called hoarsely, "are you there?"

Michael waited on the path. The girl balanced the tin of water on her head and carried it round to the back of the house. Smoke drifted up against a tall coconut palm that towered over the yard.

Noah was roused from sleep by his wife, Yebu. "There's a white man to see you," she said.

Momodu called again, "Noah!"

Two children appeared in the doorway and leaned against the jambs, licking grains of rice from their fingers stained with palm oil.

Noah came to the door and greeted the familiar figure who stood on the porch leaning on his cane.

"*M'fa, i kende?*" Noah asked.

"*I kende iko konke,*" Momodu replied. Turning to Michael, he beckoned him up on to the porch. "I told Noah here that I am as well as hunger," Momodu explained. "You see, hunger never wearies in trying to make our lives miserable."

Michael shook Noah's hand. "Hi," he said, forgetting to use the Kuranko.

Noah invited the visitors to come inside to share his evening meal. They sat in the shadowy parlor, observed by several curious children. A piebald dog with a festering ear flopped at their feet on the broken linoleum. It looked up balefully, its eyelids heavy with fatigue, then dozed off to sleep with three flies busily reconnoitering its running sore.

Yebu set down a large enamel platter and two covered basins on a table in front of the men, and called to one of the children to bring the white man a spoon. The girl with honey-colored skin, whose name was Musukura, handed Michael an aluminum spoon and a piece of taffeta to wipe it on.

Just then an old woman mounted the back steps, hesitated for a moment in the doorway, and entered the room. She took a seat opposite the men and greeted Momodu in Krio.

Noah carefully spilled rice from the large basin onto the platter, and dribbled over it groundnut soup from the small basin. The soup seeped through the mass of congested grains, and Momodu and Noah began rolling up balls of rice, which they skillfully slipped into their mouths. Michael spooned up small portions, eating without appetite.

"Bring water!" Noah called.

Musukura brought a chipped enamel mug, brimful of water, but Michael declined to drink any.

"Well," said Monodu. "Tell Noah what you have come to Kabala for."

Michael was aware of the old woman's gaze upon him.

"I would like to make a study of Kuranko customs and learn to speak Kuranko," he said. He felt absurd. "My wife and I plan to settle here for a year. . . . I was hoping . . ."

"Noah!" Momodu suddenly declared, "you are the very man to help him. I told him this morning there is no one in Kabala more suitable. What do you say?"

Noah did not want to commit himself without knowing more about the stranger whom Momodu had brought to his house and from whom in all likelihood he had already extracted a goodly dash. At the same time he did not want to appear unhelpful.

"I think the first thing is to find a house," Noah said. Then, addressing Momodu in Krio, he asked if Pa Kamara's new house at One-Mile had been rented yet.

"Hm'm," Momodu answered, shaking his head.

"There is a house," Noah resumed in English. "Maybe we could go and see it tomorrow. I'm teaching at the District Council school, but we could go in the evening . . . if you wanted."

"Yes, indeed. Thanks."

"Then things will be easier," Noah finished.

Michael agreed, remembering the gauntlet of bureaucratic obstacles that he and Pauline had run into since arriving in Sierra Leone five weeks before: schedules, forms, clearance slips, check lists, invoices, certificates, and approvals. He had spent three exasperating days at

Cline Town, trudging back and forth among various Port Authority offices, trying to get possession of his Land Rover, which had been shipped from Tilbury on the *Lobito Palm*. In the heat and dust of water-front sheds he doled out money for this or that certificate, or signed his name innumerable times on multiple copies of forms, permits, and declarations, until he had accumulated a filing cabinet full of bills of lading, dock receipts, waybills, receipts for freight charges and lighterage, consignment notes, import duty exemption authorizations, customs clearance certificates, set surcharge forms, insurance schedules, shipping notes, delivery and condition reports, certificates of importation and release. In Freetown he had passed entire mornings lining up outside some ministry with scores of others whose stoical or woebegone faces suggested that they had become habituated to the hopelessness of their petitions. At the bank he vied for the attention of counter-girls whose slatternly manners nullified the effect of their immaculate coiffures and manicured fingernails. He would arrive at some dismal office at the end of a lane that reeked of urine, and find everyone slumped over their desks, asleep. He became accustomed to being told by drowsy clerks that he needed to fill in form F3/515B, or that he had come to the wrong counter, or that the office that supplied the said form F3/515B was closed on Wednesday afternoons. Letters of affiliation to the university, residence permits, vehicle registration and insurance, a Sierra Leone driver's license . . . all took weeks to complete. Then one day, on the spur of the moment, he and Pauline had stowed their belongings into the Land Rover and headed north, vaguely in the direction of Kabala, whose name had captured their imaginations. Open vistas of grassland under cloudless skies lifted their spirits. They even felt a little nostalgic for the City Hotel in Freetown, though they had been kept awake night after night by the shouts of taxi drivers in the street and the din of a downstairs bar. Tatty vultures used to alight in the backyard of the hotel and hobble about like armless Oxbridge dons. They spoke of the prospect of Kabala and of a people called Kuranko, whom Michael had first heard of only two weeks before.

Now he was following Momodu along the path from Noah's house, with Musukura walking ahead with a lantern to light their way. The night air was cool, and Michael looked up at the star-filled vault of the sky with sudden exhilaration.

Over in Yogomaia the rapid improvisations of a group of drummers made an overture to a dry season festivity, and in the market people were milling around in shashlik sellers and cake stalls.

"Awa," said Momodu, "ma sogoma yo. Goodnight. I am going home now."

"Goodnight."

Michael bought two bottles of cola and wandered back to the guest house through boisterous streets.

As soon as the visitors had gone, Noah told his mother what they had talked about.

"Be careful," Aisetta said. "Don't let your life get mixed up with these white men. Remember what your father used to say? *Bamba ka ta, n'kul la sisi sa m'bolo:* the crocodile won't have you in mind if you don't keep chickens. Careful what you say . . ."

"I'll take care," Noah said.

"To mingle your destiny with the white men is like throwing in your lot with a djinn. Do you remember that story I used to tell you and Abdul when you were children? Well, that is it: the djinn may favor you at first, but finally you will have to pay the price of its favors."

✖✖ Chapter Fifteen

"IN 1954, WHEN MY FATHER DIED, I left Firawa and came to Kabala to go to school . . . the same school I'm teaching at now."

Beyond the house, weaverbirds flocked around the palms in the dying light, squabbling for access to their upside-down nests. Palm-wine vendors slipped past along the road, casting furtive glances at the new house where, every evening, the white man sat on the porch talking to the teacher.

"Then you must have been quite old when you began school," Michael said.

"Yes. My father had not wanted me to go away to school at all. He wanted to keep me with him in Firawa. He was very attached to me. I slept with him, moved about with him . . . in fact, I hardly saw anything of my mother. Until my father died . . ."

Noah hesitated. The weaverbirds filled the sky with their clamor.

"It was a hard time, a real struggle . . . in Kabala. I stayed with my half-sisters, Sira and Mantene. They were married to the town chief. Remember, we went to his house yesterday. Then . . . in 1958 I think it was, I sat the selective entrance exam, and passed, and went down to

Magburaka Boy's Secondary School the following year. But I left after the fourth form. Hardship stopped me going on."

"You mean you couldn't afford the fees?"

"No, it wasn't that. There were other difficulties. Family problems. I'll tell you about it some other time."

"How did you manage to become so proficient in English then? If your schooling was cut short like that."

"Well, I read a lot. Books I picked up here and there. At one time I got interested in law and used to borrow books from the district officer. In fact, it was D.O. Macdonald who got me my first job."

"Teaching?"

"No, before that. After I left secondary school I came back to Kabala. Times were terribly hard and I had nothing but my name. Then, one night I went to Lansana Kamara's shop to buy some kerosene. Wing Commander Macdonald was there, drinking on his own, and he asked after me and wanted to know if I was interested in a job. I said of course I was, but there were no jobs. Then he told me to find him in his office in the morning. I went to see him, just as he'd asked, and he offered me a job as court clerk in the Native Administration at Musaia in the Fula Saba Dembelia chiefdom. I wanted to accept his offer at once but was embarrassed by my lack of money. I did not even have the truck fare to Musaia. But Wing Commander Macdonald must have realized my difficulty. He lent me ten pounds there and then. I bought a plate, spoon, toothbrush, a bar of soap, and a suitcase, and went to Musaia that very afternoon."

"How long were you there?"

"Four years. Then I came back to Kabala and took up a teaching appointment in the District Council school. I've been here since 1964."

At that moment Musukura walked out of the dusk, bearing a tray of rice and soup that Aisetta had sent, as she did every evening, for the newcomers at One-Mile.

"My grandmother says to greet you and your wife," Musukura said shyly, and set down the tray on a rickety table in front of Michael. Then she went into the house to find Pauline.

As Noah tipped the rice out onto the tray, Michael asked, "How much do you earn, Noah, teaching?"

Noah spread out the congested rice on the tray.

"I get thirty seven leones a month—not much more than a road worker. Out of that, thirty leones goes on our rice alone. You can see why no one goes teaching!"

Michael had a vision of weary men with wheelbarrows, pickaxes, and shovels, filling in potholes on the Makeni road with soil that would be washed away with the first rains.

"How would you feel about quitting teaching and working with me as a research assistant? Helping me as you have already, especially with the language, but full time." He paused. "I could pay you sixty leones a month. . . ." He broke off, embarrassed by the mention of money, by the way it determined an inequality between them. As if to forestall Noah's negative response, he stumbled on, "But of course, Pauline and I will only be here for a year and you . . ."

Noah had expected the proposal and knew exactly how he would answer it. But he did not want to seem rash or avaricious.

"Give me a day or two to think about it, Mike," he said.

Later, to his mother, he justified his decision.

"It's not just the money. I'm thinking of the children. Na and Kaima are only small now, but if I stay here they will grow up cut off from Kuranko. Father always urged us never to lose touch with Barawa, but we have. Now there's a chance for me to spend more time in Firawa, and to take the children there too. Yebu can be with you here."

"And will you all go to Firawa to live? Pauline too?"

"I will go with Mike, at first. We'll stay a few weeks, then come back. Pauline has her own studies and says she will be all right on her own at One-Mile. Anyway, it would be too hard for her, traveling all the way to Firawa on foot."

"Why?"

"She is pregnant."

"Eh!" Aisetta sat forward and threw up her hands. "Then you must work for him, Noah. *Hun!* All this talk! And when you go to Firawa, Yebu and I will take care of Pauline. You assure her that she will be all right."

That same night, Michael wrote in his journal: "Now that Noah has decided to throw in his lot with me it seems certain that, despite all my misgivings, I am actually going to *do* anthropology. We're trekking to Firawa, Noah's hometown, this Friday—my initiation into 'the field.' "

Daunted by the prospect, he stopped writing. Only a few weeks ago he had thought that his research would come to nothing, that he would end up back in Freetown at the City Hotel, drinking Guiness in a dingy corner bar with Krio clerks and derelict coasters—a cheap imitation of a Graham Greene character.

What worried him most was the idea of *interrogating* people, addressing absolute strangers in a language he could not speak, through an interpreter whose motives were obscure to him. He still could not cast himself happily in the role of ethnographer. Conrad's lines—about curious men who go prying into places where they have no business, and coming out with all kinds of spoil—haunted him. Yet he found himself compelled to pursue his original design—to go into the unknown and see what would become of him.

He resumed writing:

Before Noah and I went to Dankawali last week I had a strange dream which, on reflection, betrays many of my anxieties. I was in a bare room, a bit like one of the classrooms at the D.C. school where Noah taught. Suddenly a corrugated iron door opened into the room and a book was passed through the doorway as if by an invisible hand. For several seconds the book hung in midair, and I made out on its cover in bold type the word ETHNOGRAPHY. I had a definite impression that the book contained only blank pages. Then the door swung open again, and a tremendous presence swept into the room and lifted me up bodily. I was borne aloft, as if in the hands of a giant, and carried out of the room. The pressure of the giant's hold against my chest made it hard for me to breathe. I woke up, afraid.

At Dankawali I got Noah to recount the dream to Fore Kargbo who told me it signified that I would become an important person. The book signified knowledge, the giant was a djinn who wished to help me, flying like a bird was a sign of happiness, being high up was auspicious, and being in a strange place among strange people signaled imminent prosperity. I didn't know whether to take Fore's remarks as sympathetic reassurances or straightforward Kuranko decipherings of common dream images. Maybe both processes are linked. In any event, Fore's remarks *did* reassure me, *and* they led to a fruitful discussion about Kuranko dream interpretation.

I've been thinking a lot about the status of the knowledge I acquire in this way. In one sense, it is merely data, because its value does not depend on my believing it to be true or on making use of it in relating to other people. But, for the Kuranko, that same knowledge has value precisely to the extent that it mediates social relationships and gives intellectual certainty. It is as if the anthropologist denies the *social* value of knowledge in order to bestow upon it a purely *personal* value as data for a research project.I keep wondering, do I want to acquire Kuranko knowledge in order to live among them or in order to further my own purposes which, it goes without saying, are quite alien to theirs even when not actually antithetical? Up to now I have been gathering data. Even my language learning is motivated less by a desire to mix socially than to know intellectually, and Noah has become quite impatient with my attempts to write a grammar when I should be just listening and responding. My favorite phrase has become *a l moi ma di; a gbele* ("It isn't easy to hear; it's hard"). But why should it be like this, when I am not bent on producing academic work and feel downright skeptical about anthropology? Is it because the data that I amass on paper make a mask for the void, keeping alive a sense of self which at home is sustained by the continual presence of familiar words and things? Is it, therefore, that the data help maintain an illusion of a bridge between myself and Kuranko people, while in reality increasing the gap?

When he finished writing he closed the shutters. The night was noiseless except for a solitary insect somewhere in the swamp. Its indolent trilling suggested that it had mistaken for daylight the fluttering light of the kerosene lantern in the window of the house at One-Mile.

In Kabala

Hardly light, cold mist in the town streets,
when the muezzin cries us out—
he not long roused from the bed
of the merchant's wife, his call her husband's
steps on the gravel, banging
of a corrugated iron gate.

No guilt here, and the occasional outburst
for public show always ends
with money passing under a counter;
not even incongrous, and we allow
coldness of January nights
against the heat of noon.

And speaking of trust . . . the tailor's wife
smuggles her daughter to the bed
of the prayer-caller one night in ten;
he having made bargains with the merchant
for cut-price cloth, ribbons
and a cheap bridal dress.

🌊 Chapter Sixteen

A LATERITE ROAD from Kabala—often no more than a walking track with impenetrable brakes of elephant grass on either side—twists and turns with every gully, boulder, and tree twenty-six miles to the Seli River.

Just as topography has determined the course of the road, so the road in its turn has determined the layout of villages. Houses are aligned along it, no longer enclosing circular courtyards; some are rec-

tangular rather than round, roofed with galvanized iron sheets instead
of thatched; and occasionally a concrete step or cement façade suggests
that someone has been away and worked in the diamond districts for
more than a pittance.

Whenever a vehicle passes, mangy dogs and flustered hens scatter
from under its wheels, and as dust billows up against the houses, villagers who have been waiting days to hitch a ride to Kabala fly gesticu-
lating from porches to flag down an anonymous truck, which almost
never stops.

Michael's Land Rover was already crammed full of people when
he left Kabala. Most were Barawa people who had heard of "Noah's
white man" and had begged a lift to the Seli, together with seed rice,
kerosene, and other provisions they had bought in Kabala after selling
rice at the market.

In the packed and overladen Land Rover the heat was stifling.
Michael's head pounded from the effort of negotiating the tortuous
track—down eroded gullies, across log bridges, over scabrous granite
outcrops, against an unflagging background noise of laughter and expos-
tulation.

"What's that?" Michael shouted.

"They say you should call your Land Rover 'Apollo,'" Noah said.
He'd noticed the word painted on truck cabs up and down the
country.

"Why 'Apollo'?"

"Some people think the Americans have gone to the moon."

"They have!"

"Yes, but they don't see how they could. The moon's so small.
How could you get out of a rocket and walk on it?"

"It only looks small because we're so far away from it."

"I know, but they don't see that. And they say that the American
rockets have disturbed the moon and sent showers of dust spilling
down on us. Specks get in people's eyes. That's why there's so much
conjunctivitis. They call it Apollo."

"You mean the eye disease?"

"Yes."

The conquest of space, he mused, reduced to the cause of an eye
disease! So much for that particular venture.

"Ouch!" The Land Rover lunged and grated through a deep hole
in the road.

"What's everyone talking about now?" he shouted at Noah.

99

"A schoolgirl—called Elizabeth," Noah shouted back with difficulty. "She was given into the care of her uncle." Noah turned round and fired a question at a wiry, taciturn man in the back of the Land Rover: *"I be an berin, nye?"*

"Ohun!" the man responded emphatically.

"Yes, her uncle," Noah resumed, "in Kabala . . . so she could go to school. But she's got two suitors: a Mandingo trader from Liberia and a clerk in the D.O.'s office in Kabala who already has a wife and is notorious for the numer of sweethearts he has up and down the country. The Liberian has heard about his rival and has written to the girl's father accusing him of prejudice, saying he tied kola for her, that his good name is being spoiled, that he's been treated unfairly. The father has sent the letter to the uncle and asked him to deal with the matter. Now the uncle is asking us what he should do."

The talk went on, boisterous and unabated, but Michael showed no further interest in it and concentrated his attention on the road.

A straight stretch opened up. He accelerated, and whirling dust enshrouded a woman on the roadside who hastily stepped back into the grass, startled and angry, steadying the basin on her head with an upstretched hand.

He felt a tap on his shoulder, and glanced back at one of his passengers, who was gesturing furiously with a loose-wristed flapping motion.

"A to, a to," he called, patting the air.

"We must stop," Noah said, "it's his sister."

"Christ! We can't get anyone else in."

"It's his sister," Noah repeated, but saw from the agonized expression on Michael's face that he would have to explain further.

"In Kuranko you have to be very respectful of your sisters. More than of your wife, in fact. We'll have to stop and pick her up, even if the man has to walk."

This ethnographical snippet seemed to appease the anthropologist, who jotted something down in his notebook as the woman clambered aboard. Dust filled the vehicle and a trussed-up rooster squawked lamentably as it was trodden on.

At the Seli river-crossing Michael ran the Land Rover into the shade of two immense cotton trees, alongside some Bailey Bridge sections that lay half-concealed in the grass.

"Is a bridge going to be built here?"

"It was," said Noah ruefully. "When S.B. was in parliament . . ."

"That's your brother, Sewa?"

"My elder brother. When he was an M.P. in the Margai govern-ment after independence he brought a lot of changes to the north . . . dispensaries, schools, roads, the generator in Kabala. The bridge would have linked Kabala and Barawa. Our people even brushed a road from Firawa to the riverside here. But it's all been overgrown now, you'll see."

"You mean S.B.'s no longer in government?"

"His party lost at the polls in 1967."

"And the bridge?"

"It's being taken away bit by bit to some other part of the country."

Everyone was organizing their belongings for the trek to Firawa: knotting cloth bundles, binding suitcases that had broken latches, twist-ing kerchiefs into pads to cushion the headloads. Michael was about to take up his pack when the young man who had forced him to stop and pick up his sister hurried forward and by gesture made him understand that he should not carry any load. He relinquished it gladly, but was guilty that he had resented his extra passenger.

After crossing the Seli on a bridge of logs lashed with lianas, they made their way to Yirafilaia Village and thence through forest to the first plateau of Barawa. It was nearly noon and the air smelled of dry grass. Flies buzzed lazily and momentarily, and in the distance came the *drrrt, drrrt, drrrt* of a woodpecker.

In farm clearings, harvested rice was piled high in golden wheels. Women, mending large circular fishing nets, glanced up at the white man and called "Heh, *tubabune!*" in tones of surprise and amusement. Knowing that he was being addressed, Michael tried out his few stock phrases of Kuranko greeting, only to have the women break into laugh-ter and hide their faces behind their hands.

The travelers pressed on across the sun-hardened earth of the pla-teau, occasionally exchanging pieces of gossip or stopping to adjust their headloads. But mainly they were silent, mindful only of the steady rhythm of the walking and the balance of their loads.

The anthropologist did not fall easily into the pace of the others. He was suspicious that people were talking about him, and the very mention of the word *tubabu* became a vague irritant. He found himself seeking Noah's assurance.

"They weren't talking about you," Noah said, "they were telling me about an Englishman who came here last year collecting butterflies . . ."

"A lepidopterist?" Michael interrupted. "When I was a kid I thought it was leper doctoress!"

"They wanted to know why he killed butterflies," Noah went on. "I wasn't sure what to say."

"They pin them in boxes and name them—after themselves if it's a new species—and file them in museums."

"Yes," returned Noah, "I know that, but it's hard to explain it to them." He hesitated. "They said he was looking for blue ones especially; blue like your eyes, they said."

Senekonke appeared, though it seemed to recede rather than loom larger as they approached it.

"Let's stop here," Noah called.

Michael gulped lukewarm boiled water from an old army flask, flopped back on a bed of dry leaves, and shut his eyes. Cicadas pulsated and jangled like a million miniature bracelets and anklets.

Noah sat apart, studying the far elephantine tor, remembering the times he had trekked across the same worn path with his father or been borne along on Yeli Pore's shoulders, the times they had rested from the noonday sun under the same *lenke* trees that now shaded the person whom everyone called his white man.

The anthropologist opened his eyes. Gaunt pods dangled like wizened tongues from the branches above him.

"What's the name of this tree, Noah?" he asked.

"We call it lenke. The seedpods explode in the dry season and scatter seeds over the ground. But none fall directly beneath the tree. That's why we say the lenke does not benefit its own kind."

While the anthropologist wrote down the Kuranko adage in his notebook, Noah fell back into reverie, and for a few moments the idyllic ambiance of his childhood returned to him and the prospect of Firawa was like sunlight when the shadow of a cloud passes suddenly from the face of a hill.

It was mid-afternoon when they crossed the expanse of granite that marks the northern entry to Firawa. Most of the village was asleep or resting, but praise-singers soon hurried out with xylophones and flattery to meet Noah and usher him to the chief's house.

Noah straightened his back and smiled in acknowledgment at

Yeli Pore, agile and spirited as ever, hammering away at the xylophone keys and calling with exhilaration the names of Noah's fathers.

"Nomor, nomor," the praise-singers cried, as Noah distributed coins among them. "Nomor, Marah, nomor!

Yeli Pore sang the song that had been Tina Kome's favorite: "Ayy-yeee, you will know a person best; ah, you will know, you will know a person best . . . in his own house, his own, in his own house . . ."

As the visitors crossed the Woldugu courtyard, Feremata and Tilkolo, two of Abul's wives, hastened up to them and bowed low, clasping Noah's hands. "*In sene, in sene*, welcome, welcome," they enthused, and clapped as the company pressed on into the heart of the town.

Michael hung back at the edge of the crowd and rejoined Noah only when the elders had been summoned by drum to Tala Sewa's house and chairs had been brought out onto the porch.

He felt awkward under the watchful gaze of Tala Sewa and his councilors, and tried to appear as if he understood and appreciated the drift of the ensuing discourse.

Finally Noah turned to him. "I've explained that you are an old pen friend of mine, that you've come to visit me here and see the place where I spent my childhood. I thought this would be the best way to explain your presence, at least for the time being. Chief Sewa says you are welcome and that you will come to no harm while you are among them. He gives you these gifts." Noah nodded toward a winnowing tray piled high with rice, and two russet hens, which a young man held compressed between his knees. "They are the customary way we give hospitality in Kuranko."

Michael looked at the elders, whose perplexity seemed greater than his own. "Ko baraka baraka," he essayed, "thank you."

Delight transformed the faces around him. *"Inwali inwali,"* the man exclaimed, "he speaks a bit of Kuranko!"

It was decided that the stranger should be lodged in the sergeant's house. This was the grandest house in Firawa, built of concrete with a galvanized iron roof, a dozen rooms, and furnished European-style with tables, chairs, and beds. It belonged to a police sergeant who hailed from Firawa but lived and worked in the diamond districts of Kono. The anthropologist did not realize it, but among the freight he had reluctantly carried from Kabala to the Seli river-crossing were two bags of cement that the sergeant's family had been trying to get to Firawa for several months. When the elders impressed upon their guest that a favor done to one is ipso facto done to many, and therefore deserving of appreciation, he failed to understand the context of the remark and thought he had been given a room in the sergeant's house because he was a European or because the chief wanted to keep an eye on him. Noah was too weary to disabuse him.

Feremata prepared food for "Noah's stranger" and sent her younger co-wife down to the sergeant's house with it. Mantene found the anthropologist sitting on the steps, surrounded by children. The older ones had overcome their initial trepidation and were propelling their terror-stricken younger siblings toward the tubabu as a way of vaunting their own superior pluck. Mantene shooed them away, and they withdrew to the end of the porch from where they watched, wide-eyed, as the tubabu ate his rice with a spoon.

When he had finished he repaired to his room and shut the door, unsure of whether it gave offense but exhausted enough by the day's commotion not to care. On the bedside table stood a vase of plastic flowers and a packet of mosquito coils that Abdul had told Mantene to put there.

He sat on the edge of the bed, scribbling in his notebook and glancing up from time to time as the children scuffled and tittered outside the door until a stern voice dispersed them. He threw the notebook aside and lay down under the torn mosquito net, studying the map of rain stains on the cardboard ceiling. The iron roof ticked and pinged in the heat.

He waited for darkness, then left the house and found the path out of the village. On the granite outcrop he had crossed earlier in the day he stretched out and gazed up at the stars. From the village came the sound of a child coughing, then silence. Already the night mist was invading the valley, but the stone retained the sun's warmth. He heard the quicksilver singing of insects, and far off, like wind chimes, a vague tinkling swept through the cobalt reaches of the night sky.

On the porch of Tala Sewa's house, the elders were interrogating Noah.

"Where has he gone?"

"White men like to be alone. They like to be quiet."

"In the bush! At night!"

"Mnhn, sometimes it is the only quiet place, he says."

"Perhaps he's gone to shit."

"Perhaps."

"What does he do when he's on his own?"

"He writes things down. Things he has seen or heard. It's his way of learning the language."

"Why does he want to learn the language?"

"So he can live among us . . ."

"Well said!"

"And understand our customs . . ."

"Well said!"

"Do you know of any white man who has ever learned our language, who has come to live here in Firawa, who eats our food, who will eat with us?"

"Well said, Noah. Nomor!"

"Do you know any white man who has come to Firawa on his own, without carriers, without his own food, just to live with us?"

"Marah, nomor!"

"Do you see?"

"All right, Noah. What harm can come of it. Perhaps your white man will help bring us the bridge."

"The bridge was there, ready to be built," said another, "but as soon as we made the road to the river they came and took it away. The pangolin works but the porcupine profits!"

"It was our government that took away the bridge, not the white men," said Noah.

"Ha!" rejoined the other, for whom there was no distinction. "When you dig a hole to make a place to live, Noah, make sure that someone else doesn't steal it from under *your* nose!"

⚜ Chapter Seventeen

FIRAWA WAS A MAZE of dirt lanes connecting circular yards called *luiye* around which houses were built so that their front porches always opened onto public space.

Noah explained: "The front of the house is the men's area; the back belongs to the women. That's why seven days after birth a baby boy is brought out of the house through the front door. A baby girl is always brought out the back door, into the *sundu kunye ma*."

"The backyard?"

"Yes, where the women cook . . . and where rubbish is put."

Gaps between houses were usually sealed by a fence of elephant-grass canes, and male and female areas of the house were thus clearly divided from each other.

With Noah's help, the anthropologist was trying to make a map of the village, and they were strolling from one luiye to another identifying the clans associated with each one.

"Who owns this luiye?"

"This is also Woldugu," Noah said, referring to his own lineage. "Namisa Bolo founded it, I think. That's where he's buried, over there." He indicated a forked branch standing in the middle of the luiye, beyond which was a rectangle of laterite gravel, edged with upturned bottles.

"Is it only the founder who is buried in the luiye?"

"Usually, yes. Other burials are on the edge of the town, or behind the houses."

An old man, sitting in the shadows of a porch, had been eyeing them ever since they entered the luiye.

"Noah!" he shouted, when it became clear that Noah had failed to see him.

"M'fa inwali inwali," Noah hastened, as he tried to identify who had called his name. "Ah, Fa Bala! *Tana ma si?"*

"Yes, I slept all right. Did you sleep well?"

"Tana wo ma si," Noah answered.

"What are you doing, Noah?" the elder asked after a pause. "You and your young white man."

"N'fen fen ma" ("Nothing").

"Nothing!" exclaimed the bemused elder. He turned to Michael. *"Al tembi yan"* ("Come over here").

"He wants you to go over to him," Noah said.

Michael approached the porch, which had recently been resurfaced with gray mud. From the shadows under the thatch the old man scrutinized the stranger's face as if trying to guess something from his expression. The old man's eyes were the color of mahogany, yet his gaze was fervent and Michael smiled in an awkward attempt to meet it.

"I tala minto?" ("Where are you going?") the elder asked abruptly.

Relieved to have understood the question, Michael answered at once: *"Mi tala sue ro"* ("I'm going about the town").

"Huh? You're going about in the town?"

Michael was perplexed; should he have said something else? Noah called out from the middle of the luiye, answering for him. "He's come to visit me and learn Kuranko. We're old friends, but he's never been in our country before. I have brought him here so he can see the town where I was brought up."

"Yes, they've told me as much," the old man grinned, assenting to Noah's words in a spirit of good humor rather than serious acceptance. Then he dug into the triangular breast pocket of his gown and took out a red kola nut, which he broke apart with his thumbnail. He handed a cotyledon to Michael.

"Woli a sa wore la," he said.

"He says that is your kola," Noah called. "Say *'ko baraka.'*"

Michael did as he was told, and the old man smiled: *"Wo ara gbe."* Then shaking his head at Noah, who had remained standing in the middle of the luiye, he added, "You and your white man, Noah."

Michael and Noah crossed the luiye and picked their way along a dusty path between straggly cotton bushes and a stand of withered cornstalks.

In the next luiye a house, gutted by fire some weeks ago, had been pulled down. Apart from the roof poles, nothing much was salvageable, and work had already begun on a new mud-brick rectangular house. Hundreds of mud bricks were stacked around the site, and bundles of poles, stripped of bark, rested against the thatched roof of an adjoining house.

"Why don't people build round houses any more?"

"I don't know, Mike. We'll have to ask."

Michael was now used to this way in which Noah prefaced any remark that was opinion and not common knowledge.

"Perhaps," Noah continued, "it's because people want to roof their houses with iron sheets sooner or later. You can't fit iron sheets to a round roof."

The anthropologist thought that tin roofs were ugly, and a betrayal of tradition, a degeneracy, and Noah found himself having to remind his friend that practicality was more important than appearance.

"It's hard to maintain a thatched house, Mike. You have to cut and carry thatch every year, and the rain gets through even then."

"But what about the heat that comes off roofing iron? My room at the sergeant's house is like an oven during the day."

107

"I suppose people get used to that," Noah said. Then, realizing it was nearly midday, he proposed they go back to Abdul's to see if a meal was ready. But the anthropologist was not hungry.

"I want to take a few photos, Noah. You go; I'll see you back there soon."

At that hour an indolent atmosphere hung over the village, and the heat haze was intense. Many of the men were out on farms, attending to the final harvest and grain storage. The older children were either with their fathers or at the swimming hole. (Michael had seen the boys yesterday, slithering down a greasy slope into a murky river hole and clambering out, hands clutched over their genitals as they watched the white man passing.) And the village women, having prepared the morning meal, were sleeping or sitting about, chatting in the cooking yards.

But although the village seemed almost deserted, the anthropologist succeeded in taking a few photos: a man weaving, another man making a mat, a woman winnowing (her child asleep on her back). And one of Chief Sewa's jelibas, who spent much of his spare time weaving, showed the anthropologist how he prepared a shuttle by winding cotton thread onto it from a bobbin that his wife had spun. Michael admired the dexterity with which the couple accomplished their task, and found himself envying their companionship.

On his way back to Abdul's house he passed the half-constructed courthouse where Chief Sewa and some elders were discussing a young man's petition to make a cassava garden on a patch of village land to which another man had made a claim, yet still lay fallow a year later.

The men greeted the white man: "Tubabu, inwali!" He cheerfully called an answer: "Inwali yo!"—unaware that the town chief was at that very moment saying that they should call the white man Sewa because of the ingratiating smile he wore on his face all the time.

"Shall we eat?" Noah asked, as Michael climbed the concrete steps to Abdul's porch.

The heat was oppressive, and Michael could still not arouse any interest in food. But he dipped his fingers into the parboiled rice, steeping it in the groundnut and chili soup, and told himself that he would have to eat something and that he had, after all, resolved to eat as the locals did.

"Did you get any photos?" Noah asked.

"Some. But I feel a bit awkward pointing a camera at people. What do you think?"

"I don't know Mike, but I think it's all right. Unlike down the line.

People in Freetown say that the Peace Corps workers take photos of village women, you know, with bare breasts, and then send the photos back to America to show how backward we are. That way they can keep their own black people in poverty."

Michael did not know what to say to this, and simply asked, "But what about here, in Firawa?"

"I think it's all right. Besides, I've told them that one day you'll come back and bring the photos with you for them to see."

That afternoon Michael managed his first daytime sleep since coming to Firawa, an accomplishment he liked to regard as a sign of his adaptation to the place.

When he wandered back to Abdul's in the evening, women were filing up the path that entered the village from the east. Michael felt refreshed by his sleep and the coolness of the evening, and he stood awhile under a mango tree at the edge of the luiye, watching the women. As they drifted by him, not glancing aside at all, their eyes slightly lowered as if for concentration in balancing the heavy pails of water on their heads, moving along with languid strokes of their hands, he felt as though he were witnessing a privileged and idyllic event that would never occur again. One woman, whose litheness and comeliness seemed miraculous, approached and passed him, and he saw to his amazement that she was elderly. Suddenly he felt clumsy and intrusive, and as quickly as the moment of grace had come, it passed away, and he was overcome by an unfathomable sadness.

At Abdul's he waited impatiently for Noah. Along the porch, Kakumba was bathing her four-month-old daughter in a basin of cold water. The infant's face was screwed up, and she was crying in protest as her mother deftly splashed water over her back and belly, then with supple fingers cleaned behind her ears, around her eyes, and between her legs.

When Noah appeared, Michael grabbed his attention before anyone else could do so. "Where do the women fetch the water?"

Noah was preoccupied by a dispute in which he had become embroiled that afternoon: A young man called Benko had demanded money "as bridewealth payment" from his elder brother's daughter's husband, saying that if he did not get the money he would "spoil the marriage." Noah considered that ample bridewealth had already been paid and that the demand was unreasonable; he had decided to threaten Benko's elder brother's son's marriage—to Noah's clan sister—as a way of making Benko come to his senses. But when Noah saw

Michael's impatience, he told Saran Konkuron, against whom Benko had made the claim, to come back and see him in the morning.

As Saran Konkuron dolefully sauntered off, the anthropologist, ignorant of what had just happened, again pressed Noah to answer his question. "Is that a place banned to men?"

"Just as I told you, Mike," Noah began wearily. "The women fetch water and do laundry at one part of the stream, and men are not allowed to go there, ever. And the same with the men's part of the stream; it's out of bounds for women."

"What if a man went to the women's part of the stream without realizing what he was doing?"

"If it was an accident?"

"Yes. How do you say that in Kuranko?"

"Well, in a court case you could plead *'ma l wuli a ma,* I didn't start on it,' that's to say 'I didn't mean to do it,' or *'ma l wuli a ma, a sa ra m'bolo ma le,* it lay on my hand.' In other words, it just happened without my intending it." Saran Konkuron, who had in fact stayed within earshot of the house, sidled back to the porch and asked Noah if they were talking about his case.

"No," said Noah, "he's asking me what would happen if a man went to the women's part of the stream."

A look of anguish came over the young man's face. "Ah," he said gravely, looking at the anthropologist as if this stranger were bent on self-destruction, "he would get elephantiasis; his testicles would swell up. He would die."

Noah interpreted, and Michael, apparently impressed by the gravity of this offense, asked what other things were prohibited to men.

"A woman's room, her trinket box, and domestic gear . . . a house where a woman is giving birth, and the girls' initiations, of course." Then, seeing Michael begin to write down his remarks, Noah turned to Saran Konkuron and asked: "What makes men separate from women?"

Saran Konkuron imagined the question had come from the white man. "*Sumafannu!*" he answered.

"Seed things, secret things, the secret societies," Noah translated, speaking slowly so that the anthropologist could write it down.

The Coleman lamp that Noah had brought out to the porch gave little light, and Michael found it hard to distinguish between his ball-point pen and its shadow.

"How?" he asked. And again Noah put the question to Saran Konkuron.

"Because men never see the secret things that women own."

"What else?" Noah asked. He realized that it was his schoolroom voice.

"Only the different ways that Allah made us," Saran Konkuron replied.

Noah translated, and the anthropologist's pen moved within the blurred shadows of the page.

"Is it true that men are braver than women?" he asked, without looking up.

Saran Konkuron enthusiastically recited examples: "If there is a fire, women will shout and cry, but the men will fight the flames. And if a snake is found on a farm, the women will cry out and run away, while the men attack it. And in marriage it is always the woman who is married to the man. It's the man who pays the bridewealth, and the woman who is given to him."

"Could a woman ever be brave, like a man?"

Noah ventured a reply. "If a woman is seen working very hard, men might say of her 'ke l tinyane ke la,' meaning 'she is spoiling maleness.' On the other hand, if women see an unmarried man cooking they'll say 'He'll never get a wife,' because they expect men to behave like men, and women to behave like women."

Saran Konkuron, who had been hoping his problem might still be discussed, was baffled by this return to English and walked away into the night. Kakumba had finished bathing her infant, who was fast asleep on her hip. She had listened closely to what the men had been saying, though pretending indifference and keeping a discreet distance. Now, as Noah jokingly enjoined her to take part in the conversation, she giggled with embarrassment but immediately stepped closer to where the men were sitting, though remaining outside the penumbra of the lamp.

"Do women ever try to become like men, and get that bravery?" Noah asked.

It was the kind of familiar question no man would ordinarily put to a woman, but Noah exploited the joking relationship he had with Kakumba, and knew that she in turn would avail herself of the latitude it allowed.

"No," she smiled.

"Are women cowards then?"

"Yes."

Michael interrupted Noah for a translation, then asked a question of his own. "If men acquire bravery, what virtue do women acquire?"

Kakumba demurred. "That is prying too much into women's affairs. No woman should answer such a question. She would die if she did so."

111

"That is something they learn during initiation, Mike. It is secret," Noah explained.

"Then could we ask what happens when a child is born?"

It was now Noah who hesitated. He bent forward and trimmed the wick of the lamp. The circle of light became fainter and smaller, and the anthropologist was now writing blind.

Finally Noah said to Kakumba, "He asks: What do the women do when a child is born?"

Standing against the wall in the darkness, Kakumba laughed nervously and hitched her baby higher on her hip. Because these absurd questions were not those of Noah, but of this tubabu whose Kuranko was that of a child and who kept coming into the women's cooking yards during the day, she felt that maybe rules of decorum no longer applied. Gradually, though not reluctantly, she spelt out details of child delivery, then Noah gave the anthropologist a summary of what she had said.

"After a child is born they bathe it with soap and water and rub burnt palm oil on its body. If the infant is sickly they boil up some leaves—any leaves at all—and bathe the infant, and give some of the liquid to the child and mother to drink. They cut the cord with a small knife, a *lilian*, unless there isn't one available, then they use a blade of elephant grass. Oil is rubbed on the cord and when the cord comes off, the navel is coated with milky sap from the *nonke* tree to heal the wound. Then the cord is buried with a kola nut, so a tree will grow and mark the place."

"What of the placenta?" Michael asked.

Noah knew the Kuranko word, and used it, though men were supposedly ignorant of all such words relating to childbirth.

Kakumba's expression was of mingled amusement and outrage, and she suddenly fled through the front door into the house from where, moments later, came the sound of raised voices.

Abdul's first wife, Ferema, appeared before Noah and began berating him.

"Men don't know these things. No man knows about these things," she cried, her body stiffening with annoyance. "Even a woman who has not borne a child knows nothing of these things. We do not speak of these things in the presence of children, or of men. There will be scandal, Noah, if you go further with this. The way you talk of these things, you have become a tubabu! You have overstepped the mark!"

Noah said nothing, but was deeply chagrined and hurt.

112

"What is it?" the anthropologist asked innocently.

"Nothing," Noah said tersely, and as Ferema stalked off, he realized not so much the depth of his error but that it had been utterly inescapable.

The Red Road

The red road led to nowhere I could go
Nowhere was a village I would never know
For days I drove companionless along it
The forest had no horizon
I wore a mask of red dirt
The wheel steered me
My body ached
At night I lay awake in terror at the night
People everywhere
Saw to me with the same indifference
They shared their food
I passed through country
Only on a map
And came back along the same road
Nothing in particular fulfilled
The red road led to nowhere I could go
Nowhere was a village I would never know.

✖ Chapter Eighteen

HE AWOKE from a nightmare of empty halls and corridors. The building could have been a cathedral, a government office, or a university college, and he had been wandering around in it searching for the room where he was to enroll.

The sounds of the village gradually edged out the dream images. A cock crowed raucously . . . a child was crying . . . snatches of conversation . . . bare feet shuffling on the porch . . . someone sweeping the parlor floor with a switch. He tugged the hem of the mosquito net from under the mattress and reached for his journal.

A profound repining came over him. He could not fathom its source or even be sure of its object. He missed Pauline, terribly, and worried about her, but the longing was for something else, there or away from there he did not know. For the last few days he had felt increasingly lonely and vulnerable. And utterly fatigued. He was sure it was not the heat or the sleepless nights or the lack of privacy or the monotony of the food. Some deeper malaise was sapping his energies. He kept thinking about the contradictions in his position there. Occasionally, like a few nights ago, dancing with villagers outside Morowa's house, he felt completely at home, and could slip into the rhythm of things with an almost somnambulent carelessness. But most of the time he was irritated by the clamor, the jostling bodies on verandahs, the strange language that enveloped him, which he strained to hear, and he wanted only to escape to the solitude of his room and hide under the gauze tent and read a book. He wanted to become a part of this energetic and voluble society, yet felt just as strongly compelled to withdraw and recollect himself in isolation from it. He wanted to shuck off his skin, yet also to take refuge in it. The painful thing was to realize that as long as he kept up this kind of separation between himself and the villagers, he would be passive in contrast to their activity, which made it inevitable that they would seem a threat to him.

"Honk honk!" Michael recognized Sewa's eccentric greeting outside the door. Sewa was Abdul's son, and though he'd never seen a vehicle, he mimicked a truck's horn as a way of greeting the anthropologist, and spent hours each day wheeling around a skeletal vehicle that he had made out of raffia spines and old umbrella wire. "Tubabu!" he called, "I've come to greet you."

Michael opened the door and listlessly returned the greeting, whereupon Sewa handed him two eggs. He placed them on the bed beside his journal, wondering if they, like the other eggs that Sewa had brought him, would also have embryos in them and be inedible.

Sewa led the way to Abdul's house. A chill mist hung over the village like a mosquito net. Women were filing down the lanes toward the stream, basins or buckets on their heads, stroking the air with their free hands, walking with infinite grace. The anthropologist yawned. At the edge of an old cassava garden a small boy was tethering a goat to a mango tree whose lower leaves had been scorched and buckled by a recent grass fire. Sewa shouted, "Honk honk," and ran to join his friend.

The anthropologist wearily climbed the steps to Abdul's porch, greeted everyone, then took up his usual place at the end of the verandah and waited for Tilkolo to bring hot water for his tea.

On the western side of the courtyard two coconut palms caught the rising sun. It crossed his mind that it was strange that coconut palms should be growing so far north, but when Noah appeared he forgot the palms and turned his attention to the day's work.

With Noah's help he was interviewing all the household heads in Firawa, completing a census that might reveal vital connections between kinship, residence, and marriage patterns.

Noah felt bored by the work—perambulating around the village in the heat of the day and having to field the awkward questions that elders put to him. Why did the white man want to know where their wives hailed from or whom their sons had married? Did he work for the government? Did Noah work for the government? Was there going to be a new tax on households? One old man, who had known Tina Kome, had not masked his discontent. "Why don't you talk to us as a person, not as a stranger, a tubabu," he had said to Noah. "A person will fight for what his grandfather decreed; but what his grandfather did not decree, should he fight for that?" Noah had been stung by the old man's rebuke, and recoiled at the prospect of yet another day translating questions he could not see the value of.

The anthropologist was talking to him. "I'm not making the kind of headway I'd like, Noah. In fact, this bloody census is driving me up the wall! Can't you give me a better idea of when you're free . . . so we can work together . . . without distractions?"

"If you're referring to yesterday, Mike, I told you, I got caught up in that palaver over my sister's marriage. I explained it all to you last night."

"I don't mean just that," Michael said, unsure of what he *did* mean. "I want us to come to some kind of understanding," he continued vaguely, "about when you're with me and when you've got other things to do. After all . . ." He was on the verge of saying something about money but stopped himself.

Noah was thinking of a night three weeks ago, not long after they'd first arrived in Firawa, when Michael had refused his help and ineptly tried to fill his lantern without using a funnel and spilled kerosene all over the place. He'd said they could easily buy more when it ran out! Then he had tried to show him how to trim the wick, but to no avail, and Sewa had to go down to the sergeant's house every night and clean the glass mantle so that his lantern would give enough light to read by. What did his father always say? *Hali morgo may yi ke gbile ro a to a yi la a bolo:* "If you can't put water with the pumpkin, then let it cook in its own juices."

"You decide when I should be with you," Noah said, but he saw from the fretful look on Michael's face that this was not enough. "Perhaps if we spent more time on the language we could get more done," he added tentatively.

The anthropologist suddenly detested himself for his caviling and condescending, for making Noah bear the brunt of his frustrations. "You're right, you're right," he said, and drank his tea, which had gone cold.

"Let me get more hot water," said Noah.

"No, no, it's O.K., unless you want more."

"I've had enough, Mike."

The census was shelved, and the anthropologist took to strolling about the village on his own, greeting people, amusing them with his stock phases, picking up words.

He stood in the full glare of the open courtyard, pointing into the shadows of a porch where some dusty bottles, crinkled horns, and strings of cowrie shells were tied across the lintel. *"N'fen bi wo la?"* he asked the old man who was sitting near the doorway.

The old man looked at him quizzically. *"Bese,"* he answered, then got up, took his staff from against the wall, and walked resolutely away from the house.

"What does the white man want?" a neighbor called out.

"He wants to know about the medicines!"

That evening Michael asked Noah if he knew the old man who lived at the far end of the village and always walked around with a staff.

"He's my uncle, Saran Salia Sano."

"I saw lots of things tied over his doorway. On other houses too. . . ."

"Medicines. He's a *besetigi*, a medicine-master."

"Do you think he'd mind if we asked him sometime to talk about these medicines?"

"No. But you have to understand that some of this medicine business is secret. He may not want to say much."

Next day Noah took the anthropologist to Saran Salia's house. The old man was sitting on the edge of the verandah, leaning on his staff.

Noah greeted him, *"M'berin, inwali,"* and Michael muttered in turn, "Inwali."

Saran Salia glanced up at the anthropologist, frowned, then

looked hard at Noah. "Ha! Noah," he breathed, as if his visit confirmed some unspoken and negative intuition.

"The white man asks will you tell him something about the medicines you make and use," Noah began.

"You use them, Noah. Why don't you tell him about them?"

"He wants you to."

Saran Salia spat on the ground. "What does he want to know?"

"What do you want to know?" Noah asked, turning to the anthropologist, who was staring at the spot in the dust where the old man's spittle had landed. Three young men stood a few yards away with puzzled expressions and folded arms.

"Why does he put medicines over the doorway?"

Noah put the question to his uncle and translated the reply. "He says they are there to protect the house, *ka bon kandan*. It could also mean to enclose the house. They are usually put over the door, the mouth of the house."

"So the house is like a person?"

"Mnhn."

"What does he need to protect the house from?"

Again Noah translated.

"From witches!" Saran Salia replied huskily, much to the amusement of the young men. Saran Salia glared at them and waved them away with the back of his hand.

"Why would witches want to attack his house?"

The old man listened gravely as Noah translated the question. He made no reply, but took out of his gown pocket a small tobacco tin, the lid of which had been punched with a nail to make it serve as a kola grater. He rubbed a red kola nut across the lid, then conveyed the grated nut to his mouth with his cupped hand.

"I am not a witch," he said at last, "therefore I do not know why they do what they do. But you have to take precautions."

The anthropologist pressed Noah to ask if the different medicines on the lintel had different purposes, or whether they were all to protect the house from witches.

"It is customary to make them like that," Saran Salia said, "it is what our elders taught us."

"But custom isn't a reason . . . or is it?" the anthropologist appealed to his companion.

Noah, who awhile ago had felt silly putting Michael's simplistic questions to his uncle, now found himself intrigued by these medicines he had always taken for granted, and was gratified by Michael's earnest interest in things that Europeans generally derided. He asked Saran Salia to explain the use of the miniature raffia gate.

Saran Salia's face betrayed neither animosity nor impatience. "Ask the white man a question," he said, "ask the white man why he writes our names down in his book. Why does he do that?"

To save Michael embarrassment, Noah did not translate the question but instead suggested they continue their inquiries another day. The anthropologist, pleased with the headway he thought he had made, ingenuously said to Noah, "Please thank your uncle for his time."

"There's no need." Then, to Saran Salia, Noah explained, "The white man wants to know who belongs to which family so that he will feel more at home in Firawa."

As his visitors walked away from the house, Saran Salia gazed after them with an expression of both incredulity and bemusement.

That night, from the verandah of Abdul's house, Michael watched a group of girls performing their preinitiation "happiness dance." He had begun the day in lassitude and boredom; now he watched enthralled as girls came forward singly within the full circle of their age-mates, stamping more and more rapidly as the accompanying drummers lifted the tempo, letting their supple arms beat the air behind them as if in imitation of birds, bending forward, paced by the momentum of the drums and by their companions clapping and calling their names.

After a while the group moved off into the darkness and Michael slumped back against the wall. Noah was again in altercation with Yeli Kulako over the matter of a belated bridewealth payment. At the far end of the verandah, Abdul's treadle sewing machine jabbered away as he stitched together white strips of country cloth to make Doron Fina's initiation gown. Children leapt about on the steps, tagging one another and shouting taunts. To Michael the language was no less intimidating than it had been a month ago. He remembered Sewa's coming to him one morning with a scrap of paper covered with a scrawl of wavy lines. It was the child's idea of a letter, and Sewa had thought the scribble conveyed his thoughts. The palaver, cries, and chatter on the porch seemed just as confused—a seething mass of sound whose drift he could only guess at. He tried now not to hazard guesses or even cultivate interest, for if he did he invariably wound up with the unhappy conviction that he was the subject of all the talk. He glanced again at Noah, envious of the ease with which he moved among his own people. And Abdul, taciturn and patrician, was still sewing, his lips sealed on a row of pins.

When he got back to the sergeant's house he lit a candle and picked up Nabokov's *Despair*. He had been stuck at page 23 for two days, but tonight he managed to get as far as "An author's fondest dream is to turn the reader into a spectator" on page 26—his own recipe for successful writing.

The spluttering candle threw the vague silhouette of his unusable lantern onto the wall. He jotted down on the cover of his journal two reminders: "the theme of the double—kerosene," then blew out the candle. Its acrid lingering smell swept him into a memory of his childhood, and sleep.

In the morning there was a visitor at Abdul's house, a hunter who'd come into Firawa from a remote Barawa hamlet to present Tala Sewa with the foreleg of a bushbuck that he had shot along the Sunguru River at dawn. Sinkari Yimba wore a country-cloth tunic and leggings, and the three-cornered cap of a master hunter, dyed dark russet like the rest of his outfit.

Through Noah, the anthropologist asked the hunter the name of the cap.

"*Konkodangbe!*" Sinkari Yimba exclaimed, then, stabbing at the cap with his forefinger, he rattled on, "Only when a hunter has killed seven buffaloes is he allowed to wear konkodangbe. These tassels here, at the sides, these are the ears of the buffalo, the most dangerous of all the animals. And see here, this middle tassel, this is its horn."

Noah's own interest quickened as Sinkari Yimba related details of a hunter's apprenticeship and described the rules and techniques of hunting. Head down, the anthropologist scribbled in his notebook, and Noah was relieved that he appeared to be getting the kind of information he wanted.

—ventures into the wilderness at night—uses *besekoli* to ensure protection—hunters in bush must regard one another as brothers—take care of one another. Some have darkness—can make themselves invisible—so if you're attacked the hunter with the gift of darkness can interpose between you and the animal so animal won't see you. This why amicability so important: you may have to rely on man with gift of darkness to save your life. Or, if wounded and attacked—play possum—since by offering no resistance animal will think you dead and go away.—

By mid-morning, as the sun dispersed the last vestiges of mist on the hills around the village, Sinkari Yimba was still talking. Indeed, he was now engrossed in an account of Mande Fabori, the ancestral hunter, and considered it a matter of some urgency that they go and see the shrine to Mande Fabori on the outskirts of Firawa.

The shrine was a yellow clay effigy, sheltered by a canopy of palm leaves. Blackened by blood and bristling with pieces of bone and horn, the original hunter overlooked a small pile of recent offerings: rice, bananas, kola.

"When we kill an animal," Sinkari Yimba explained, "we come here, smear some of its blood on the clay, and say, 'Teacher, this is your share.' If there are no fresh blood stains it means that we've been having a hard time finding game."

"What makes the game scarce?" the anthropologist ventured.

"Hah!" Sinkari Yimba laughed. "A hunter should not worry about his wife at home or have anything on his mind except hunting. You've got to be patient and respect the rules of hunting, otherwise you'll never find game."

When Noah had translated the hunter's answer, Michael could not help wondering if it was meant as some oblique reference to his own concerns, but before he could say anything he was distracted by a dark-blue bird with an enormous bill; it flew up into a mango tree beyond the shrine.

"What's the name of that bird in Kuranko?" he asked Noah.

Noah asked the hunter.

"*Gbulangbulan*," said Sinkari Yimba.

After its ungainly flight the bird settled among new foliage high in the tree. The anthropologist wrote down the name and a description of the bird, which would later lead him to identify it as an allied hornbill.

The sun had now climbed clear of the haze, and Noah's head ached from the heat.

"Let's go back to the house for some food," he said.

The anthropologist, pleased with the wealth of information he had gathered in a single morning, readily assented.

He ate the stringy chicken and glutinous rice with an appetite that surprised him, and it was only when he and Noah were finishing the meal that he thought to remark on Sinkari Yimba's absence.

"I think he's eating with his own people," Noah said.

Then Michael happened to glance down the lane that led to Tala Sewa's, and saw his informant coming toward them, a rifle in one hand, and in the other a dangling matted object.

As the hunter neared the house, Michael was aghast at what he now recognized.

120

Sinkari Yimba stepped up onto the verandah and flung down the dead hornbill. It skidded across the porch, leaving a smear of watery blood on the clay.

"Gbulangbulan," said the hunter, smiling. Then he said something to Noah that Michael could not understand.

Noah translated: "He says you will now know the bird that belongs with the name."

Cattle Egrets

Every dusk from the swamp
the cattle egrets
fly up
from their day's stilted
wading at the blind
beasts' feet.

Villagers won't say
where these birds go
at night:
only that, as we have
angels, invisible to us,
so the beasts have theirs:

And against the flight
of angels, men lock
their doors,
put fetish gates and
knotted grass
across the lintels.

I've seen the cattle
huddled by the hill
beyond our house,
felt wings as palpable
as fronds
against my face.

And once at dusk,
the wind fallen
in the bush, heard
the threshold sound of angels
leaving, and the laughter
of a djinn.

⚉⟫ Chapter Nineteen

ON HIS RETURN to Kabala, Michael found himself again assailed by doubt. His approach to knowledge seemed to contain within it a morbid impulse. Under his gaze the vital, elusive, and unifying qualities of existence shriveled and died. Yet it was not so much the incident of the dead hornbill that oppressed him, but the tension in his relationship with Noah—an unspoken resistance that sprang from a deep contradiction between his quest for knowledge and his desire for friendship. What kind of dialogue might open up the possibility of amity rather than produce bits of information sealed off from life? He had peeled away layer after layer of the onion—to be left with nothing but tears.

Noah, meanwhile, relieved to be back among family and friends, had already forgotten how he'd been compromised in Firawa by broaching matters like magical medicine and sexuality, which verged on the secret and were quite impolitic to pursue. But whatever misgivings remained, he confided them to no one. Instead, he decided upon a stratagem that might provide the anthropologist with something useful and at the same time satisfy his own interests.

One night he took out the letter his father had written in December 1946 to Makeni, the commissioner of the northern province, submitting his name as a candidate for the Barawa chieftaincy and setting out his grounds for doing so. Noah pondered his own place in this scheme of things—in which war, invasion, colonization, death, and political rivalry had eroded all sense of predictability and justice. His father had urged him to take pride in his heritage, to come into his birthright. "If you do not know where you have come from, how will you go anywhere?" And he had hammered home the integrity of that heritage. "It is *our* Barawa, and we are true Kuranko; we have *never* mixed." But it was a divided house to which Noah was heir, exactly as it had been in his father's time—as the last lines of Tina Kome's letter made clear: "Apart from the fact that I have laboured for Government satisfactorily since 1907, I feel that justice should be done by appointing a candidate for Morowaia House this time."

But Noah vacillated between a dream of somehow fulfilling his father's ambition in Barawa, and a dream of following in his elder brother's footsteps and making his mark on the national political scene.

The day Noah arrived at One-Mile to show Michael the letter and suggest they embark on a study of Barawa history, he found Michael entertaining Mamina Yegbe, an old man whom Noah had introduced to the anthropologist a week ago.

Undaunted by the old man's presence, Noah gradually moved the conversation around to Barawa, chieftaincy, and succession. Finally, he drew out the letter.

"I've brought this to show you—something my father wrote in 1946. . . ."

While Michael read the letter, Noah exchanged polite words with Mamina Yegbe. But by the time Michael returned the letter to Noah, the old man had become edgy; rather than cloak his awkwardness in silence, he decided to take his leave.

"Do you think we should work more on history, then?" Michael asked, returning to the room after seeing off the old man down the road.

"I think it's important," Noah said.

But his optimism was dampened almost immediately when the anthropologist showed keenest interest in the most remote of the Marah ancestors—in particular Yilkanani, whom praise-singers described as "the first father," "the first ancestor," and who was attributed formidable powers, fabulous wealth, numberless progeny, and outstanding virtue—who, in time, the anthropologist would identify as Alexander the Great.

In the course of this event, both their interests were frustrated. When Michael, for example, insisted they seek out Mamina Yegbe as a source of information, the old man proved to be more inclined to recite personal recollections than historical facts. Meanwhile, although Noah pointed out that Mamina Yegbe was generally regarded as a bit touched in the head, and tried to dissuade the anthropologist from relying too much on what he was told, he saw finally that Barawa—and politics—would have to wait.

MAMINA YEGBE was at least seventy. He knew the names of Palmer and Captain Leigh, who built the barracks at Gbankuma before the British moved to Falaba. As a small child he had fled his village with his parents to avoid the white men, and he remembered the first barracks at Kabala—on the site that Michael knew as the town's market. He remembered the creation of the frontier, of the Court Messenger Force, and of the Chiefdom Police, and he knew that the first taxes, which people paid to Warensi, were two shillings and sixpence per house, and later rose to five shillings, then to nine shillings, and finally to one pound five shillings and one pound ten shillings per head.

"In the old days people were happy," he told the anthropologist. "We were happy with our government. All the chiefs had their favorite music, and whenever the chiefs assembled, the jelibas would play. Beli-koro, Konkofa, Sinkerifa—I knew them all."

Mamina Yegbe was small and spry, and always looked slightly bemused. The anthropologist felt at ease in his company and began seeking him out at the town chief's house near the market, taking him packets of tobacco to show his gratitude for the old man's tolerance of his fractured Kuranko.

One morning he was at the district officer's office, working through a stack of intelligence diaries and daybooks from the colonial period, to search for corroboration of what Mamina Yegbe had told him about local history. Around him the clerks were busy with their own bureaucratic chores, filing memoranda, moving dog-eared files from the "out" tray of one desk to the "in" tray of another, sharpening pencils, or fetching iced Coca-Colas for the D.O.

Before being allowed to look at the records, he had been obliged to submit five copies of an application, all typed, signed, sealed in offi-cial envelopes, stamped, and countersigned. But he was already losing interest in the musty volumes, and figured he had spent more time get-ting access to them than in actually reading them. He stared at the whitewashed wall where two wasps were adding yet another accretion of moist red clay to their nest. Outside the barred windows of the office, the leaves of an enormous mango tree hung limply in the heat. He closed the daybook and made to go.

Two clerks immediately deserted their desks and asked for a lift to the market.

As he switched on the ignition he caught sight of Mamina Yegbe sitting on a rock under the mango tree, smoking his Bavarian pipe with the hinged metal lid.

"Do you want a lift?" Michael called, and motioned with his hand in the direction of the market.

Mamina Yegbe clambered up into the front seat of the Land Rover, beside the clerks. As usual he was wearing an embroidered tunic and a blue silk cap with a tassel, and looked like a Mandarin. He sat bolt upright with an almost smug expression on his face, holding against his chest a large manilla envelope marked in capital letters "On Sierra Leone Government Service." The envelope was covered in ornate signatures and sealed in several places with red wax; it resembled something out of a Saul Steinberg cartoon.

The clerks were clearly amused by the envelope, and their guffaws began to annoy Michael.

"What's the joke?" he demanded.

The first clerk winked at him, then nodded toward Mamina Yegbe, who was gazing straight ahead. The other clerk dodged the question by suddenly recognizing two friends sauntering along the road.

"Mosquito!" he yelled. "Heh! Peacecorps!" he called, and hung his arm out the window of the Land Rover.

A thin, gangly youth who answered to the first description, and his companion, wearing faded jeans with frayed cuffs, lifted their arms to wave, but the dust in the wake of the vehicle enveloped them.

After dropping the clerks at the market, Michael sought to satisfy his curiosity about the envelope.

"What is it?" he asked.

The old man continued gazing straight ahead, but raised a finger to his lips as if to enjoin silence. He then got down from the Land Rover and without a word disappeared into a crowd around the kola-nut traders.

That night Michael drove back into Kabala from One-Mile to buy some cold Fanta at Lansana Kamara's bar. The bar was a shabby and poky corner room that opened onto a verandah and the marketplace. It was furnished with several warped and dusty shelves, a battered deep-freeze, and five armchairs with polystyrene foam stuffing bulging out through rents in its red vinyl upholstery. The jangling strains of the latest hi-life hit issued from a dilapidated record player at one end of the bar: "I really love you, Fati Fatiii . . ."

Lansana Kamara did not particularly like hi-life tunes, and whenever business was slack he would get out his records from Guinea and, with tears welling up in his eyes, would listen to the stirring refrains of praise-songs of ancient Mali.

On the walls of L.K.'s bar were several fly-specked calendars, showing beaming Africans in open-necked shirts holding aloft bottles of Vimto, Fanta, or Star beer. L.K. disdained such drinks.

With a lugubrious air he poured himself another large Martell brandy and chaser of Guiness.

Michael bought what he wanted and was about to go when he saw Mamina Yegbe in the corner, surrounded by a dozen boisterous youths, among them the two clerks from the D.O.'s office. One of them made a remark that was inaudible to Michael, but it drew a burst of taunting laughter from the others, and the old man shrank back as if from a blow. Michael saw that Mamina Yegbe was still holding the big envelope, only now it was ripped open, and bits of sealing wax littered the floor among the beer-bottle caps.

When the old man saw the anthropologist he seemed to regain his composure, but before either could greet each other one of the clerks confronted Michael with bloodshot eyes and beery breath.

"He says it's from Seku Toure and Siaka Stevens!" the clerk roared. "That envelope! He says they've given him a big country in Guinea and a million pounds, cash! He says he's coming to the D.O. tomorrow to collect it!"

Everyone broke into laughter. Then they looked at the anthropologist, waiting for his reaction. He appeared to be quite nonplussed.

The clerk became angry. "He says he's going to be appointed to a high position, in the government!" he shouted. "It's all in the letter!"

Michael glanced at Mamina Yegbe, who raised a finger to his lips and smiled ingenuously. He then appealed to L.K. for a clue to what was going on, but L.K. simply smoothed his knitted singlet over his enormous stomach, lowered his eyes, and took another sip of brandy.

The clerk, exasperated by the stranger's stupidity, lurched over to the old man, wrenched the envelope from his grasp, and shook out its contents onto the bar. L.K. dolefully moved his glass to one side as his customers pawed at the sheaf of papers, spreading them out so that the anthropologist could see what they were.

He recognized several old G.C.E. examination papers, some official memoranda and letters, and a page of his own field notes. He could not think how it had come into the old man's possession.

Stabbing at the papers, the clerk drew Michael's attention to a bundle of leaflets, all advertisements for Surf washing powder.

"This is the letter from the prime minister!" the clerk hooted. "Can't you see what it is either?"

Michael recalled a Volkswagen that had turned up outside the market a few days before. A huge display packet of soap-powder had been fitted to the roof rack, and a loudspeaker blared out hi-life tunes. Four or five men in sunglasses and pale blue shirts had gone about distributing leaflets and occasionally giving away sample packets of Surf. In the afternoon the vehicle, still crackling with canned music, disappeared in a cloud of dust up the road toward Falaba.

"Yes, I can see what it is."

126

He knelt down and started picking up the papers that had fallen on the floor. They were already smudged with red dirt from the clerk's shoes.

The jokers appeared embarrassed by the crazy show of sympathy for the old man. They backed out onto the porch, making half-hearted gibes and clutching their bottles of beer. L.K. stared morosely at his glass of Guiness.

"Do you want a lift home?" Michael asked Mamina Yegbe.

"Awa."

"I really love you Fati Faaati . . ." followed them out into the night, strangely louder than it had been in the bar.

Michael looked down the unlit street, thinking "The generator's gone again," and wanting to say this to Mamina Yegbe but unable to work out how one might refer to an electricity generator in Kuranko. He also wanted to ask the old man, now sitting in silence in the Land Rover beside him, if he still intended to present his letter to the D.O. and claim his fortune, but this question, too, proved difficult to phrase. "Anyway," he thought, "it might seem like another taunt." And then he remembered the page of his field notes and was curious to know where Mamina Yegbe had got it—but he was suddenly struck by the simple faith they all placed in the power of printed words, these fetish-ized leaves—the clerks, this benignly mad old man, and himself no less.

The headlights picked out the mosque and the grove of palms beyond it.

"I'm going back to Barawa on Friday," Michael said, "with Noah— for the initiations."

Mamina Yegbe made no response.

"I'll come and see you before I leave."

In the darkness the town gave forth the sounds of its invisible life: a dog yelping, shouts, a radio badly tuned, an inconsolable child crying, a motor scooter spluttering down a potholed lane, the taut drubbing of an initiation drum.

Michael drew up outside the house with the broken verandah where Mamina Yegbe lived.

"Ma sogoma yo, goodnight," he said, as the old man got down.

Mamina Yegbe stood on the roadside in the glare of the head-lights.

"In the old days people were happy," he said. Then he turned and drifted into the darkness.

📚 Chapter Twenty

AT THE END of his first day back in Firawa, the anthropologist installed himself in his usual place at the end of Abdul's porch. Against the rose-red western sky were silhouetted several conical thatched roofs and the harsh metal ridge of a western-style house. Shadows from the twin coconut palms extended across the Woldugu luiye toward him, broken by a jumble of mud bricks lying on the ground to harden. From the yards came the husky thud of pestles.

The warm night enveloped the hill and invaded the village, suddenly seeming to animate it. Laughter and brisk movements countered the coming of darkness, and a distant sound of drumming signaled yet another round of dancing and visiting in preparation for the girls' initiations.

A small child toddled along the porch, naked except for a string of black and red beads around her waist. Her mother had just finished bathing her, and her oiled skin glistened in the twilight. Beaming, Mantene walked behind her child, ready to catch her if she fell.

"Matan, Matay, Matay . . ." the child called.

"Man . . . tene, Man . . . tene, Mantene," her mother replied, teasing her.

"Matay, Matay . . ." repeated the child, swaying a little as she saw the white man smiling at her.

"Mantene," her mother insisted, then burst out laughing.

The child's sister came out onto the verandah and swept up the child into her arms. "Ah, little Matay!" she teased, rocking the child on her hip.

The dried-mud surface of the porch was still warm from the day's sun, and Michael spread out his cane mat and leaned back against the wall.

It was now quite dark. Across the courtyard a kerosene lantern flared into life then settled to a steady glow. Nearby, a group of children were clapping and dancing around an orange tree, the older children leading the younger ones by the hand. Mantene went into the house, intoning her name. "Matay," said the child, delighted at the game she had learned to play with her mother.

Noah appeared with a lantern and radio. "I thought you might want to hear the news, Mike."

Through surges of static came the measured voice of a BBC broad-caster announcing that Palestinian guerillas had hijacked a Pan-Ameri-can airliner.

"I thought we'd got away from all that," Michael said querulously. But Noah did not hear him, and turned the volume up further.

"To regain the tranquility of the night, Michael wandered through the house to the backyard. It was unconventional for men to spend time in this zone of domesticity, but Abdul's wives had got used to their guest and his various eccentricities: wasting firewood by overstoking the fire, wasting palm oil frying his rice, wasting time boiling his water.

As his eyes became accustomed to the dark he recognized Tilkolo, and greeted her. She and the others had not long arrived back from the Seli river-crossing, toting supplies for Abdul's shop. They were talking about the bridge they hoped would be built someday to join Barawa with the road to Kabala. Everything had to be brought in to Firawa as headloads: roofing iron, cement, kerosene, palm oil, hoes. And if they wanted to market their rice they had to tote it out the same way. The bridge was a recurring subject in Barawa conversations.

Michael listened awhile as he kindled the fire to boil some drink-ing water, then he asked if they had ever considered the disadvantages a bridge might bring.

"Hah," Tikolo exclaimed, "if you had seen us when we got back you would have pitied us. If the Seli were bridged do you think we would suffer sore necks and aching limbs? If it were possible to ask an unborn child what it most desired in the world, it would say 'the bridge,' so that trucks could come to Firawa."

"But I've seen the villages where trucks come. Strangers arrive. Everything changes."

"Are you not a stranger! Strangers may tell us about new ways of doing things. If their ideas are good, we will take them up."

"What about bad ideas?"

"We will spurn them!"

"What if your daughters all went away, as the young men have done? What if they go and lead useless lives in the big towns?"

"That would be bad, of course. There is indolence in the big towns. People are shiftless; they steal rather than work."

"Wouldn't a bridge to Barawa lay it open to these changes?"

"That depends on us, upon what we decide. Even in Freetown there are people who maintain their customs."

"Have you ever been to Freetown?"

129

"No, but I'd like to go there. I don't know anybody there, but if you ask me I'll go with you!"

The women laughed at Tilkolo's audacity. She helped Michael fill a country pot with water and set it on the three clay hearthstones.

He squatted on a hearth stool, watching wisps of wood smoke drift across the surface of the water. In the darkness Mantene murmured, "He can light a fire almost as well as you, Tilkolo."

Then Tilkolo and Mantene began to sing quietly:

> *Muse dila den koe le la:*
> *ni i wara ba denke sorona*
> *i kana fo i ma lui soron;*
> *ni i wara dimusu*
> *i kana fo i ma bon soron .*

The anthropologist did not understand the song, but when Noah came out to look for him he asked what the women had been singing.

Noah questioned them, and Mantene laughed at the curiosity of the tubabune.

"He even tried pounding rice when he first came here!" she said.

"And winnowing!" Tilkolo added wryly.

"The song means," said Noah, "that if a woman cries for a child, and she gets a son, she should be thankful because she gains a courtyard. If she gets a daughter she should be just as thankful because she gains a house."

"Which is more important, courtyard or house?" the anthropologist asked.

The women smiled to themselves. "It is the courtyard, of course," said Tilkolo, "because the house is contained within the courtyard."

Michael caught a hint of irony in Tilkolo's voice, and changed the subject.

"You seem to get on well together," he observed.

"In our place everyone does her share. Everything is sweet. We are all friends."

Noah confirmed Tilkolo's remark. "Abdul has seven wives, though some are inherited wives, but they do get on well together."

Michael asked Tilkolo if co-wives in other households were as happy together.

"No, there is often discord."

"People who are close often quarrel the most," Mantene put in.

"What prevents discord in your own household?" Michael asked.

"Our husband says that we should not quarrel." Tilkolo began, "and besides, he treats us all fairly according to our relative seniority. Our children, ourselves, and our husband are one. And as you know, it takes three hearthstones to balance a cooking pot."

The anthropologist was thinking about a court case he had attended in another village. A young wife had run away from her husband, who had then traveled to the girl's parents' village to fetch her back. Throughout the lengthy litigation, the errant girl had sat with downcast eyes, never addressed but continually referred to, as the elders debated the rights and wrongs of the case.

"Do you resent having no say in whom you marry?" he asked.

"Ah, a woman can always kick against that by eloping with her lover. Some of us came to our husband that way, though I was inherited."

Next morning women from other Barawa villages poured into Firawa for the "day of the rice-flour sacrifice." Dressed in colorful lapas and headkerchiefs, the visitors sought out kin with gifts of rice, salt, cloth, and money to help defray the expenses of the initiation festivities. The village filled with the noise of ebullient greetings, the rhythmic thud of pestles, and the unflagging beat of drums until, at dusk, the hubbub ceased and families gathered to offer rice-flour sacrifices to their ancestors.

For two days the anthropologist did not rest. As groups of performers appeared he scurried about taking photographs and notes.

A line of young men, their cheeks pierced by porcupine quills, faced him brazenly. A young girl, her body daubed with red, white, and black ochers, stood before Abdul's house with an immobile face. Wearing a man's gown and carrying a cutlass, she held a pad of cloth clamped over her mouth. Near Tala Sewa's courtyard a group of boys sang and drummed around a comical figure trussed in moss who danced in mimicry of a chimpanzee. Each group of entertainers prompted the anthropologist to ask Noah further questions.

"But it's just as I've told you," Noah repeated wearily. "It's just a way of adding to the enjoyment of the occasion, nothing more."

(The masklike expressions—are they a way in which these girls sympathetically strive to induce in their older sisters some measure of self-control? Is this impassivity a way in which they seek magically to countermand or neutralize the emotional turmoil in the hearts of the neophytes? These songs the women sing, assuaging fear and urging calm—are they ways in which the village tries to cool "the bush"? These girls in men's clothes—do they want to assimilate something of men's fortitude and fearlessness, or is this muddling of quotidian roles simply an expression of the confusion surrounding the moment of mid-passage? And the chimpanzee boy, falling to the ground and lying there utterly still before being roused by the drumming and resuming his dance—is this an image of death and rebirth?)

Questions that could neither be asked nor answered succeeded one another in his mind, and his notebooks recorded a chaos of self-interrogations.

Toward noon on the third day, when Noah went back to the house to escape the broiling heat, Michael said he would stay out in the village in case anything happened.

"But it is the middle of the day," Noah protested, "nothing will happen now until the evening."

The anthropologist wanted to stay anyway, and Noah left him.

Tilkolo had been pounding rice all morning with some friends, helping prepare the meal that the initiates would eat after the operations. On her way back to the house, she saw the white man against the simmering heat haze of the hill. He was taking notes.

She sought Noah's help.

"Why is he so excited about crossing the water?" she asked, alluding to the girls' initiations.

"In his country, men and women are more open with each other. They do not observe the same restraint in public that we do. Often you see them sitting together. Even holding hands. Besides, they do not have initiations in their country."

"Eh! Then how do they become adults?"

"They have schools . . ."

"Like ours?"

"No, different schools. They teach different things. It is all very different.

Tilkolo suspected Noah might be teasing her, and she let the matter rest. Anyway, she had much to do before nightfall.

In the gathering dusk the women began to drift down the path that led to the secluded bush clearing where the initiations had taken place. Behind them the village was soon lost in the bluish twilight.

The men talked in low voices in the shadows of verandahs. Everyone was tense and listening.

Then far off came the ominous music of the women's cult. Children, followed by the men, rushed indoors. *"Segere, segere . . ."* they whispered, as if the white man would at once comprehend the reason for their alarm.

Behind locked doors and bolted shutters they waited, huddled together, listening to the dark surging of the women as they approached the village.

The music came closer. Children panicked and clung to their fathers' gowns as the rhythmic shuffling of feet and the muffled pulse of the music was heard in the lane outside.

A solitary figure seemed to race by beneath the shuttered window, dragging something wooden along the wall. The children shrank back in terror. When the white man began to peer through a chink in the shutter, Sewa pulled him back, crying "Segere, segere!" Later on, the men would tell him that any man who saw segere would die.

As soon as the seige was lifted they went out onto the verandah again. Above the village the stars were like a crust of salt at the bottom of a blackened pan. No one spoke much. Everyone was affected by the absence of the women, the deserted hearths.

They fell to listening to the white man who was pressing Noah to explain why the male initiations no longer took place.

"What is he saying?" one man asked Noah.

"He says that we should still organize men's initiations."

Some of the men laughed. Saran Salia, the medicine-master, was astounded by the white man's view.

"He must surely know about these things," he said. "The white men induct people into the army don't they? Isn't that how they cross the water into manhood? Tell him it is just like that for us. That is how a person acquires fearlessness."

Noah translated, adding something another man had said.

"We go into the army now. You become brave there. It makes you a man, it gives you force. In the old days a soldier in the villages was like a white man. He commanded great respect. Tell the tubabu that most of the men in the army are Kuranko."

But the anthropologist had other ideas. He wanted them to talk about the old days. And so, as the night wore on they gradually turned to reminiscences of their own initiations, of journeys around Barawa to tell kinsmen of the forthcoming festivities, of arrivals in strange towns and challenges issued to the local boys to wrestle, of trysts at night with new girlfriends, of the trepidation everyone felt during the long night in the ma'bon, of their awe of the cult spirits.

Noah translated, but Michael did not write down a word of it.

133

Instead he wrote: "They share something I can never know. Their anecdotes seem to conceal the very particulars of event and mood I want so much to capture."

As Michael wrote, Saran Salia was saying: "It was one of my happiest days, the day I gave away the gown of initiation and donned the clothes of manhood—the cap, the gown, the trousers. You become important . . . everyone says how fine you look."

The anthropologist had now finished writing. As he looked up from his notebook he suddenly noticed that Saran Salia's right hand was badly swollen.

"What's happened to his hand, Noah?" he asked.

"Your hand," Noah said to Saran Salia, "is it hurt?"

Somewhat nonplussed by this interruption, Saran Salia unraveled a strip of grubby cloth and peeled away several leaves to expose a septic ulcer on his forearm.

Michael immediately disappeared toward the sergeant's house, returning with penicillin tablets, which he made the old man gulp down with a beaker of water.

Each morning for the next four days he gave Saran Salia more tablets to take, using his visits as excuses for conversation. He half expected the medicine-master to show some willingness now to talk about his own medicines, but Saran Salia tactfully evaded all the anthropologist's questions.

One afternoon Saran Salia appeared at the entrance to the lane that ran alongside Abdul's house. He greeted the anthropologist with a broad smile. Michael returned the greeting and asked, "Is it better?"

Unhooking his arms from the staff he was carrying across his shoulders, Saran Salia waved his hand about. "It's fine now, you see. Fine."

Later, when Noah gave Michael the news that Saran Salia wanted to meet them at nightfall on a granite outcrop outside the village, the anthropologist felt sure that he was about to be initiated into a mystery.

They waited until after dark. The hills began to be invaded by a chilling mist rising from the swamps. Saran Salia did not turn up.

"You must not take it amiss," Noah said flatly, but the anthropologist believed that the old man was testing him in some obscure way. Or warning him off. He had already learned that Saran Salia was or had been a master of the men's *kome* cult, and he found it disquieting to try to reconcile the old man's geniality with images of fierce transfigurations and bizarre alliances with bush spirits.

134

As they started back to Firawa, Noah said, "He was probably held up."

"Perhaps it's better if I stop asking so much about medicines."

"But there's really not a lot in it, Mike. This medicine business . . . it's not what you think."

🎗️ Chapter Twenty-One

THE BAGBE RIVER marks the southern boundary of Barawa. In the dry season its water is murky and inert. Overhanging trees and lianas cast shadows across the water as if goaded and shoved by the vast clamoring forest behind. Crocodiles lurk in the deep pools, but only the dapple of sunlight and fallen leaves animate its sullen surfaces.

The river is crossed by a hammock bridge not far from the forest hamlet of Momoria. Each year an association of young Barawa men rebuild the bridge, a feat of engineering skill and strength that they celebrate obliquely in the name they give themselves: *konke*, meaning mountain.

Once inside the neighboring chiefdom of Woli, the forest becomes dense and overpowering. The narrow path is aswarm with ants, and myriads of butterflies illuminate the occasional shafts of sunlight that fall from the forest roof. Tree snakes slowly unwind in the foliage along the trail, and the spoor of animals can be seen everywhere. In the forest canopy, monkeys bark and birds screech, summoning one another from danger; but along the path there is a ban on speaking too much lest a person chance to mention his companion's name and a djinn steal it for bedevilment.

The two travelers had left the bridge. Michael was limping worse than ever, and Noah urged that they turn back to Firawa. The prospect of climbing the Loma Mountains unsettled him, and the forlorn isolation of the Woli villages aroused in him old anxieties. But the anthropologist would not give up. He maintained that the paralysis in his right leg was merely an aftereffect of the antivenin he'd been injected with in Kabala a week ago after being bitten by a night adder. He said it would get better and that they should press on.

Late in the day, dragging his useless leg, the anthropologist reached Bandakarafaia under the mountain wall.

Chief Damba Lai Marah was used to having white men lodge in his village and make it their base for scaling Loma *mansa*. He was also accustomed to the way they preferred their own company and their own food; to avoid rebuffs he no longer tried to extend to them any sort of hospitality. As for the opinion that some of his people held—that the white men were seeking the mountain djinn to forge alliances with them—he reserved his judgment. He was sure that the *tubabunu* really did gain a kind of satisfaction from toiling up the granite slopes of the Loma for two days and then taking photographs of themselves on the summit. Confronted now by a solitary white man who had arrived without carriers or food, the chief dismissed the visitor from his mind as yet another harmless aberrant.

The anthropologist lay down on some pit-sawn plants stacked in front of the house the chief had provided for his use. His head ached and his ears were ringing. The heat clamped down on him like an iron band.

A desultory search for a container in which to boil water had yielded only a broken calabash. Noah had gone to look for some relatives, hoping they might prepare food for them. But the village seemed to be deserted.

Michael dozed off but was startled awake by two skinny sheep nibbling the grass at his feet. As he propped himself up on his elbow they staggered away, bleating. One of them had a deformed hind hoof turned back upon itself, and the creature limped as if in pain across the barren laterite of the street. It took refuge with the second sheep in the shadows of a house, hovering there, trembling like a scrap of soiled cloth.

Noah turned up with a bunch of bananas and a handful of groundnuts.

"Why is the place so empty?" Michael asked, ignoring the food and looking toward the dark, cupped hand of the escarpment.

"I don't know," Noah said, who did not want to relate what he had seen.

When he had gone looking for his uncle's house he had come upon a group of grave and taciturn women in a lane. Suspecting a death, he passed them with only a cursory greeting. He located the men of the village in a nearby courtyard, crowded outside a derelict house, many of them standing right up against the doorway, peering into the gloomy interior. Again the same bleak expressions. Among the men was his uncle, who hardly seemed to recognize him.

"Danke," he explained when Noah stood beside him, then turned back his eyes toward the house.

Noah made his way to the doorway and saw on the earth floor of the house a stricken man. Under the impassive gaze of the elders, the victim of the curse threw himself from side to side, his body oddly rigid, his eyes dilated and anguished, his nostrils flared. He could have been in the grip of an invisible tormentor who was forcing the breath from his lungs or trying to wrench a confession from his soul.

The older men were reluctant to speak about the cursed man lest they become part of the affliction, but gradually Noah pieced together what had happened.

Some weeks before, the young man had run away with another man's wife from the village of Bandankoro. When the chief's court ordered him to send the woman back to her husband he defied the injunction. Realizing that legal processes would get him nowhere, the aggrieved husband traveled to Kunya, some forty miles away, where he hired a renowned sorcerer to place a curse on his wife's lover. Not long afterward, while working on his elder brother's farm, the young man was gripped by terrible pains in his neck and chest. He felt as if a great weight were bearing down on him. At night he could not sleep, and he cried out for the stone to be lifted from his chest. It was clear to everyone that he was under a curse, and his brothers sent to Kunya to plead for his life, only to be told by the sorcerer that the matter would first have to be settled in court.

It was too late. The young man was dying, and his kinsmen now fell under the same shadow, unable to show concern or grief lest they become accursed by association. They could do nothing but keep vigil until the end.

Noah left Michael the food he had found and returned to his uncle's house. The last of the daylight slipped over the crown of the escarpment, plunging the village into darkness.

Michael tried to sleep but his body kept moving over the forest path, and the mountain was moving away as he neared it, and then the beginning of Dylan Thomas's *Poem on His Birthday* came into his head and he found himself compelled to remember it all.

Feverishly he scraped a hollow in the hard ground for his hip and pummeled his rucksack into the shape of a pillow, but still he could not break the momentum of walking or quell the images of mustard seed, thistledown, waves, and blackberries that crowded into his brain like memories of another existence.

137

Then he began to pick up noises from the far end of the village—a flat wooden clapping, followed by a dull, hoarse muttering as though someone were stuffing words into the mouth of a horn. His fretfulness gave way to fear as the sounds came nearer, but silence again enclosed the village and he heard only the unsteady thumping of his heart and the sirens ringing in his ears.

The night dragged on. He became plagued by a skin rash that quickly spread to every part of his body. Desperate for sleep he scratched and clawed at himself, struggling to think what leaves he might have touched or what mite could have caused the allergic reaction. He cursed himself for having brought no medicines.

As dawn broke he got up and paced about, shivering with cold and tearing at his skin. From outside the house came the strained, gravelly crowing of a rooster: *er er er err.*

He stumbled into the street. A pallid sun glimmered through sluggish wastes of mist. Here and there across the granite face of the mountain, trees snatched at the swirling vapor, teasing it out until it disclosed for a moment the black wall behind.

Some boys were sitting on stones around a dying fire, reciting a sura:

Praise be to Allah who has revealed the Book to His servant shorn of falsehood. . . .

We have decked the earth with all manner of ornaments to test mankind and to see who would acquit himself best. . . .

Did you think the Sleepers of the Cave and Al-Raquim were a wonder among Our signs? . . .

You might have thought them awake, though they were sleeping. We turned them about to right and left, while their dog lay at the cave's entrance with legs outstretched.

Michael sat down with the boys as they chanted by rote verses that neither they nor he understood, and stretched out his hands toward the cone of embers.

Suddenly a bundle of faggots was dumped on the fire, and as smoke poured up around the sticks the anthropologist found himself staring at a boy who had no nose. There was only a hole in the middle of his face, and a pink finger of flesh flickered there as he mumbled a greeting to the white man.

Michael staggered to his feet and strode away.

138

He found Noah standing at the edge of the village, looking into the mist-bandaged forest. Anger and irritation overwhelmed him.

"Where the hell have you been? I've been looking all over for you."

"Someone died," Noah said.

He had died in the night. Noah had just seen the cursed man's kinsmen leaving the village, carrying the body in a mat. Now he was here, confronted with his friend who was weeping and trying to explain away his anger.

"We should go back to Firawa," Noah said calmly.

The anthropologist controlled his sobbing and scratched at his ribs. "We'll give up climbing the mountain," he said, "but I still want to do something here. We haven't come all this way to leave empty-handed."

They went back to the chief, who told them stories of the mountain, but the anthropologist was barely able to write and his attention kept straying to Damba Lai's drum, which was carved with breasts and a navel. It was the first sign of carving he had seen and he wanted to know why the drum had been made to resemble a woman.

Damba Lai smiled. "I do not know," he said, "I inherited the drum when I became chief."

The anthropologist passed the rest of the day in a guilty stupor, alone in his room. The skin rash burned, and he was bleeding where he had torn the skin with his fingernails. He longed for might to come, and sleep.

But he did not sleep that night either. He lay in a delirium, a sodden log drifting downstream, air warm and cloying on his face, feeling slight vertigo as the current rolled him slowly from side to side, panic when he heard the sound of rapids, then uncanny calm. He thought, "I am not lying on the earth, my lying on the earth is being done. I am disembodied now watching myself lying on the ground, but I am not lying here. I am being made to feel the darkness, claustrophobic, hot, and the shrilling of a single cicada in the rafters, but I am not feeling anything or hearing anything. These things are happening to me, I am having them happen to me." Then he was looking down on his own supine body, his awareness drifting away from it like smoke, upward toward the rafters and the stars, looking back with a kind of calm pity on his exiled self, thinking "I am dying, is this dying?" because he knew he could choose, and that he could go back into that prone form if he wanted to. Suddenly he heard as if from a distant room in a great house, Noah calling his name, and gazed down again at his immobile self with its placid and empty eyes and Noah bending over it. As he gradually returned to himself he realized that the room had gone dark and that Noah, whom he had seen a moment before in what seemed to be full daylight, was now talking to him through the darkness, saying, "We must leave, Mike, we must leave."

"Yes," he found himself saying. "Yes."

"Now."

"Yes."

"I'm going to borrow a lantern and then we can go."

"Yes."

"How's the leg?"

"Fine. And the rash is better too."

In the lantern's dull penumbra, dark forms stirred into life, while out of the depths of the forest, howls and shouts gave voice to scampering shadows.

Each man guarded his thoughts, and it was not until dawn that Noah broke the silence to unburden himself of the events surrounding the death of the cursed man.

Michael immediately stopped and rummaged in his rucksack for his notebook, only to find he had left it in Bandakarafaia.

"Shouldn't we go back for it?" Noah asked cagily.

"Not on your life," Michael said, "forget it."

As the daylight began to penetrate the forest, the travelers extinguished their lantern and pushed on. Insects trilled wearily along the path.

"How long shall we stay in Firawa?" Noah asked.

"A day or two maybe. I don't feel like going on to Kabala right away, do you?"

"I'll be happy to get home," Noah said after a while, "I've missed the kids."

"I've been thinking about our child too."

"Next time you come to Barawa she will be born."

Michael smiled. "How do you know it'll be a girl?"

"I don't, but Yebu says she wants a sister for Ai."

The forest now gave way to patches of open grassland, and the mist was lifting. Noah walked ahead along the narrow trail.

"I've been thinking all night about that drum," Michael said, "at Bandakarafaia."

"The chief's drum?"

140

"Yes. How it was carved. Like a woman."

Noah was silent for several minutes, then hesitantly said, "There's a story about a drum. You might like to hear it when we get back."

Michael murmured his interest.

"I'll see if there's anyone in Firawa who can tell it to you."

As the Bagbe River came into view among the trees, a palm-wine tapster overtook them and offered them fresh wine from a gourd. They drank.

A moment later, seized by a sudden urge to bathe, Michael clambered down the riverbank, undressed, and waded into the turbid water.

On the sandy beach, swallow-tailed butterflies quivered and flapped, settling back to feed on animal droppings, and in the shade, like a delicate cage, lay the sloughed skin of a snake.

Chapter Twenty-Two

A DUSTING OF MOONLIGHT covered the hills around Firawa, and on the verandah at Abdul's house no one had bothered to light the lantern. Under the soft pollen-fall of the starry night the children listened spellbound as the storyteller began.

I am going to tell you the story of the *yimbe* drum, the drum that the youngsters play and dance to at the time of their initiations.

Once upon a time the yimbe drum was in the hands of the hyenas in the deep forest. Every evening they used to play it, play it, play it. On moonlit nights like this you could hear the sound of the yimbe drum far-off in the forest. And every evening people strolling in the town heard the melodious music of the drum.

One day the elders assembled and went to the chief. "Chief," they said, "you know that we have been affected by the music we hear every evening. If you do not get the drum for us to play, then we will leave the town and go into the forest."

The chief was much concerned, and he sent a message around the chiefdom, saying that he would give a hundred of everything to whoever brought the yimbe drum from the forest to the town.

Now, between that town and the deep forest there dwelt a *tutufingbe*. This djinn lived on human flesh! Whenever it saw a human being, it cut off his head and ate him.

But there was one young man who decided to brave the wilds and go in search of the drum. He said farewell to his mother. "Mother," he said, "it does not matter whether I return or do not return. I have to go."

His mother said, "So be it then. I wish you well."

He set off. He reached the part of the forest where the tutufingbe lived, but it was not there. It had gone foraging for food. The young man sat down on a pile of skulls, and waited for it to return. When the tutufingbe came back and found the young man sitting on the skulls, it cried out, "Heh you, what have you come here for?"

The young man kept cool. "I have come to beg your pardon," he said. "I am journeying to the deep forest in search of the drum that the hyenas play every evening, and I have come here to ask that you forgive my intrusion and let me go on my way in peace. The chief of my village has promised a hundred of everything to the person who brings the drum back to town, so if you please, I beg you to let me continue on my way and do what I am resolved to do."

The tutufingbe listened patiently. Then it said, "I accept your apologies for invading my domain. Furthermore, because you have shown such courage in coming here and meeting me face to face, I am going to give you something to help you in your quest."

The tutufingbe made him a fetish. Then it asked the young man for his name. "My name is Sarafin Marah," the young man replied.

The tutufingbe gave him the fetish. "Take this. If you get into trouble, consult it. You should address it with the words 'Sarafin Marah greets you.' Then it will reply, 'Greetings to you,' and tell you what you want to know." The tutufingbe also gave him some charcoal, an egg, a piece of bamboo, and a stone. It told the young man to put them in his pocket.

The young man traveled on until he reached the deep forest where the hyenas lived. In the middle of the hyenas' village was a courthouse where the yimbe drums were stored. The young man noted its location and greeted the female leader of the community, whose name was Hyena Sira. "Blessings to you, Hyena Sira, and to your husband, Hyena Tamba," the young man said. Then he announced his intention of spending a night in their village.

Hyena Sira summoned all the hyenas to a meeting. "Heh!" she exclaimed, "This young man has come here with only one purpose in mind—to steal our yimbe drums."

"Hah," replied another hyena, "enough of such talk. Do you think a mere human being could steal our drums? Even if he did get hold of one and made off with it and went as far as Freetown with it, it would take us no time to catch up with him. Let's not worry about him."

So they showed the young man to his lodgings and left him alone. That evening, the young man was heard crying out, "I am sick, I am sick. I took some medicine but it has done me no good. Please let me lodge in the courthouse. I will sleep better there."

The hyenas said to themselves, "All right, anything to keep him quiet." And they lodged him in the courthouse where the yimbe drums were stored.

The hyenas gathered in the courtyards to drum and dance. They beat the yimbe drums and made sweet music. The young man took care to remember which was the loudest and most melodious of the drums.

When the dancing was over, the hyenas put the drums back in the courthouse and went to their houses. But Hyena Sira was still worried. "Haven't I warned you that this young man has come to steal our yimbe drums?" she said.

"We have told you not to worry," the others replied. "Do you really think that a mere human being could make off with our drums?"

As soon as the village was quiet, the young man took out the fetish and said, "Sarafin Marah greets you."

The fetish answered, "Greetings to you, Marah. Lie down for a while longer. Hyena Sira is still awake."

After a while the young man took out the fetish again. "Sarafin Marah greets you," he said.

The fetish answered, "Greetings to you, Marah. Now take the yimbe and go!"

He seized the best drum and ran from the village: . . . *gbaramgbaram, gbaram, gbaram.* Hyena Sira woke up immediately and roused the other hyenas. "He has stolen one of our drums," she cried. The hyenas rushed to the courthouse and, sure enough, the man was not there and the best of the drums had been taken. They set off after him: . . . *barabarabara, barabarabara.*

Rapidly they began to narrow the gap between themselves and the young man. As they were about to overtake him, he took out the fetish. "Sarafin Marah greets you," he said breathlessly.

"Greetings to you, Marah," the fetish answered. "Throw down the bamboo and run for your life!"

He threw down the piece of cane and a wall of bamboo sprang up from east to west. The hyenas ran east along the wall and west along the wall, but there was no way through. "Didn't I tell you that this young man came to steal our yimbe drums?" Hyena Sira said.

Hyena Sira began to gnaw at the bamboo: . . . *wado, wado, wado, wado.* She quickly forced an opening in the wall, and the hyenas set off again in pursuit of the young man.

The young man saw a cloud of dust on the horizon. He took out the fetish and said, "Sarafin Marah greets you."

The fetish answered, "Greetings to you, Marah. Now throw down the stone!"

He threw down the stone and a granite wall sprang up from east to west. The hyenas ran east along the wall and west along the wall, but there was no way through. "I told you that this young man was going to steal our yimbe drums," said Hyena Sira, "but you all said no, such a thing could never happen."

The hyenas said, "We were able to gnaw through the wall of bamboo, but how will we get through this granite wall?" Hyena Sira put her mouth to the rock and ground at it with her teeth: . . . *morto, morto, morto, morto.* The wall collapsed. The hyenas burst through.

Again the young man saw the dust of the hyenas on the horizon. He took out the fetish and said, "Sarafin Marah greets you."

The fetish answered, "Greetings to you, Marah. Now throw down the charcoal!"

He threw down the charcoal and a wall of fire sprang up from east to west. The hyenas ran east along the wall and west along the wall, but there was no way through. "I warned you, I told you," Hyena Sira said.

The hyenas said, "Ah, we were able to gnaw through the bamboo wall and grind down the granite wall, but how will we get through this wall of fire?" Hyena Sira turned around and pissed on the flames: . . . *sa sa sa sa.* The fire went out, and the hyenas set off again in pursuit of the young man.

The young man was now within sight of the town. But the hyenas were catching up with him. He took out the fetish and said, "Sarafin Marah greets you."

The fetish answered, "Greetings to you, Marah. Now throw down the egg!"

He threw down the egg and it became a great river that stretched across the world from east to west. The hyenas ran east along the river and west along the river, but there was no way across. The man went on into the town and gave the yimbe drum to the chief.

He received his reward—a hundred of everything. And the townspeople danced and sang in celebration of his return.

Now, when the tutufingbe gave the fetish to the young man, it had also given him certain instructions: "As soon as your search is over, you must kill a red bull as a sacrifice to the fetish. You must dip the fetish in the blood of the bull so that, thereafter, it will do whatever you ask of it." The young man had agreed to do all this, but once he was safely back in the town he forgot his promise.

Hyena Sira transformed herself into a human being and crossed the river.

Late in the afternoon a strange girl arrived in the town The young man described her to his mother. "Beware of her," his mother said. "She is really one of the creatures from whom you stole the yimbe drum. Do not go anywhere near her." The young man agreed to do as his mother said. But all the other young men had gathered around the strange girl, marveling at her beauty. The girl was scanning the faces in the crowd, looking for the young man. Suddenly she glimpsed him standing in a doorway.

"That is the man I love," she exclaimed. "I love no other man but him."

The young man went to his mother and told her what had happened. "Mother," he said, "that strange girl says she loves me."

His mother again told him to take care. "Do not go anywhere near her."

The young man's mother went to his house. A dog was lying on the ground in the yard. She said to the dog, "My son is in your care." Then she spoke to the door, "My son is in your care." She said to the hearth, "My son is in your care." She said to the bed, "My son is in your care." And she said to the smoking-basket over the fire, "My son is in your care." She placed her son in the care of all these things.

That night, Hyena Sira, in the shape of that strange girl, came and made love to the young man. So great was his pleasure that he afterward fell into a deep sleep. Hyena Sira got up. She was about to kill the young man when the bed said, "No!" Then the smoking-basket over the fire said, "Leave him alone!" The door said, "I will not let her pass!" The hearth said, "I will burn her unless she lies down." So the girl went to sleep.

In the morning she told her lover that she was leaving. She asked him to accompany her some of the way. Mindful of the penis of the bush, the young man took a machete from the wall. "What's this!" the girl cried, "do you mean to do me harm?" He took a cudgel instead. But the girl cried, "Why are you taking a cudgel? Do you mean to beat me?" So he went with her weaponless.

A little way along the path from the town he said, "I will leave you here."

But the girl said, "I think you do not love me. Why leave me so soon? If you love me you will accompany me at least as far as the river."

At the riverside the young man said, "Well, I must leave you here."

The girl pleaded with him, "Eh, do you want me to have to cross the river alone? Please come with me a little further." So they crossed the river.

No sooner had they reached the other side than the girl shouted, "I have returned, and the infidel is with me!" The hyenas sprang out from the bushes and Hyena Sira returned to her animal form. The young man fled, and climbed a tall tree.

"Now let us fell the tree!" Hyena Sira cried. The hyenas began to gnaw at the trunk.

The young man was desperate. He put his hand in his pocket and felt for the fetish. He took it out and said, "Sarafin Marah greets you."

The fetish made no reply.

He repeated the words. "Sarafin Marah greets you."

The fetish was silent.

In desperation the young man cried out. "Oh, what can save me from this terrible plight? If my misfortune is because I failed to sacrifice a red bull to you, fetish, then I promise to sacrifice two red bulls if I am saved."

The fetish spoke at once. "You did not heed your mentor, nor did you heed your mother. But take hold of one of the branches of the tree." The young man eagerly seized a branch. It turned into a rifle. The fetish spoke again. "Take some leaves." He did so, and they turned into cartridges. He loaded the rifle. "Now shoot!" said the fetish. The young man began firing at the hyenas.

After a while he took out the fetish and said, "Sarafin Marah greets you."

The fetish answered, "Greetings to you, Marah. Hyena Sira is still alive. Shoot her again." He shot her dead.

The young man climbed down from the tree and went home. As soon as he arrived he sacrificed two red bulls to the fetish and dipped it in the blood.

And that is how people began using magical medicines.

The storyteller paused and glanced at the children, many of whom had fallen asleep in the shadows of the porch. "That's all," he said, "until another night."

As he settled back in his hammock, the wide-awake children roused those who were drowsing, then noiselessly drifted away to their homes. Michael switched off his tape recorder.

He walked slowly back to the sergeant's house with Noah, who summarized those parts of the story Michael had not followed. The moon was high now, and the whole village bathed in its supernatural brilliance.

But his thoughts were muddled. He had begun to imagine a parallelism between the story and his trip to Bandakarafaia. And already there was the suspicion of a link between the wild, futile quests of Laing and Reade and his own. Suddenly he asked Noah, "Why did the story end with that reference to magical medicines?"

"Well, we'd have to ask . . ."

"But what do *you* think?" Michael demanded.

In fact, Noah had also remarked on a parallelism—his own life of going forth into the wilderness of the world, getting an education at his father's behest, struggling to make a living, to come to terms with the unpredictable winds of political change . . . hoping always to find renown yet at the same time bring honor to Barawa and fulfill his birthright.

"I suppose," Noah began slowly, "it's because bese can sometimes cure, sometimes kill . . ."

"Like knowledge!" Michael interrupted. "I mean, knowledge is like the yimbe drum—it has the power to initiate us into manhood, to make us responsible . . . and yet, distracted by its music, we can easily be led into using it for private gain."

They had reached the sergeant's house.

"Yes," Noah breathed. "I'll see you in the morning, Mike."

The same milky light that flooded the village poured through the open window of his room. He lay awake, the thoughts set in motion by the story now ceasing—pooled in a sudden and overwhelming desire to return to Kabala and Pauline. Noah's repining for his children made sense now, merged with a need in him for the hearth that alone gives point to the journeys men make away from it.

As he fell asleep he heard a child crying faintly in a nearby house. On the table beside his bed his medicines and notebooks were covered with a thin layer of red dust.

✖ Chapter Twenty-Three

"WHY DON'T YOU GREET ME?" Don't you know who I am?"

He looked up and saw Tilkolo standing over him, smiling.

"Ah, Tilkolo, inwali inwali," he stammered. "Did you sleep well?"

"I slept well," Michael replied.

He had been absorbed in watching the fire-finches flickering around the yard, searching the ground for broken grains of rice from the winnowing. He had not been able to get out of his mind the thought that each bird was a place of exile for the spirit of a child who had died in infancy.

When Doron Mamburu Sise, the diviner, got back to Firawa from his farm that afternoon, he found the white man waiting for him.

"M'fa inwali," Michael said.

Doron Mamburu answered the greeting, acknowledging the white man's respect. He laid down his machete on the porch and took some kure fruit from his pocket. He was about to offer some to his visitor when Michael forestalled him.

"I've come to ask you to look at the stones for me," he said.

The diviner had already guessed that something was bothering the white man, and he beckoned him inside the house. The two men stooped to pass through the low doorway into the cool darkness of the central room. It smelled of stale wood smoke.

Doron Mamburu dragged shut a rickety cane door whose daubing of mud had all but flaked off. He waited until his eyes had become accustomed to the gloom before spreading out his mat on the earth floor. He ordered the white man to sit down opposite him.

"Why have you come?" he asked.

"I've come to find out about my wife. She is expecting a child sometime around the beginning of the rains. I've been worried about her. Can you tell me if all is well, if all will be well?"

The diviner emptied some stones from a small monkey-skin bag, and spread them out across the mat with the palm of his hand. Most were river pebbles: semilucent, the color of rust, jasper, and yellow ocher. Among them were several cowrie shells and pieces of metal. Michael handed Doron Mamburu his fifty cents consultation fee, and the diviner mingled the coins with the pebbles.

"What is your wife's name?"

"Pauline."

Doron Mamburu found difficulty with the name but did not ask for it to be repeated. In a soft voice he addressed the stones, informing them of the reason why the white man had come. Then he gathered up a handful and began to chant. At the same time, with half-closed eyes, he rhythmically knocked the back of his cupped hand against the mat.

With great deliberation he laid out the stones, some in pairs, some singly, others in threes or fours.

"All is well," Doron Mamburu said quietly, his attention fixed on the stones. "Your wife is well. She will have a baby girl."

Without a pause he proceeded to lay out a second pattern.

"There is nothing untoward. The paths are clear. The birth will be easy."

In order to see what sacrifice the white man might have to make, Doron Mamburu laid out the stones a third time.

"Your wife must sacrifice some clothes and give them to a woman she respects. You must sacrifice two yards of white satin and give it to a man you respect. When your child is born, you must sacrifice a sheep."

The diviner looked quizzically at the white man, wondering if he would do what the stones suggested.

"To whom must I address the sacrifice?" Michael asked.

"To your ancestors," Doron Mamburu said flatly. Seeing that his client was still nonplussed, he added, "You must give those things away, do you see?"

"And in doing so, will I gain . . . blessings?" Michael asked, not sure if he had found the right word.

"You do not do it to gain, but to give away. Whatever follows, follows. Do you see?"

Doron Mamburu began to collect the stones. He had been clearing his farm site since dawn, and was famished. The dull clang of the lid of a cooking pot in the yard had already distracted him, and he caught a whiff of chicken and red pepper sauce.

Michael had been reassured by the diviner's insights, but as he reflected on the way the insights had been gained, he began to have doubts.

"How can the stones tell you what you told me?" he asked.

"They speak, just as we are speaking now. But only I can hear what they are saying. It is a gift that I was born with."

"Could I acquire that gift?"

"A person cannot tell if a bird has an egg simply by watching it in flight."

"I don't understand."

Doron Mamburu fetched the loose sleeve of his gown up on to his shoulder and frowned. "You cannot go looking for it. Not at all. It comes of itself."

Michael said nothing.

"Eat with me," said Doron Mamburu, getting up from the mat. He stowed his bag of stones between a rafter and the thatch, then wrenched open the door. The sunlight was blinding.

Doron Mamburu's wife brought them rice and sauce in a chipped calabash, and the two men sat on the verandah, eating in silence. Michael struggled to phrase the question he wanted to ask.

"How did you get the stones?" he said at last. "And the words you say to them—surely someone taught them to you?"

Doron Mamburu finished his mouthful of rice. He was amused by the childlike curiosity of the tubabu.

"If you find fruit on the ground, look to the tree," he said. Michael still looked perplexed, so Doron Mamburu continued. "What a person has is never his to call his own. In my case, I began divining a long time ago, in the days of Chief Pore Bolo. I was favored by a djinn. I saw a djinn, and the djinn told me it was going to give me some stones so that I would be able to help people."

"Where did you see the djinn?"

"In a dream. They came in a dream. There were two of them. A man and a woman. They had changed themselves into human beings, and were divining with river stones. They called to me and told me their names. They said, 'We are going to favor you with a different destiny.' They showed me a certain leaf and told me I should make it into a powder and mix it with water in a calabash. Then I was to get some stones from the river and wash them in that liquid. When I woke up next morning I went at once to the Bagbe River and found that leaf and those stones. I did everything the djinn told me to do."

"Would I be able to find that leaf?"

"Eh! I cannot tell you about that."

"The djinn then, did you see them again?"

"Yes, I see them often. Every Thursday and Friday night they appear to me in a dream. Sometimes they say to me, 'Are you still here?'"

"Do the djinn speak to you through the stones?"

"Yes," said the diviner emphatically, pleased that the white man seemed at last to understand.

"When you address the stones, you are not speaking to the djinn?"

"No! I am speaking to the stones." Again a frown creased Doron Mamburu's forehead. Hitching up his sleeve he scooped a ball of rice from the calabash and stuffed it into his mouth.

Michael had finished eating. "Do you ever give anything to the djinn?"

Doron Mamburu swallowed the rice and washed it down with water. "From time to time I offer them a sacrifice—of white kola nuts."

Michael got up to go. "I have eaten well," he said.

"You are going?"

"I'm going home."

The dry season was almost over. The dusty cobalt of the sky turned to ultramarine, and huge white stacks of cumuli came up from the south; each afternoon the collapsing shadows of the clouds made the air sticky and oppressive. At night, thunder caromed and grumbled far away, and along the horizon the sky flashed its filed teeth.

Michael listened to the first rain drumming on the iron roof of the sergeant's house, and went out and stood on the verandah. The village lanes had become small streams, and children were dancing in the warm downpour, shouting with delight.

While the rain fell steadily, householders who had put off their thatching complained of leaking roofs, and on the verandah at Tala Sewa's house the Firawa elders sat on tin chairs looking out into the rain that had stolen all speech. On far farmsteads, tender shoots of germinating rice were beginning to overwhelm the scarred hillsides and beseige drab farm huts and fences with greenness.

Michael went indoors and packed his things, knowing it would be some time before he came back to Barawa.

Leaving the village, the last person to whom he said farewell was the old medicine-master, Saran Salia, who was standing under the eaves of an unfinished house, his stave across his shoulders, smiling through the curtain of rain.

"We will see each other again, Uncle," Michael called.

"Awa! we will see each other."

As soon as he reached Kabala, Michael told Pauline about Doron Mamburu's divination. Pauline collected clothes to give to Aisetta, and Michael bought two yards of white satin as his gift to Noah. Their daughter was born in May and was given Aisetta's name.

150

In her first few months of life, the infant may have been so instilled with the memory of warm rain and rolling thunder, the touch of clammy bodies, the odor of a straw paillasse, and the various shadows of faces, that years later she would understand Aisetta's embrace and why the African woman kept saying to her, over and over, "You have come back, you have come back. . . ."

Fieldwork

Even now they file at first light
through the elephant grass, along
the red path to their farms, leaving
me behind. I used to follow them
and ask if I could hoe or weed,
stack unburned branches beyond
the outer fence. They used to
laugh outright, though some said I
could try my hand, knowing it would
provide for more amusement later
when I tried to keep in line.
At last I gave up going. I passed
the day learning new words from
women. At dusk the men returned
and granted me an hour or two of
conversation. "Ask what you want
and we will tell you what we know,"
they said. And so I queried them
on this and that, and learned about
their farms that way, and what they
did among the trees along the ridge
at harvesting (a sacrifice to keep
the spirits off), and for a year
my work went well. But then I found
myself describing them with words
they would not use, and could not tell
the way the drummers held the line
that moved, hoeing and chanting,
down the further slope, or how
the old man sowed the seed, and how
the pitch of women's voices flowed
across the valley as they closed
the earth. These gestures are
like rain. The crops will grow
out of these acts. There is no
book in it, no facts, no line
that leads to some result:

but it holds good like any truth
and I have learned to write as
they might sow, scything the grain
against the downhill wind. We
do not make it grow, we point the way.
In this I go along with them.

Part 3

✖️ Chapter Twenty-Four

THE RAINS that germinate the rice also breed mosquitoes.

The Barawa chief, Tala Sewa Marah, was not sure exactly what the government in Freetown did, but in Firawa it made its presence felt after harvest with the arrival of tax collectors and magisterial clerks who removed court cases from his jurisdiction and took them to Kabala for settlement. The elders charged that a people's tithes should be repaid by benefit. "In the old days," they said, "our heads were in the hands of our ruler. Now who is it holds our lives in fee?" The brash functionaries ignored such questions, and hid behind cheap sunglasses, counting the days that remained between themselves and a city.

For ten years there had been coups and countercoups in Freetown, news of which reached Barawa as rumors of bungled conspiracies and brutal retaliations. But when the smoke cleared, it always became evident that nothing had changed the government's indifference toward the north.

Only once did there seem the merest chance that the Seli might be bridged, and that year Tala Sewa brought together all the young men of the chiefdom to cut a vehicle track from Firawa to the river. But the bridge did not materialize, and within two years the earthworks washed away, the log bridges, so laboriously made, collapsed under their own weight into the streams, and grass and scrub reclaimed the path, reducing it once more to a single, worn line of laterite winding around outcrops of stone, blindly honoring the oldest contours of the land.

Tala Sewa then trekked to Freetown and presented gifts of rice, cloth, and cows to government ministers as rulers give gifts to rulers, but was obliged to take his place in lines of listless petitioners, waiting for an audience that could only increase the sense of humiliation. He came away from the city with the memory of men in tailored suits and dark glasses who were perfumed like women and did not conceal their annoyance at having to pass the time of day with an illiterate country-man wearing sandals.

Finally, to save his own dignity as much as to fulfill a promise to his people, he took matters into his own hands and began the construction of the bridge. "You cannot cross a river on the bridge that is in your mind," he said, and urged his people to contribute money, cows, rice, cement, and labor to get the bridge started.

When Michael returned to Barawa in 1979 there were four box pillars of reinforced concrete standing on the bedrock of the Seli. Negotiations were under way with the government for funds to complete the bridge span and build a road to Firawa.

"Too bad you don't have a Land Rover any more," Noah said. "You could have been the first person to drive to Firawa."

Michael watched his daughter playing with Noah's children at the edge of the river. He was glad to be beyond the noise of traffic and the dust of roads. The morning journey by truck from Kabala had been exhausting, and with Pauline and Noah he was sprawled in the shade of a giant cotton tree, resting before going on to Firawa.

Abdulai Sano, who hailed from Firawa, was making the journey with them. He was telling Michael about his bad luck in the diamond districts of Kono.

"I'm going home now, to see a diviner and find out what is wrong," he said.

"And then what will you do?"

"Go back to Kono."

Michael turned to Noah. "You see, Noah, while I spend all my energies trying to get to Barawa, you people spend yours trying to get away from it!"

Abdulai asked Noah to translate the remark, and was not amused. "The lizard and the bat do not eat from the same dish," he said, getting up to go.

When they set out for Firawa it was nearly noon and a dry stifling heat had taken hold of the plateau. Emerging from the remnant forest of the river valley, they looked eastward across a succession of hazy ridges covered with dun-colored grasses and stands of knotted lophira. Large areas of elephant grass had been burned, and charred canes had fallen on the path. Filaments of ash lay in small whorls in the dust.

As the children ran ahead, pushing through the blackened canes, Abdulai called out after Heidi, "Come here Heidi Aisetta, you are my wife!" He had teasingly claimed her as his betrothed, and promised to settle the matter that same day by tying kola and giving it to Michael.

The children hurried out of sight, and Michael and Noah fell to talking over events of the past few years, clarifying things that had become obscured through long periods of separation, letters gone astray, and political upheavals.

"Do you remember," Michael said, "how people used to call me your white man, and expect you to benefit in some fabulous way from associating with me?"

They entered a glade and crossed a small stream. Blue butterflies danced over a bank of wet sand.

What Noah remembered was the way people had warned him to beware of any involvement with the anthropologist, who would pass through Barawa, as others had done, pressing the grass down in one direction but never returning. "You are right," he said, "in one way. When you first came here, most of us were skeptical about you and what you wanted. My friends advised me against working for you. But now, everyone is only too pleased to help you. You'll see that. Everyone knows about your book—what you've done for us."

It was late afternoon when they reached Firawa, and as they crossed the expanse of granite at the edge of the village, Michael recalled the elusive medicine-master, Saran Salia. But before he could ask Noah about his uncle, the thump of the town chief's drum signaled that their approach had been observed, and Noah called the children so that they would all enter the village together.

In Tala Sewa's courtyard a great crowd was assembled. People had come from villages and hamlets throughout Barawa, and there were visitors from the neighboring chiefdoms of Woli and Yiraia. The verandahs were thronged, and children shinnied up the mango trees to gain a view over the crowd.

Tala Sewa and the Firawa elders were sitting in the middle of the

157

courtyard. A passage had been forced through the crowd by a group of young men, all dressed in red shirts emblazoned with the motif of the one-party state.

Surprised by such prepared ceremony, the visitors moved slowly toward the elders, followed by praise-singers who had accompanied them from the edge of the village with xylophone music and flattery.

Noah glimpsed Yeli Pore, on whose shoulders he had been carried as a boy. Remembering his father, he peered beyond the crowd to the coconut palm that marked Tina Kome's grave. The second palm, which had grown from Tina Kaima's grave, had been felled in a thunderstorm two years before.

After paying their respects to Tala Sewa, the visitors sat down while praise-singers relayed the ruler's greetings to them.

It quickly became clear that the welcome had been staged partly in error. A young man whom Michael and Noah had dispatched from Kabala several days before to announce their arrival had garbled the message. Tala Sewa had been led to expect a visit from the minister—S.B. Marah—as well as the assistant district officer and a bridge engineer. But he did not betray his disappointment, and told Michael that the people of Barawa were mindful of what he had done to try to secure S.B.'s release from detention in 1976, and of the book he had written. Turning to the crowd and ignoring his speaker, he declared, "We want this man to make Firawa his home, and to live here in peace with his wife and daughter, not just as our friend but as our brother."

Shrill refrains of women mingled with jangling triangles and pulsing xylophones. The air was filled with dust, and people jostled and pressed to see the white woman and her child. Michael scanned the crowd for familiar faces. He had heard of so many deaths, and children he had known were now young men and women whom he could not recognize unless they gave their names.

As the crowd began to disperse, he saw Saran Salia standing against the wall of the sergeant's house, gripping his stave and grinning broadly. Michael pushed his way through to the old man and embraced him.

"Inwali inwali. M'fa inwali."

"Ah!" Saran Salia exclaimed, shaking Michael's hand. "Ah!" He grasped Michael's forearm and looked at him wryly. "You are here again!"

Saran Salia insisted that the newcomers have the use of his house. He would move across the courtyard and lodge with his son.

While Saran Salia gathered together his medicine horns and pouches, which seemed to be all he possessed and were jammed into every nook and cranny of the house, Michael made arrangements to have the walls and floors resurfaced with white and gray mud, and a ceiling of raffia matting installed. Tala Sewa gave the visitors a table, Alhadji Hassan loaned them a chair, Tilkolo brought them hearth-stones, and then, one day, the mat-maker turned up with an old wire-wove bed frame to go with the sacking and straw mattress they had brought from Kabala.

Outside, Michael leveled the backyard and with the help of neighbors dug a latrine and built an enclosure of woven elephant grass for bathing. A platform of lashed bamboo served as flooring.

They were soon settled in the village, though the local children, less obedient than their parents to the chief's warning that tubabunu preferred privacy and quietness, kept drifting in and out of the house, their curiosity aroused by the white tents that draped the beds, the books and packets of dried beans that littered the table, and the white man who sat on the porch in the evening, typing. It was a djinn, they whispered, that made the machine work. But as Heidi became more used to the village children and let herself be enticed into their company, the strangers seemed less and less interesting and the children seldom ventured unbidden into their house.

Going about the village, Michael was struck by the number of political posters everywhere, pasted on doors, walls, and shutters, yellowing and worn but still constituting a rough record of the events of 1977.

There were the ubiquitous All People's Congress posters: a rising sun surmounted by the words "A.P.C. Live for Ever," and there were campaign posters of various Koinadugu candidates in the 1977 elections. Most conspicuous were those that proclaimed the independent cause of S.B. Marah and *ferensola*.

When Michael asked Noah what had persuaded S.B. to return to politics, Noah responded enthusiastically, for in the winds of change that had swept through Barawa he saw the hope of some niche for himself; moreover, he was pleased that at long last Michael was showing an interest in things that mattered.

"You know, S.B. was an M.P. in the Margai government after independence?"

"Yes."

"Well, after the Southern Leone People's Party lost the polls to the A.P.C. in 1967, he vowed to keep out of politics. The stress . . ."

159

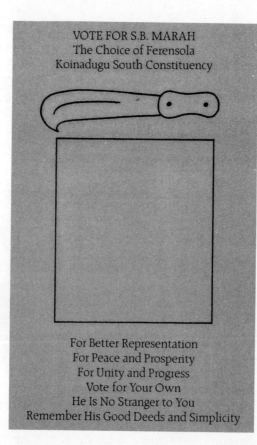

VOTE FOR S.B. MARAH
The Choice of Ferensola
Koinadugu South Constituency

For Better Representation
For Peace and Prosperity
For Unity and Progress
Vote for Your Own
He Is No Stranger to You
Remember His Good Deeds and Simplicity

"Was it being in prison those fourteen months that changed his mind?"

"I don't think it was that so much as the people's urging. I remember back in 1973 he turned down the nomination for Koinadugu South. He was adamant then that he didn't want anything more to do with politics. But the whole of ferensola became determined to return him to power, to have a Kuranko in parliament. He was no longer his own man. The movement of the people was incredible. Everyone wore the ferensola cap, the ferensola gown. Jelibas composed songs to stir people's hearts. Your ferensola book was part of the movement."

Michael was about to ask Noah to explain more about ferensola when he was interrupted by Fore Kande, an old man, once a renowned wrestler, who was suffering from conjunctivitis and had come to Michael earlier in the afternoon for eye ointment.

"We are all in this ferensola business," Fore said. "We all stand united behind S.B. Marah."

160

Michael saw that S.B. had become a folk hero for Barawa, but he could not reconcile this with all these allusions to a unity greater than the chiefdom. It seemed to him that behind the rhetoric of political representation and prestige lay more eternal concerns—for a sense of place in the wider world, for some kind of assurance of personal power—the same concerns that led people to place suras and magical medicines over their lintels, to consult diviners about their dreams, to make sacrifices in seedtime and times of uncertainty to Allah and their ancestors alike.

But it was time for them to pay their respects to Tala Sewa, and Noah suggested they move in the direction of the chief's house.

Tala Sewa smiled when he learned of Michael's interest in ferensola. "When you first came here you were a child and moved about with the children. Now you are one of us. Well, there is conversation that has a seed and there is conversation that is mere chaff. Without germane talk, there is no way of knowing another person's mind. Therefore, I'm going to have a certain man speak to you and tell you what you should know."

That night, Yeli Maliki Kuyate came to Michael's house and announced himself. "I am Yeli Maliki, S.B. Marah's jeliba from Firawa. I am going to tell you how our country came to be called ferensola, and how power in our country was returned into our hands."

Yeli Maliki had brought his four-stringed *konne*, and against its droning accompaniment he sang the praise-songs of the lords of Barawa, naming the rulers from Yamisa to Morowa and Balansama, upon whose ruling houses the dawn still broke. He remembered Manti Kamara Kulifa, Tina Kaima, Tina Kome, S.B.

"They were born into a ruling house. In the beginning, chieftaincy was with them. In the end, chieftaincy will still be with them. This is not the first time that the Marah have been the protectors of ferensola.

"In this our Barawa, Tina Kome went away to the army in order to open up the country and make it prosper. He alone did that. Ferensola depended on him. Now his son, S.B. Marah, has restored this country to its people. It was his ancestor who first ruled here, and it is through him that ferensola has been returned to its true lords.

"If you hear of ferensola, you should know that Barawa is the seed of ferensola.

"The word *ferensola* means 'twin town.' But not twin in the literal sense of the word.

"There were four founder rulers—Mansa Morfin, Mansa Yira, Mansa Borsingbi, and Yamisa. Yamisa ruled in Barawa. Yet Barawa was the most powerful and impregnable of the four countries, so the first three rulers placed themselves under Yamisa's protection. When Yamisa accepted the overlordship, he declared that the whole country should be known as ferensola so that he would not appear to hold the prestige of chieftaincy all by himself. Thus, the countries of Morfin, Yira, and Borsingbi came to be one moiety in the twinned lands. When we say ferensola we mean oneness, despite our differences. And the four corners of the ferensola mark the boundaries of Kuranko itself."

There was a dance that night in Firawa—in part an acknowledgment of Michael's return, in part a celebration of ferensola. As he picked his way through the dark lanes of the village to where the dancing would be, Michael pondered the fate of Marin Tamba, who had killed himself after the invasion of his country almost 250 years ago. He found himself contemplating all the equations implied in Yeli Maliki's recitation—of self as part of a village, of village as part of a chiefdom, of chiefdom as part of a country . . . the seed always within its husk, the part always connected to the whole. And with sudden exhilaration he began to see that he too was part of Barawa, and that by dint of an allegorical bridge he might compare his own struggles for adequate understanding with the struggles of Noah, of Tala Sewa, of Barawa itself—the quest for a fusion of person and place being, in each instance, existentially identical.

By the light of kerosene lanterns, jelibas were striking up on their xylophones, and the crowd began to form a circle to dance.

Pressed together, they shuffled round and round on the coarse laterite of the courtyard, while Senewa Kamara sang the song that had become the anthem of ferensola:

"*Be ara kanye*," he made out, "We are all one . . . *ma I koinya*—our cause . . ."

He approached the dancers, and the close-pressed circle assimilated him easily. He let his body move with the lulling shuffle, his arms swaying limply, his head tilted back, his eyes half-closed.

The music swelled as Senewa Kamara's shrill voice rose above the clamor of the courtyard. They danced until they lost track of time in an ecstatic commingling of xylophones, flutes, and singing. They danced until the beat of the gourd rattles and bells was no longer necessary to cajole them into moving as one. And so at last the kinship of the circle lifted them from themselves.

✖ Chapter Twenty-Five

ABDULAI COULD NOT decide whether or not to return to the mines. A Qur'anic diviner had told him his luck would improve, and Abdulai had dutifully sacrificed a sheep to Allah, sharing the meat among his neighbors. Years ago, when he first went to the mines, the diviner had advised him well, and he had made enough money to fund his elder brother's pilgrimage to Mecca. But now doubts nagged him, and he kept delaying his departure from Firawa, avid for further insights into his fluctuating fortunes.

When Michael showed an interest in Kuranko augury, Abdulai seized the opportunity of asking how white people interpreted dreams. It was not long before the two men had begun hazarding interpretations of each other's dreams.

Michael related a dream he had had the night before. He had been drawn toward a river by the sound of rapids. The night landscape was filled with fireflies, as if all the stars in the sky had fallen to earth and been dashed to pieces. He heard hippos laboriously climbing the river-bank, and saw them moving out to graze, wading through the shimmering grass, black holes in a disintegrated sky.

Abdulai quickly explained that the dream presaged esteem and prosperity. He then told what he had dreamed the same night.

"I was up in the sky, near the moon. I went up like an airplane, and came down to earth again. While I was in the sky I was not afraid, but as I came back to earth I became very scared and called out, 'I am falling, I am falling.'

"In the next dream I was praying. It was the middle of the night. I was praying and counting my beads."

"I think you want to go to Mecca, just as your brother did, but that you fear you may not make it," Michael said.

"*A ko sebe!*" Abdulai exclaimed. "That's true. That *is* what is in my mind."

But Michael had held a lot back. He had assumed the first dream to signify that Abdulai feared losing command over his own life; the second dream, accordingly, suggested the notion that in Islam some sense of mastery over one's own destiny could be regained. In his view, Abdulai's failure to find wealth had led him to seek spiritual fulfillment and power as a kind of compensation. But was this interpretation apposite, or a mere projection of his own preoccupations?

163

Some days later Abdulai related another dream. "I was lying in bed, drawing my wife toward me, when a *musu gbe* came up to her and began pulling her away from me."

Michael assumed musu gbe—pale-complexioned woman—to mean "white woman" and thought the dream betrayed a desire to sleep with a European woman; he suggested this to Abdulai who abruptly sat up straight and clapped his hands together once.

"Eh! Not at all. That is not what I had in mind. The woman resembled no one I know."

"But Alhadji Hassan told me the other day that if you dream of a person, then that person really does exist somewhere in the world."

"Yes, that is so. But it is not as you say. You see, I have two wives. One is pale-complexioned and one is dark. You know that paleness signifies good luck. Well, I had intended on taking my dark wife with me when I went to the mines. Now I will take the other one, because in the dream she was pulling the dark one away. It means that she will draw the bad luck away and bring me good luck."

Michael was abashed by his own revealing misinterpretation, and tried to turn the conversation in another direction.

"What if things do not go well for you, Abdulai, despite all the good omens?"

"That depends on Allah," replied Abdulai casually. "A person's destiny is in the hands of Allah. The Qur'an is Allah's word, and the Qur'an shows us how to understand our dreams."

Reflecting on the extent to which Islam had taken hold since he had last been in Barawa, Michael recalled what Fore Kande had said a few nights ago: "Conversion to Islam is just like the ferensola business. Where everyone goes, there you will go also. Would a sensible person turn his back on what everyone else was doing? Would he invite snubs and ill-feeling, or risk losing the help that neighbors give in times of need?"

At the time, Michael had felt that the winds of political change would inevitably die down—to be replaced by older ways of asserting one's command in a world so aleatory and bewildering that it could never be explained solely in political terms. Abdulai's fluctuating fortunes were a metaphor for the uncalm destiny of Barawa itself.

"Do you ever go to pagan diviners?" Michael asked, thinking of Doron Mamburu, the diviner, who had remained staunchly if quietly pagan and still saw his spirit allies in dreams every week.

"Sometimes I do," said Abulai, shifting awkwardly on his folding chair. "Indeed, I once went to a Qur'anic diviner and a pagan diviner on the same day, and they both saw the same sacrifice for me."

"You respect both Islam and the old way then. I mean—you acknowledge other powers that can be tapped."

"Mnhnn," Abdulai responded dubiously. He paused, slapping the palms of his hands together as though ridding them of dust. "Let me tell you a story."

"You can't tell stories in the daytime!"

"Why not?"

"Your parents will die, won't they?"

"Hah—my parents are dead," Abdulai laughed. "Besides, that's only a ruse to keep children at their farm work. I'm not a child and I don't have a farm. So—shall I begin?"

"Awa."

There was once a man and his wife. He was called Ferenke, and her name was Mariama.

They were gray haired and had no children. But Allah made it possible for the woman to conceive.

She told people she was pregnant, but they said she was lying, that she was ill, that a gray-haired woman could not bear a child.

When she gave birth, Mariama told everyone, "Friends, since Allah has given me this child I will call it Alama, 'of Allah.' "

Alama grew up. But his father was very old. One day he called his wife and said, "Mariama, we have got only one child. I have never learned Arabic and you have never learned to pray, so let us send our child to a Muslim teacher."

So they gave their child to a *karamorgo* who said, "Let him stay with me for seven years."

The woman said, "But during those seven years who will feed us? And how will we be able to pay the teacher his fee?"

The husband said, "I have told you that we should send our child to learn the Qur'an. I am not a learned man, and you do not know how to pray. We will benefit from sending him."

The woman said, "I agree. Since the day I married you I have never argued against you. But how many months will he be gone?"

The husband said, "Do not ask how many months; rather, how many years." The child was sent away for seven years.

During those years the woman fetched water for people in return for rice. Her husband said, "Hnn, my wife struggles to support us. But when the time comes for the karamorgo to claim his fee, what will we have to give him? My wife has no family, I have no family, and our neighbors laugh at us." The man decided to plant a tobacco garden. The tobacco flourished, and the old couple had enough to eat because the woman pounded rice for people in return for a little food. But the thatch on their roof was rotten because they had no one to mend it.

The boy now reached the last stage of his schooling, and the karamorgo decided they should visit the boy's parents. The karamorgo refused, however, to lodge with the boy's parents because their house had a broken roof. He went straight to the chief.

The chief summoned the old couple and said, "The man to whom you entrusted your child has come. The boy's schooling is finished, and the teacher says you must repay him the cow and sheep he sacrificed when your child passed the penultimate stage of his schooling."

The boy's father said, "All right. I gave my child to the karamorgo because I did not know the Qur'an and my wife did not know how to pray. We hoped our child would bring us blessings. Now that his teacher has come, he should lodge in our house, no matter how rotten the roof.

The chief said, "Karamorgo, have you heard?"

The karamorgo said, "All right, so be it."

The man and his wife prepared thirty-six basins of rice. The teacher ate well. He had not expected such hospitality. The next day the man gave the karamorgo a sheep. He said, "This is for you." The following day he gave him another sheep, and said, "This sheep is to repay you for the sheep you sacrificed when my son passed the penultimate stage of his schooling." On the third day the man gave the karamorgo a seven-year-old bull, and said, "I gave you my child to teach. Now that he has finished his schooling, I give you this bull in payment."

The karamorgo was very pleased. He said, "I have forty-six pupils. I will send them to cut thatching grass and repair your roof. You have made me very happy." He took the boy's hand, and blessed him, saying, "Your parents do not know how to pray, so when you go to pray take them with you, write your suras on your slate, and teach your parents to recite them. That is all they will need to know."

Three days after the karamorgo's departure, the boy called his parents to pray. But his father said, "My son, this year I have made my farm in the same place as I made it the year you were born. Tomorrow morning I want you to go there."

The boy said, "It is not proper to travel on a Monday. I will go on Friday." So after Friday prayers, he set off.

On his way to the farm he came upon three wells. The first was at a place like Firawa, the second at Kabala, the third at Koinadugu Town. The water from the Firawa well flowed into the Koinadugu well, and the water from the Koinadugu well flowed back into the Firawa well, but no water flowed into or out of the well at Kabala. The boy saw this, and traveled on.

He then encountered a group of monkeys who were praying. He said, "Aha, this must be another reason why my father sent me to the farm where I was born." He traveled on.

He came upon a dead buffalo, one side of which was fresh and edible, the other side putrescent and covered in maggots.

He traveled on and came at last to the farm where he was born. He found a young woman standing there, as pale complexioned as a European. He thought she was a djinn, and became afraid. But just as he was about to flee, the girl said, "Wait, come here. I am your wife. Though if you fail to hold me I am not your wife." The man took off his cap and tried to catch the girl. But she easily outstripped him, and at the end of the day he gave up the chase and went home.

On returning home he went to pray. Afterward he went to his father and said, "Father, you sent me away to learn the Qur'an, and today you sent me to the farm where I was born. On my way there I saw three things that confused me greatly. Can you explain them to me?"

His father said, "Yes," and the boy then told him about the three wells, how water flowed freely between two of them yet no water flowed into or out of the third.

His father said, "My son, I bore you. You are now learned in a way I am not, yet I still possess the intelligence I had when you were born, and this intelligence is not a matter of what can be said in words but of what can be seen in actions. Let me therefore explain what you saw. What you saw is that today the wealthy look after their own interests and neglect the welfare of their kinsmen. This is why so many people are poor."

The boy said, "Father, that is true. But what about the monkeys I saw praying?"

His father said, "That is a sign that in time to come Muslims will say to us, 'If you convert to Islam we will give you power!' But people must do things for their own reasons, and not let themselves be bribed into aping others."

The boy said, "Father, that is true. But what of the buffalo I saw whose one side was healthy, whose other side was putrescent?"

His father said, "Well, my son, the buffalo is the head of the family. He endures much distress. Some of his sons are shiftless and negligent. They deny their father clothes and food, yet seek his help when they find themselves in trouble. The putrescent side of that buffalo was the father's distress. But some sons help and respect their father, and this is what you saw on the healthy side of that same animal."

While telling the story Abdulai had sat very still, his eyes lowered, his hands loosely clasped between his knees, an unlit cigarette between his fingers. Now he lit the cigarette and glanced up at Michael with a look of worried expectation.

"What about the pale-complexioned girl on the farm?" Michael asked. "Who was she?"

Abdulai scuffed the floor of the porch with his sandal. "What do you think?" he said, exhaling smoke through his nostrils.

Michael did not hazard a guess, and thought of asking Abdulai about the names. He knew Ferenke was a name given to a twin male and Mariama was Mary the mother of Jesus; the doubling intrigued him.

But the dull thump of the mosque drum interrupted his thoughts, and Abdulai pinched the end of his cigarette to extinguish it, and hurried off for evening prayers.

"I'm coming," he said, meaning he would come back.

From every quarter of the village, men and women drifted separately toward the mosque, among them Saran Salia, the medicine-master.

As he went through the house to help Pauline prepare their evening meal, Michael wondered if the old man had been converted, like so many others, by the promises of a new age.

✖◆ Chapter Twenty-Six

IN THE BRIEF FALSE DAWN, Saran Salia made his way round to the back of the house.

He had been awakened, as usual, by backache and the cold, and had lain curled up on his mat listening for the familiar creak of a door across the courtyard, the signal that Michael was up and would be lighting a fire.

Entering the yard through a gap in the withe fence, the old man began, slowly and stiffly, to collect straw and twigs that had been kept dry overnight under banana leaves. Beyond the gully, a clammy mist still hung over the hills, and a rooster crowed drearily on the far side of the village.

Michael and Saran Salia greeted each other with the same phrases every morning.

"M'fa, did you sleep well?"

"I woke up because of the cold."

"How is the back?"

"It aches."

"Let me get the fire going then."

While Saran Salia wrenched rotten branches from the yard fence, Michael set the fire, utilizing at last the skills that Noah had given him.

He first formed a tiny pyramid of dry twigs and grass, then laid three lengths of wood so that the splintered ends met between the fire-stones. Too much firewood would prevent the fire from breathing and burning economically.

As Michael filled a pot with water and balanced it on the hearth-stones, Saran Salia eyed him askance, unable to get used to the way the tubabune performed a woman's chores. As soon as he could he took a brand from the cooking fire and lit his own pile of straw a few feet away, warming his hands in the smoke.

"That's better," he said.

Michael was watching termites escape from the smoke-wreathed wood under the cooking pot, and he reminded himself, as he did every morning, that he must go to the bush and cut proper firewood, regardless of Saran Salia's objections, else the entire yard fence would be burned up within a month, and it would then be impossible to keep the neighbors' goats out of the garden.

"I'm going to cut firewood today," he announced.

"No!" replied Saran Salia emphatically, "I'll tell the kids to bring some. Don't you do it."

The old man promptly attacked another section of the fence, struggling to disentangle the lianas that bound the withes together. To prevent Saran Salia from exhausting himself, Michael promised him, as he did every morning, that he would not cut any firewood but would wait for the boys to bring some.

When the tea was made, Pauline and Heidi joined Michael and Saran Salia on the back porch for breakfast.

"Tana ma si?" Musu Salia, their nearest neighbor, greeted Pauline diffidently across the broken fence. She was worried that the tubabunu might have overheard a bitter altercation she'd had with her husband during the night over whether or not she had a right to the money she earned toting water from the stream for Pauline. Pauline and Michael, however, had slept through the argument and were ignorant of their part in causing it. Pauline returned her neighbor's greeting, and Musu Salia smiled in acknowledgment and relief.

The sun was now rising above the mist, and Saran Salia took his stave and returned to the hadji's house for a rest before beginning his fire rounds. A few weeks ago, two houses had caught fire when sparks from cooking fires were blown into the thatch. Tala Sewa had imposed a dry-season ban on fires during the middle of the day, and it was Saran Salia's task to supervise the ban.

No sooner had the old man gone than Noah came by with his children—Kaima, Aisetta, Ibrahim, and Jeneba—who at once took Heidi off to play.

Michael poured Noah a cup of tea. Then he broached a matter that had been on his mind for a long time:

"I've been trying to get your uncle to tell me more about himself," he began.

"Saran Salia?"

"Yes. I want to get him to tell me his life story. But my Kuranko isn't good enough, and I wondered if you might be able to get him talking."

Noah sighed. "That's difficult, Mike. For one thing, there's no word in Kuranko for life story."

"Does that mean that people don't think of their lives as we do, as something self-contained, that you can tell like a story?"

"No, I don't think they do."

"Then what if we asked him about his childhood, or his initiation, or his marriages? Or when he was master of the kome cult?"

"We could try. But as I say, Mike, people don't like to talk about themselves in that way."

It was late afternoon when Saran Salia reappeared. He stood in front of the house, stooping slightly under the weight of a stave that he held across his shoulders, and peered at Noah and Michael sitting in the shadows of the porch.

"M'berin, inwali!" Noah said.

"Noah!" answered Saran Salia cagily. He knew by the earnest expression on Michael's face that Noah had been set up to ask him questions about something or other.

As Noah began outlining what Michael wanted to know, Saran Salia sidled nearer the porch, listening intently while scrutinizing an ambiguous diagram the children had scratched in the dust. At the mention of kome he looked up and grinned, exposing his few remaining kola-stained teeth.

"Hah, I've always known he was intrigued by those things," he said, nodding toward Michael. "But you know, Noah, I am like a woman now. I'm too old to farm, and I depend entirely on Alhadji Hassan for food and a roof over my head. I'll have to beg his permission to talk about those things."

As the days passed it seemed that nothing would eventuate. One morning, however, Saran Salia, looking unusually somber, turned up at Michael's place with Alhadji Hassan and Abdulai, his two "sons."

This time Noah exercised great caution in explaining Michael's interests, but the hadji's face clouded as he listened. He tugged at his djellaba, frowned, and shook his head.

"It is not good to talk of those things," he said grimly. "It is wicked to walk on that path and wicked even to speak of it. He who makes idols denies Allah's revelations!" Then, turning to Michael, he emphasized his point in English. "Jujus. Bad," he said, "very bad."

"But why not let the old man speak of what he *used* to do?" Abdulai interjected.

The hadji ignored his younger "brother" and went on. "Everyone here believes in the Qur'an now. All the medicine-masters have thrown away their fetishes. In our grandfathers' time everyone made use of fetishes. In our fathers' time a few people embraced Islam. But now everyone has converted to Islam and turned away from those things."

"In that case there can be no harm in talking about them," Noah said. He glanced at Michael, and added, "Alhadji is taking a hard line because Abdulai is willing to compromise. But if we're patient, he'll relent."

As they talked on, Saran Salia sat in the hammock, seemingly indifferent to the discussion, grating a kola nut on the lid of his tobacco tin.

When Alhadji Hassan finally consented to having Saran Salia answer Michael's questions, it was on condition that the old man speak only about his childhood. Abdulai applauded his elder "brother's" sagacity, and Noah gently urged Saran Salia to begin his story.

The old man filled his mouth with grated kola, chewed for a few minutes, then spat into the dust beyond the porch.

"From the day of my birth," he said, "I was in my elders' hands. My parents petted me. I ate sweetly with them. And in the hands of my elder brother, Malfore Sano, I was also happy and well cared for. We made our farms. We made our farms until the year I donned the clothes of manhood. When they died . . ."

"Your parents?" Michael interrupted.

"Yes. My father died about ten farm seasons after I was born. My mother died not long after my initiation. My elder brother too."

Saran Salia leaned out over the edge of the porch and spat into the dust again. The hammock ropes creaked against the worn poles of the verandah.

"When they had gone from my mind, I went in pursuit of kome. I drew the kome tether for twenty-eight years."

"What is the kome tether?" Michael asked Noah.

"Women and boys are told that a man draws the bush spirit along by a rope, just as you lead a cow or horse."

Saran Salia threw Michael an uneasy glance, and resumed his story.

"Then my child, Alhadji here, said 'Leave it.' So I left it. Gave it up. That kome business.

"After that, Chief Sena Lai of Bandakarafaia gave me a job as messenger. I was happy there. When he died and his younger brother Damba Lai became chief, I was again appointed messenger. I lived sweetly through that time too. Then this child of mine, Alhadji, called me to Firawa. He said, 'You'll live sweetly here with us now.' He made me a farm, cooked rice for me. Up to this very day there has been no hardship upon my head."

"Your wife was dead?" Michael inquired.

"My wives died. But Alhadji here, and Abdulai, built me this house and said, 'Father, live here. Father, you are too old to work, so live here and take it easy. Let us feed you. You are old, so let us take care of you.'"

Saran Salia paused, and smirked at Michael.

"You too I like very much. You like my 'sons' and my 'sons' like you. Because you've come and asked me to tell you all I know from the time of my childhood up to the present time, that is what I'll tell. There's nothing else."

Noah felt the old man was drifting off the subject.

"We want you to tell us about how you went in pursuit of kome, and what made you do that."

Abdulai laughed nervously and the hadji cleared his throat loudly and sank his head in his hands, but Noah pressed on.

"You should keep nothing back. You should explain everything you did in the past because, after all, it is custom."

Abdulai turned excitedly to Michael.

"If it was night we would let you see kome at once! But you would flee in terror if you saw it."

Noah had noticed that the hadji had become gloomy and apprehensive.

"I don't think the old man will speak freely in your presence," he said.

"I told him to repudiate all those things he's been involved with since his youth," retorted the hadji. "We told him to renounce all that. So let the white man be satisfied with what he's been told so far. It is too hard on the old man to expect him to explain everything he's done and how he did it. He's an old man! Let the white man be satisfied."

"But why *not* let him explain everything?" Abdulai broke in. "How he sought kome, what he used to do. I beg you to allow it, Alhadji."

"Surely there's nothing to fear in telling Michael about these things," Noah added quickly. "Those of us who know Saran Salia will perhaps be able to read about him, and those not yet born will one day be able to read about him, as well. Even the tubabunu . . ."

Noah hesitated, and took another tack. "If you see an ulcer on your grandfather's leg, should you tell him you find the smell offensive? Isn't it a good thing to maintain our customs, the things our forefathers did? Can that be bad? Do you know that in my trunk I have a cap and gown? Do you think it is an ordinary cap? Or that my gown is an ordinary gown? They have been steeped in magical medicines, and even my wife knows not to open the trunk in which I keep them. Even if one of our children was sick and about to die, my wife wouldn't dare open that trunk to look for medicines, for she knows what would happen if she did so!"

Nothing Noah had disclosed was new to Michael, but he was struck by Noah's vehemence and conviction. Were there also doubts, encapsulated within Noah's express belief in political power, that could only be allayed by the use of magical medicines?

Noah's eyes were on the hadji, who said nothing.

Saran Salia noticed that some boys had shuffled up to the porch to satisfy their curiosity about the conversation that had been going on all morning; he shooed them away with an abrupt shake of his arm, then straightened his sleeve and muttered something to Noah that the others did not hear.

Noah translated for Michael: "He wants to know if he should tell you about kome or about medicines."

"Aren't they the same thing?"

"No, a medicine-master is not necessarily also master of the kome."

"Perhaps we'd better keep to the subject of medicines."

When Noah translated Michael's response, Saran Salia looked perplexed.

"But he knows all that! You've told him all that!"

"Yes, but he wants *you* to explain it to him," said Noah.

Saran Salia glanced furtively at the corner of the porch where there were several old horns and grimy bottles plugged with raffia that he had still not taken to the hadji's house.

"To speak of badness," he began, his voice almost a whisper, "the first thing we can use to do ill is *nyenkafori*. If we put it on your skin you'd be scratching yourself all day and all night. If we didn't rub the antidote on your skin you would not get better. Well, that one is over there; the bottle is there in the corner. I can prepare that one."

Michael suddenly remembered the skin complaint that had plagued him so terribly on his trip to Bandakarafaia years ago. He'd always explained it psychosomatically—thinking it was induced by his craving to exchange his closed and willful self for a greater openness of being. But could the allergy have been some kind of sorcery?

Saran Salia had paused, his head tilted back as though he were listening to something far away.

"Nyenkafori doesn't know its owner," he resumed. "If the wind blows it back on the man who's using it, he'll end up scratching himself, just as if the wind had carried it to the intended victim.

"Then there is *gboye*, which makes the body swell up and split open. And *koli*, which if dropped on the ground in a person's path, gets into the foot and causes it to swell up."

"How do you prepare it, the koli?" Michael asked.

"Uhun!" exclaimed Saran Salia, shaking his head. "I do not make that one. But if you wanted some I could get it for you."

"I've heard that it is made from broken glass and special leaves," Noah said.

Saran Salia seemed not to notice. "Sometimes," he said, his voice falling to a hoarse whisper, "when it is dropped on the ground you will see it stirring in the dust, then making a line through the dust toward its target."

"How does it find its target?"

"You speak the name of your victim when you drop the medicine."

"Do you inform the victim?"

Everyone including the hadji laughed.

"No!"

"Why not?"

"Because people would seize you and bind you and take you to court. You are not allowed to use these things openly. Even in the old days it was so. Except during the boys' initiations. The kome masters would drop koli on the ground. But the boys would have smeared themselves with the antidote, you see, and it would be a way of showing your fearlessness to walk about where koli had been dropped. Without the antidote, however, you would be afflicted by it. It would pierce your skin. The only other thing that can nullify its power is rain. If it gets wet."

"Is there one antidote to all these medicines?"

"No, each has its own antidote."

Saran Salia studied Michael's face, and went on.

"Then there is *korte*," he whispered. "It is lethal. You die from it within ten minutes unless you get the antidote to cool you."

"How does it afflict a person?"

"Benko Yaran was a victim. His head ached, his eyes were bloodshot, and blood streamed from his nose. He even vomited blood. Then he fell to the ground, pan!, as if he'd been shot by a bullet. He lost consciousness. Everyone knew it was korte. Luckily there was someone with the antidote. They smeared it on Benko's head, washed his body with it, and steamed him in it. He got well. Whether he is still alive or in *lakira* I don't know. It was never known who used korte against him, or why."

"If you can't use these medicines openly, is it bad to use them? What if I quarrel with my neighbor and then use korte surreptitiously to kill him?"

"It all depends. It is good and it is not good."

"When is it not good?"

Saran Salia glanced wryly at the hadji. "It is good if you get satisfaction from it. It is not good because people say it is not good, and because the hadjis don't like it!"

Alhadji Hassan's brow furrowed with annoyance, and Noah quickly took up where Saran Salia had left off.

"Korte is used to take your revenge," he explained. "If someone has taken advantage of you and there is no legal redress, then you might use sorcery to get your own back. But only if you have right on your side."

Abdulai was eager to elaborate. "If you are in the wrong, and you use korte against another person, then that person's *hake* will go against you."

"Hake?"

"In Krio they say 'sin,' " Noah said.

"If you try to harm someone who has done you no wrong," Abdulai continued, "then you will fall sick or suffer misfortune. It is because that person's hake has come out against you."

"How would you stop another person's hake from getting at you?"

"You'd have to confess your ill-feeling and beg him to forgive you."

Saran Salia had fallen back in the hammock and half closed his eyes. It was almost noon and the scorching sun was oppressive, even in the shade of the verandah. Overhead the roofing iron ticked and pinged in the tremendous heat.

"Have you ever used medicines to kill a person?" Michael asked Saran Salia.

The old man grasped the sides of the hammock and pulled himself up. *Orhor!*" he laughed. "I have not, but those who tried to harm me did not live long!"

"How so?"

"Sometimes people have confessed to having used their powers of witchcraft against me. At Bandakarafaia, many years ago, Bala Kande owned up before he died: 'I went out as a witch,' he said. 'I went out and looked for him and saw his kome. It killed me.' You understand? I was immune to those powers. I had all the antidotes to witchcraft. So he died."

"Why did he want to harm you?"

"I don't know. He was born like that. . . . He never showed any dislike of me. But no one ever tried to harm me after that. Bala Kande was an example to everyone."

A scruffy hen stalked onto the porch and began pecking at the mud plaster that had crumbled away around the door jamb. Saran Salia waved his arm at it, and it jumped away squawking. He adjusted the sleeve of his gown and fell back into the hammock.

"The old man has a gown," Abdulai said gravely. "If you saw the gown, it would kill you."

Saran Salia closed his eyes. Noah yawned. The hen again encroached on the porch, jerking its head warily as it strutted to the crack in the wall where it had found the ants. No one moved to shoo it away.

Pauline came to the doorway.

"Do you want to eat now?" she asked.

The hadji smiled weakly and excused himself. Abdulai went with him, and Noah returned to Abdul's house for his siesta. Saran Salia remained in the hammock, fast asleep.

In the evening, after he had finished his fire rounds, Saran Salia rejoined Michael, who promptly took up the subject of medicines again.

"Can you give me the names of some curative medicines?"

"Ah! There are many." Saran Salia began counting them off on his left hand, pulling down each finger into his palm. "Headache medicine, stomachache medicine, medicine for ulcers and sores, chest-pain medicine, earache medicine, medicine for swollen feet, eye medicine, backache medicine, medicine for skin rashes." He grinned at Michael. "You see, there are many!"

"How did you learn about them all?"

"Whenever I see someone with a leaf that can cure an illness, I ask to be shown that leaf and how to use it. Many people are skilled in herbal curing. Abdulai's mother, for one."

"Did you learn the use of curative medicines when you became a master of the kome?"

"Eh! You ask a lot of questions! No, no. You learn only about harmful medicines there. But I use curative medicines or dispense antidotes to the harmful ones. You know that. You've seen the boys who sleep in my room, whose parents have sent them to me for protection against witches. . . ."

The stubborn thud of the mosque drum interrupted the conversation.

"I'll be back," said Saran Salia as he took up his stave and answered the summons to prayer. "Wait for me."

When he returned, Michael asked him: "Do you pray?"

"Of course."

"When you were a master of the kome, did you pray then?"

Saran Salia shook his head. "Not at all! Even though I was born into a Muslim family, no, I did not pray."

"When did you begin to pray?"

"After I stopped the kome business. The Muslims said they would not care for my body if I died. They said they would not arrange my burial unless I renounced the kome."

Saran Salia noticed the worried look on Michael's face. "But the word *fire*," he added dryly, "can't burn down a house! Do you understand?"

Michael smiled, as if he had received a gift.

Sorcerer

Made of pangolin claw and clay
this medicine
snakes through the dust
to one we all detest

Better this way
than the knife, or poison
in your food, your young
wife's infidelity

For when you're dead
they'll say the magic killed
and I'll avoid
suspicion as the old men talk

Sheltering in a smithy
from the rain. Perhaps
they'll praise the magic
for what it brought back—

Our power, our name.
We will forget
your face as though it
had been mist

Wreathing the far hills
when we farm, something
redundant as the dry months
promising harvest came.

 Chapter Twenty-Seven

MICHAEL SQUATTED on the ground, watching Keli make a mat. The
boy had hammered two parallel rows of pegs into the hard earth and
passed raffia cord to and fro between them to form a grid. Now he was
interweaving cane strips.

Michael pondered the image before him—of a dialectic of identity that moved between the poles of self-closure and openness to change. He'd been struck by the way that, although most Kuranko used *kandan li fannu*—protective medicines—some seemed able to dispense with them, to go bravely and boldly out into the wilderness. It was as though this biographical movement from the security of the village into the unpredictable otherness of the bush found an echo in the historical destiny of Barawa itself—now sealed and safe, now open and at risk . . . but in either case, the greatest powers always lay beyond—in the wild, in becoming other than what one was at the outset. . . .

His train of thought was interrupted by Keli, demanding cane. He passed the boy a bundle, then took up the cord he'd been preparing.

Keli, who was Musu Salia's son, had already taught the tubabu how to make cord by deftly rubbing threads of raffia between his hands, and how to strip narrow lengths of cane from the spines of palm leaves with a machete. Now he was teaching him to weave.

"Keli?" Michael asked.

"Nnn."

"You are often with the old man."

"I like him."

"He says he's your mentor."

"Yes. He has done many things for me. I couldn't tell you all the things he's done to help me."

"What are some of them?"

"Well, when I was initiated he sent his apprentice to look after me. And he is my teacher—and my father. . . . I regard him as my father."

"What do you do for him?"

"I mend the fence around his house."

Michael was smiling, and Keli also perceived the irony of his reference to the now almost nonexistent fence. "Well," he added hurriedly, "I fetch firewood for him, catch fish for him, bring him sweet things to eat . . . many things."

Musu Salia's daughters had begun pounding rice. The pestles fell with a soft coughing sound in the wooden mortar. Bending lithely from their hips, the girls widened their elbows as they became attuned to the rhythm of their work; alternately, each girl released her pestle at the top of the stroke, clapped twice, and took hold of it again as it began to fall. Between outbursts of giggles they broke into an impromptu song about a tubabu making a mat.

Michael crossed back into his own yard through a gap in the fence and found Saran Salia waiting for him with a bunch of bananas and a papaw.

"M'fa, ko baraka baraka," Michael said, thanking the old man for the fruit.

"Have you finished making your mat?" Saran Salia asked.

"Not yet, but I'm learning. Slowly."

They passed through the house to the front porch, in keeping with their routine, and as soon as Saran Salia had ensconced himself in the hammock, Michael took up the conversation where they had left it the previous day.

"Tell me about your children."

The verandah posts creaked as Saran Salia set the hammock swaying by pushing with his foot against the wall.

"I have one son alive—Karimu. My other three children died. One from stomach trouble, one from chest trouble, one from a head complaint. Allah brought about their deaths. I cannot blame any person for it."

"So Alhadji and Abdulai are not your real sons?"

"No. The bananas on the same stalk are not the same as those in the same bunch."

"When you were a child, were you afraid of sickness?"

"Nnhn," said Saran Salia tersely, shaking his head.

"What did you fear?"

The old man set the hammock swaying again, and his sandal rasped off some mud daub, which fell like a sprinkling of salt onto the dusty floor of the porch.

"Djinn . . . witches . . . the masters of the korte medicine . . . the dead." Saran Salia's voice was a hoarse whisper. "I feared them greatly. When I was a boy you did not dare go outside on the day a person had died."

"When did you stop fearing the dead?" Michael asked softly, accommodating his voice to the old man's gravity.

A faint smile passed across Saran Salia's face. "When I acquired common sense!"

"But how did you overcome your fear of witches and the korte medicines?"

"I got embroiled with kome and conquered my fear."

"Didn't you fear kome too?"

"When I was a boy I feared greatly," Saran Salia breathed. "Kome

. . . gbangbe . . . konke . . . all the secret things. When you are a child you have mixed feelings. You imagine what they are like, the secret things. You are told that gbangbe kills people. You are afraid. You don't know what it is. Then, after you've been initiated, you see them for the first time. And you see men! You see the secret things and you see that they are only men!"

Saran Salia hesitated. "But they are not ordinary men," he added quietly. "The power of gbangbe is equal to the power of many men."

"And kome?" Michael asked diffidently. "Is kome really a person?"

Saran Salia leaned forward from the hammock. His face was tense, and his voice wavered.

"Kome . . . does not come from the bush. I am kome. I myself. I dress myself up. If our eyes met when I was like that you would fall to the ground. If I said 'Eh!' you would fall down in terror. But I am old now. I cannot do it any more. I'm old. I cannot do it. . . ."

Michael was silent for a while. The old man's somber mien made him feel uneasy.

"What drew you to kome?" he asked at last.

Saran Salia answered eagerly. "Before I ever saw kome I feared it greatly. I did not know what it was, but I suspected it to be something extraordinary. Do you understand? Then, the very first time I saw it I wanted to be it."

"Why?"

"People were giving the kome master kola, chickens, rice. . . . I wanted to be given gifts like that as well."

"But what of the power of kome?"

"Yes. The kome fears nothing, once he has been immunized. But everyone fears him! He will appear with smoke coiling and drifting about his body, while flautists and xylophonists play his music. Why, if I were young again and dressed myself up, you'd run away as soon as you saw me! I used to be able to lie on my belly and crawl like a snake. I would disperse groups of men, moving as a snake. . . ."

Saran Salia's voice trailed off. He had caught sight of the hadji and Abdulai crossing the courtyard toward him.

Michael gave his chair to Alhadji Hassan. Abdulai sat on the porch wall, facing the courtyard. With a stick he poked at a pile of rubbish—bits of raffia, banana skins, groundnut shells—that had been swept from the house.

"What was your first wife's name?" Michael asked Saran Salia.

181

The old man responded with a knowing grin. Then a look of morose concentration clouded his face, and he touched his fist to his forehead.

"I do not know. But . . . wait. Orhor! Yes. Her name was Sayo Marah."

"Did you have children?"

"With her? None," he said bluntly.

Abdulai stopped poking at the rubbish, and half turned to Saran Salia.

"Tell him about what happened."

A pained expression came over the old man's face, and he glanced away, his eyes seeming to fix upon a derelict papaya tree that had grown up beside the house.

Finally he spoke. "They took her away from me by force," he muttered gloomily. "The girl's father abetted the lover. She ran off with him."

Saran Salia looked at Michael. "A wife might love her husband, but if her father ruins the marriage then that's that. Do you understand?"

Michael gave a sympathetic nod, and Saran Salia continued. "The lover taunted me. 'Show me that your iron can cut my iron!' he said to me. 'If you are a man, then do what you will!' he said. 'Do you mean me?' I said. 'Me!' There and then I took up the kome tether. You understand? Whoever sees kome, dies!"

"And did the lover die?"

"He died not long after that. My wife too. And her father a little later on. But I did not kill them. In the past, why yes, if someone aggrieved you, you would get up, and go and cut off his head. But that time and our time are not one. The white men banned all that. That is why we use medicines. You see? There are many ways that a bird can fly in the sky."

Just then Noah arrived, and under the sullen gaze of the hadji they resumed their discussion of kome.

Saran Salia's voice was a furtive whisper. "If you take up the kome tether," he began, "you must apprentice yourself to a teacher. You take him gifts—white rice, fowls, kola, palm oil, country cloth—to show that you want to become a master of kome. My own teacher was Yamisa, of Sigiri, in Guinea. I spent three good years with him, and worked for him to pay for my apprenticeship. . . ."

Saran Salia broke off as Musu Salia approached the porch carrying a pail of water on her head. At the doorway Michael helped her lower it to the ground. A handful of water splashed onto the mud floor, where it quickly seeped away. Musu Salia hastened through to the back of the house to greet Pauline. When she was out of earshot, Saran Salia continued.

"The immunization is the most important thing. First of all you have to wash yourself thoroughly in the river. You go downstream, and your teacher goes upstream. Then he changes into a snake."

"A real snake?" asked Michael, unsure of the Kuranko verb, *ke felen*, which can mean both change and exchange.

"Aha," said Saran Salia. "It comes like this," and he suggested the form of a snake with his forearm. Holding his hand at a right angle he then imitated a snake swimming through water with its head above the surface.

"Then it wraps around you!" He grasped his leg and held it fiercely. "When it wraps around you like this, you are afraid. But then your teacher comes back and says 'leave it,' and you look, and the snake has gone.

"After that he brings some leaves for the immunization proper. And he finds a corpse, seven days dead, and severs its head. He puts the head and the leaves in a pit he has dug, then he sets fire to them and you have to squat over the pit and be fumigated.

"Then nothing can harm you, nothing can touch you. If someone assaults you, you'll easily overcome him. If flies settle on you, they'll die.

"Then the clothes," Saran Salia said huskily, "your clothes have to be fumigated in the same way. Then I put on the clothes. I wear the sleeveless gown. If anyone hits me when I'm wearing that gown [*Saran Salia slapped his thigh*] he will die. But if I do this back at him [*another slap*] it will nullify the effect and the person will not die."

Michael looked perplexed. "Is the gown a sort of ally, a sympathetic part of the wearer himself?" he asked Noah.

"Yes it is. If the wearer is assaulted, *it* demands retaliation. When the wearer hits back at his assailant, the gown is satisfied that action has been taken and it will not use its own power to retaliate."

Noah nodded at the old man. "go on," he said.

"I drew the kome tether for twenty-eight years. But now I have stopped."

"Because you are too old?" Noah ventured.

"Yes."

The hadji suddenly roused himself and tilted forward on his chair. "Not only because of old age!" he exclaimed. "I advised him to stop."

Noah did not take his eyes off Saran Salia. "Would you prepare the immunization for anyone who wanted it?" he asked.

"Yes, if the cloth was provided."

Noah reminded Michael that he was having a gown made for himself, and that Saran Salia had agreed to immunize it.

Saran Salia pointed casually at Michael. "You too," he said quietly. "If you want, I will make you a gown that you can take with you when you leave us."

"Could you train me to become a master of the kome?" Michael asked.

"That I cannot do. You cannot take the medicines and other things to your country. Besides, you are not used to kome. If you saw kome now, and kome shouted at you, you'd be terrified!"

"I'm not afraid," Michael lied.

"Then it would cost you dearly if you went off to draw the kome tether," said Saran Salia irritably.

Michael changed the subject. "What has your mastery of kome given you?" he asked.

Saran Salia looked puzzled, and Noah rephrased the question.

"Aha," Saran Salia breathed, "I have been well paid. During the boys' initiations, fathers would each give me a shilling. And I have been given cows, rice, salt, everything. . . . But above all, I have been given affection. Even today the children follow me everywhere and offer to do things for me. Is it not so?"

"Are you sorry you renounced kome?"

"Even now, when the jelibas play the kome music and sing the kome songs I feel an urge to dance."

Alhadji Hassan got up and tugged at the folds of his djellaba. "I am going," he said.

As the hadji walked off blinking in the sunlight, Michael turned to Abdulai. "Why did you make the old man renounce kome?" he asked.

"I like it," Abdulai mumbled defensively. "It's the elders who told him to give it up. And I cannot go against them."

"Do you use the antidotes and immunize your gown?"

"Yes. Even the hadji does."

"Alhadji Hassan?" Michael said, surprised. Noah smiled.

"Yes," said Abdulai. "If they shoot the hadji with korte he'll fall to the ground and die just like any other man unless the antidote is applied."

"Is Islam unable to protect him?"

"If Alhadji offended a man who owned korte, and that man used korte against him, then Alhadji would die. The korte does not care where it goes when it dies! Hell and heaven are all the same to it."

Shape-Shifter

They said it was you
changed into a leopard, devoured
your neighbors' cattle,
and at this remove I think it likely:
you regarded even me
as part of your domain.

But I cannot prove a thing:
only that girl's death, not long before
I left, invites comparison.
I believe the boy
who glimpsed you in the bush,
half-man, half-animal,

In the dusk confirmed
something of your truth and ours:
and innocent like him
I ought to speak out now
and say I saw you too, dragging
her bloodied carcass through the trees.

Chapter Twenty-Eight

THE DAWN MIST inched back from the bush. He heard an animal crashing through the undergrowth on the other side of the Sunguru stream. Then silence.

He was sweating, less from exertion than from the thought of what was going to happen, of what he was going to make happen. For a moment he thought his thudding heart was a presence outside himself, and he jerked around expecting to confront some animal. But the path and landscape were deserted. He reminded himself why he had chosen that hour to enter the wilderness. He would be assured of solitude, and his accomplishment out there alone, girt by mist and the clammy, numbing quietness of the unfarmed hill, would be the greater. A night-jar fluttered up in front of him and flew off with whirring wings, but he did not react. He was calmer now, and his calmness gave him courage. Bird screech or the distant mutter of a disturbed djinn could no longer alarm.

He quit the path and pushed uphill through a drenched entangle-ment of elephant grass. His legs were covered in gummy seeds and smeared with ash. Panting, he gulped in the damp air until it felt like a solid core inside him.

When he gained the granite outcrop above the slope he found it overgrown with Combretum and ground orchid. But he sighted a patch of bare rock, slipped off his sandals, and padded across the creepers to it. There he closed his eyes and stood awhile to get back his breath.

He crouched down and pressed his palms onto the pitted surface of the rock to take up its density and power. His eyes were closed. He drank in the cook air. He threw out his chest, broadened his shoulders, and hardened his hands against the rock. The rock began to stir with life. He imagined molten iron pouring from a broken clay crucible, streaming into his limbs, filling him. His shoulders began to churn, and his neck muscles tightened. He felt the rock drawn up into him.

He ponderously lifted one foot off the ground, and stretched his toes. It was beginning to happen. The sensation was of blunt nails spreading, and great calloused platforms; he tensed his legs to bear the weight of his enlarging frame. Then he leaned forward, thrusting back his buttocks until the root of his tail began to swell and extend.

Now his forehead was a huge boulder, which he butted cautiously against the air. As the sun swam out of the mist his hide shuddered as if from sudden cold. He flapped his ears against the sides of his skull and awkwardly swung his trunk to and fro. Along his back the vertebrae cracked and knocked like river stones in floodwater. Again he took up strength from the rock. His skin went taut, but the enormous effort of filling and holding the vast firmament of his body made him sweat. There was a stench of leafmold, wet ash, and sweat, and he felt water trickling down the folds of his back, followed by the vague sensation of a bird pecking at the top of his skull.

Rrrrrhrauaaaa! Nnnnnnnaua!

The bush shook as he trumpeted. Swaying slightly he opened his eyes on a diminished valley, and frowned at the meager outcrop on which he stood. The rock quaked. Spangles of dew shattered and fell from the spiked fronds of raffia palms. The grass shrank back as he began to lumber down the hill.

Innnnaua! Rrrrrhrauaaaa!

It was difficult to move. Underfoot the grass was smashed into shallow pans into which reddish water oozed. His forehead collided with a low branch and he maneuvered stiffly to dodge it. A smell of scorched earth assailed him as he toppled and scraped against the runneled bark of a lophira tree.

In the bush by the stream he stopped. A gust of water showered him from the foliage he had dragged along his back. He lowered himself into the dark pool.

His feet settled in the sand. It was as if the dark water were flowing right through him, pulsating like a drum. He let himself be lulled by the pulse of the water and sink deeper into the pool, his ears flapping languidly. Under his feet he felt the current snatching away the sand.

Then his strength, too, seemed to flow from him, and he rose up clumsily, clenching his leg muscles and expanding his rib cage with desperate gulps of air. He threw back his head and tried to trumpet. But all he could manage was a weak, nasal cry.

Clambering from the water he lurched back up the hill toward the granite outcrop.

In the open the sun had already dried the grass, and a *suluku* bird had begun its monotonous daylong refrain. As he labored through the canebrake, he sensed a great shadow lying around him, engulfing him, but no longer a part of him. His power was ebbing away. The cicadas ached and shrilled with a piercing intensity.

On the rock the shadow loomed over him. He pressed his palms and the soles of his feet into the rock, but the granite gave back nothing but granite. For a moment he was nothing more than a hide pegged out in the sun for curing. He glanced downhill toward the stream and the cavernous shadow formed by the forest. Underfoot, the hard integument of the rock held trapped the now dull and faraway heartbeat of the elephant he had been.

It was hot. The grass was alive with small clicking and riddling sounds. A fly buzzed indolently, then ceased.

He regained the path and walked back to Firawa.

At Braima Yaran's forge a group of men were sitting around talking, and as the shape-shifter took his habitual place by the hearth, the others greeted him. So too did the white man, who seemed at that moment to be the center of attention. The shape-shifter tugged loose his tobacco pouch from behind a rafter above his head, and murmured greetings in return.

Braima Yaran was busy making spreaders for a hammock, and did not interrupt his work. He pummeled his monkey-skin bellows, and the coals glowed into life in a rough hollow in the ground. Then, taking his tongs, he drew a red-hot poker from the coals and forced down its tip on the hardwood yoke. The wood sizzled, and acrid smoke snaked up from the hole he was burning through.

Just as the blacksmith was about to push the poker back into the coals, the shape-shifter leaned forward on his haunches and took it from him. Squinting, he held the poker near his mouth and lit his cigarette with it.

The other men looked vaguely at Noah and Michael, who were discussing in English something Braima Yaran had said.

"So *miran* means container," Michael said, "any sort of vessel."

"Yes. But property too. Things you own, like your clothes, your house, your protective medicines, your belongings in general. These are all *mirannu*."

"From what Braima Yaran said before, miran can also mean self-possession."

The blacksmith glanced up on hearing his name, then went on punching the forge bellows.

"Yes," Noah said, "something like confidence."

"Presence?"

"Yes, or dignity. Chief Sewa has miran, for instance. When the section chiefs meet at Yifin, and Chief Sewa is late in arriving, the others say, 'Let us wait until the chief is here before we begin.' "

"Can you gain and lose miran?"

"Of course. Some people may use jujus to undermine your confidence. Or parents may intimidate their children by shouting at them or frightening them. It's the same when you're in the presence of someone with miran. Like Saran Salia was telling you the other day, when he gets dressed up properly he is so fearsome that your miran goes out of you, paf!"

"So his gown is part of his miran?"

"Yes."

"And without your protective medicines, your clothes, your belongings, you feel less . . ."

188

"Less in command of yourself, less in control of things. Sometimes, when you're walking at night in the bush on your own, you'll suddenly sense the presence of a djinn. Fear clamps you. All your confidence goes out of you . . . just like that!" Noah dashed one palm against the other to emphasize his point.

"Does miran include magical properties such as witches are supposed to have?" Michael asked.

"Yes, those things are mirannu," said Noah. "The witch-finders seize them and so disarm the witches."

"What about when a person leaves his village and goes and works in town, among strangers whose language he cannot speak?"

"Well, that could take away his miran," said Noah, and he put the question to Bala Sise, a young man who had a few days ago returned to Firawa from Freetown.

"Yes," said Bala fervently, "it is true that if you have no home, no family, then you have nothing, and your life is nothing. But when we go away we know that our village is there. We can always go back."

"If only to leave again," added Noah dismally.

"What if a person gave away all his belongings and stopped using protective medicines?" Michael asked.

"I have never heard of such person," said Noah, and passed the question on to Bala Sise. But it was Braima Yaran, the blacksmith, who answered:

"To be naked and alone! You would go mad or die," he said with finality, and chucked a handful of charcoal into the fire.

"Like a tree if you stripped off all the bark," said Bala.

"Every seed has its husk," added another man.

"But a seed can only germinate when the husk is broken through," said Michael, "and you can only eat the seed when its husk has been winnowed away."

"It is true," said Bala, "some people can lay themselves open like that. But you become changed, you risk your life, you never know what will happen."

"Are those the people who can change themselves into animals?" Michael asked.

"Yes," said Bala, "but only some people have that power."

"Do you know such a person?"

Bala glanced anxiously at the other men, but they were watching Braima Yaran burn through the last hole in the hammock spreader.

"Those who can do it don't make it public," Bala said, addressing Michael. "If you come upon someone in the bush, changing, he'll beg

189

you not to expose him. If you divulge his secret he'll die before his time. . . ."

Noah interrupted. "He will try to keep his ability secret, because he could be blamed whenever animals damage farmers' crops. Say he had quarreled with a farmer, and the farmer knew him to be a shape-shifter. Well, the farmer could accuse him of destroying the crop."

"Europeans cannot change," Michael said to Bala.

"But the tubabunu change into things," Bala replied vehemently, "like airplanes!"

Michael raised his eyebrows. The other man kept looking indifferently toward the hearth.

"When I was a small boy," Bala explained, "there was an American missionary at Yifin . . ."

"Mr. Dauda," Noah broke in. "I've heard of him, too."

"He could change. Once, he took me on a hunting trip along the Bagbe River. We saw a crocodile seize Mr. Dauda's dog and drag it down into a deep pool. Well, Mr. Dauda immediately ran to the pool and got down into the water. He disappeared for two hours, and turned up later, upriver. When we went to see the Yifin chief, Mr. Dauda explained how he'd seen a town under the water, with fine houses and many, many people. He said he'd found his dog there and brought it back. Mr. Dauda had that power, and so did the Yifin chief. He could change too. He often changed into a crocodile and went to that town beneath the water."

"What did the chief say when Dauda told him all that?"

Bala hesitated. "He didn't say anything. He just laughed."

"Then what happened?"

"Well, Mr. Dauda told the chief that he was going to shoot all the crocodiles in the Bagbe River, and he warned the local shape-shifters that they risked their lives loitering there, lying in wait for traders and cattle crossing the ford."

Michael was amused by Bala's story, but before he could ask him anything more about the legendary Mr. Dauda, the blacksmith handed him the finished hammock spreaders and he found himself struggling to thread the hammock ropes through the holes. Braima Yaran watched him for a while, then took over and completed the task himself.

"When I return to my country," Michael said, digging in his pocket for money to pay for the work, "people will admire the hammock and I'll be able to tell them who made it."

Braima Yaran gathered up his tongs, pliers, and cold chisels and dumped them in his toolbox. Praise was not part of his fee.

Michael and Noah left the forge and wandered back to the house, Michael carrying the new hammock under his arm.

"How long will you stay in Firawa after we go?" Michael asked.

"I want to buy up more rice, so I'll stay as long as that takes."

Two months earlier Michael had given Noah capital for an entrepreneurial venture, but he had not asked much about it at the time; now he had serious misgivings.

"And you'll sell the rice later this year?" he asked.

"Yes, during the rains when the demand and price are high."

"The hungry time." Michael reflected, then had to ask: "Don't you feel you're exploiting your own people, Noah—profiting from their labor?"

"Not at all. They sell some of their rice after harvest anyway, but keep back enough for their own needs."

Michael was dubious but did not want to argue. "Maybe, but it saddens me."

"Everyone sells rice now, to pay taxes, buy kerosene, cloth, blankets, seed rice," Noah went on defensively.

"But without making bigger farms, it's disastrous!"

"They'll make bigger farms."

"What about the labor, Noah? Most of the young men are going away. Look at Abdulai, and Bala. And besides, you've often said yourself that if a farmer does better than his neighbors, he's likely to be envied and lay himself open to sorcery."

"Sometimes."

The meekness of Noah's tone annoyed Michael. "Once you get mixed up in markets and money you lose your self-sufficiency, you lose control of your own world. Isn't that what Bala was saying at the forge? And Saran Salia?"

"But it also works the other way round, Mike. Nowadays these are the only ways we have of getting back control and dignity."

They had reached the house, and Michael threw down the hammock on the porch.

"I wish it were like the old days, Mike," Noah said, knowing that their disagreements could usually be eclipsed by an appeal to their shared nostalgia. "We had no worries then. But look at me now! Who would you say is the oldest—Abdul or me? It's me, isn't it? Even though

I'm younger than he is. And all because of worry! In the old days, Mike, people used to move together, work together. Whatever we wanted we bartered. We made our own salt, our own soap, cloth, pots, everything. Smelted our own iron, fashioned our own farm implements, grew whatever we needed."

Michael was half-inclined to accuse Noah of conflating biography and history but realized it was something he, too, was equally prone to do; he felt anger at himself for having challenged Noah's right to follow his own judgment in the business of buying and selling rice.

"I'm sorry to be so critical," he said, picking up the hammock. "Do you want to come in and have some tea?"

"Gladly."

A WEEK LATER, Michael and his family prepared for their departure from Firawa.

On their last evening in the village, visitors crowded into the house to say goodbye while Noah supervised the most equitable distribution of the household goods they were leaving behind.

Tala Sewa shook Michael's hand. "Next time you come, the bridge will be finished and we will have made the road into Barawa."

As the chief pushed his way toward the front door, small children pressed back against the walls, eyeing the goings-on with a mixture of bafflement and awe. Musu Salia gestured effusively to thank Pauline for her gift of the water buckets, and Keli grinned shyly as Michael pretended to give him the mat he had made. Tilkolo arrived to reclaim her hearthstones, but first she joked: "You must take them with you, Pauline. And leave little Heidi Aisetta here with us!"

Everyone took refuge in banter except Saran Salia, who stood by the back door, his face drawn, his chest heaving. It was late when he found the opportunity he had been waiting for.

"Come," he said, and led Michael out into the backyard. The last quarter of the moon gave hardly any light, and Michael stumbled after the old man's dark outline.

Just beyond the line where the fence had been, Saran Salia stopped. With a single slash of his machete he cut down a bunch of bananas from the bedraggled palm.

"They are green, but they will ripen and be sweet," he said, his voice quaking.

In the darkness Michael fought back tears. "*M'fa, ma si ma nyorgoye,*" he stammered, "we will see each other again."

Saran Salia thrust the bananas into Michael's hands.

✖ Chapter Twenty-Nine

FROM BARAWA to Freetown is no easy journey. It often involves waiting days for a truck to turn up at the end of a bush road, and usually
another day to cover twenty-five miles back down the same road—the
overladen vehicle running out of oil or water or breaking an axle or falling through a rotten bridge—until, exhausted, the traveler needs at least
a further day to recuperate before starting on the next stage south.

In Kabala, Michael and Pauline were lucky to find the government
rest house vacant, so they broke their journey there.

The entire rest house compound was made of concrete and surrounded by a high barbed-wire fence. A watchman made sure the gate
was always closed against the street; indoors he pretended to dust, with
desultory sweeps of a piece of cheesecloth, the concrete windowsills,
linoleum floors, and vinyl furniture.

All day trucks roared along the laterite street, and young men
wearing sunglasses, pink shirts, and cowboy boots sped past on their
Japanese mopeds, sending up billows of reddish dust that engulfed
women walking to market, and covered the interior of the rest house
with yet another deposit of rust-colored flour. Even the watchman,
waking from his siesta under the eaves at the back of the house, would
have to dust himself down before returning to the same endless chore
inside.

At night the babble of voices in the street rose raucously in argument or gave way to the blare of transistor radios. Greetings were
shouted in four languages. Horns tooted. Dogs yapped. Prayers were
called. Children drummed on discarded baked-bean tins. Along the
rows of kebab stalls lit by flickering oil lamps, school boys sauntered in
white shirts, painstakingly pressed, the boys' fingernails long and lacquered to show their disdain for work and dirt.

After the placid nights of Firawa, Michael and Pauline could not
get used to the noise, and only Heidi slept through it unperturbed.

They woke at dawn to the bleary thumping sound of laundry
being beaten against a concrete culvert. Later, as the sun came up, the
first trucks churned blindly down the street, overloaded with travelers
going south to the big towns.

On their second night, their fitful sleep was interrupted by what
sounded like a deranged lawn mower tearing around the compound,

followed by banging and shouting as new arrivals moved their gear into the house.

The next morning Michael shared his breakfast with the new-comers. They all wore dark glasses and sat along the bench on the front verandah, elbows on thighs, hands clasped, looking out into the yard at the Suzuki 540cc jeep in which they had driven up from Freetown.

One of them tilted his head to claim Michael's attention. "What are you doing here?" he asked.

"I've been living in Barawa for a while. Do you know where that is?"

"Sure I know." His voice was smudged with an American manner-ism, and unamazed.

"Have you lived in the States?" Michael suggested.

"No. But I'd like to. You American?"

"No."

"English?"

"No."

The man turned his gaze back to the jeep in the yard. "Barawa, eh?" he mused.

Michael felt under interrogation. "Yes," he said.

Then, as if retrieving a thought he'd almost lost, the other added coldly, "We know about Barawa."

"Oh."

"Do you know about ferensola?"

"Yes," said Michael cautiously.

"Oh yes!" the other replied, as if surprised by this sign of ingenu-ousness. "What do you know about it?"

Michael explained the etymology of the word.

"I haven't heard that before," the other said, almost cynically.

Michael imitated the tone: "Haven't heard what before?"

"Ever heard of Mau Mau in Kenya?"

"Yes."

"Ferensola," said the other, as if the connection were obvious.

Michael decided to say nothing. He scrutinized the line of dark glasses, each pair reflecting an identical silver sky.

"Do you know ferensola is an illegal political party?" the other said acidly.

"That is simply not true. I've heard malicious reports to that effect, but I happen to know they are wrong."

"Oh yeah," said the other, reverting to the spaghetti-western voice.

Now the silver sky he saw in the dark glasses had black specks in it: vultures were circling. The image was too crude, and made him think of a Graham Greene novel.

"When do you leave here?" the interrogator asked.

"Tomorrow, I hope."

"Going to Freetown?"

"Yes. How about you?"

"Kurobonla. You been there?"

"I know it, but no, I've never been there."

"Mnhn," said the other incredulously.

In a moment, without any apparent signal, the three men got up and descended the steps to their jeep. As the engine revved, the interrogator leaned out of the jeep and shouted above the racket: "It's been good talking to you. Hope to see you again before too long, Mr. . . .?"

"Jackson," Michael yelled back.

"Jackson," the other mouthed, and the jeep sputtered out toward the gate, which the watchman had swung open as if he, too, knew exactly when they had intended to go.

When the jeep had disappeared up the north road, Michael again turned his attention to a list he had been compiling, of truck mottoes: All Things Nar God, If You Worry Pass God Go With You, No Condition Is Permanent, The Black National, Destiny, Conscious Man, Please Realese Me. Suddenly the list seemed frivolous and absurd. He screwed it up and tossed it into the yard, then sat staring up the empty road, disquieted and estranged. From the culvert came the repetitious thump of laundry being beaten against the concrete.

A pariah dog limped along the roadside beyond the barbed-wire fence. It shared the color of the road: a reddish tawny pelt with black moles and pale dun patches on its belly. It was so gaunt that every one of its ribs was clearly visible. One ear had been lacerated in a fight, and had festered. Pus exuded from the blotchy pink flesh, and flies busily crawled across the wound.

The dog did not seem to see the lurching truck that bore down upon it: without having made even a surprised whimper, it was suddenly gathered up in a cloud of dust and fastened beneath the chassis. The truck did not stop, but two men clinging to the tailboard shouted back at the dog as if to admonish it.

On the canopy of the vanishing vehicle Michael made out the motto, "Look Road for 'Power-Man.' "

The dust settled. Little shivers and spasms twitched at the dog's body. Then it was utterly still.

Women were now filing along the road toward the market, carrying on their heads wide enamel basins filled with groundnuts, rice, bananas, sweet potatoes, and cassava leaf. Each group of women stopped when they came to the dog, peering at it as if to see whether it was really dead before they went on.

A group of children came down the road. One boy was bowling along the rim of a bicycle wheel, hitting it with a stick. His companion was wheeling a toy truck fashioned out of wire and controlled by a long wire handle connected to the front wheels. When the boys saw the dog they slowed down and came up to it warily. The boy with the toy truck picked up stones from the road and lobbed them at the dog. When it did not stir, the boys muttered amongst themselves and continued down the road. The skeletal hoop and toy truck left three thin lines in the dust.

At the culvert the washerwomen bashed down their sodden bundles on the concrete, wringing out the suds into the slimy water of the near-stagnant stream. None of them looked up at the passers-by.

As the morning wore on, the dog seemed to stiffen and sag. Its belly became bloated, and the scruffy skin puffed out until the ribs were no longer visible. The dog's lips shriveled, exposing a snarling line of small, sharp teeth. A trickle of blood from its broken hip went black in the sun. Flies hovered above the wound, ignoring the festering ear for more fertile ground.

A hen stepped gingerly onto the road and was making toward the dog, then suddenly flapped its wings and scampered into the grass. Two vultures clumsily swept down and, like a couple of broken umbrellas, folded their shabby wings at their sides and took up vigil on the ridge of the rest house. From time to time they shifted about, scratching their claws on the roofing iron, but they made no move to descend to the carcass.

Through the noonday and into the afternoon the vultures kept vigil. People passed down the road. Some stopped for a moment to look at the dog; some discussed briefly how it had been killed. Trucks swerved to avoid running over it. The young men on their Japanese mopeds tooted at it.

It was now swollen up and its bony legs stuck out from its body. Its teeth, bared in an inane grimace, were covered with flies trying to find a way into its mouth.

In the evening it began to stink, and the foul air carried to the rest house. Michael went out and picked up the dog from the road and hurled it far into the long grass.

🐾 Chapter Thirty

IT WAS THE BEGINNING of the rains. Above the peninsular hills great heaps of inky cumulus clouds formed and reformed a rider—now hooded, now headless, now unhorsed. At dusk, however, the skies were barren of everything except flakes of high cirri, amber in the setting sun, and random swallows.

Michael walked past the Red Cross headquarters in Brookfields; the compound was stacked with engineless VW Combis and wheel-less Land Rover ambulances rusting away in the long grass. Under its faded red crosses one made out: "Gift of the People of the German Democratic Republic, or Donated by the International Medical Aid Society."

Hill Cut Road ran from Brookfields up to Hill Station. Sewa's house was at the foot of the hill, before one reached the sequestered bungalows of the bankers, diplomats, and businessmen. The air was hot and sticky, and the traffic din from the city hammered in Michael's ears. By the time he got to the house he was exhausted.

He sat at an open window and looked out into the garden. A hummingbird hovered uncannily at the mouth of a bougainvillea bloom. Two orange-and-indigo gheckoes skedaddled from the window ledge. Under the casuarinas, three convicts in dull mauve shirts and trousers chipped weeds from the stony ground while a bored prison guard watched them from the shade of a mango tree. One of the prisoners, a convicted marijuana peddler, glimpsed Michael at the window and mimed puffing a cigarette, smiling his gratitude for the money Michael had slipped him that morning. A sluggish wind wafted in through the window, smelling of mildew and the sea. Against the flimsy mimosas, a bull the color of milky coffee swiveled its ears, swished its tail, then

stood stock-still in an attitude of weary meditation. It would be slaughtered at the end of the week.

Michael unfolded the local newspapers he had bought. One of
them had become famous for the number of typographical errors that
littered its pages—the combined product of an antiquated linotype
machine and broken fonts. He read:

HUNTER MOULDED TO DEATH BY RAIDING BUFFALO

A hunter, Momoh Sannoh, was moulded to death during search for a buffalo which has been threatening the people of Bagbo Chiefdom in the Bo
District. Momoh was killed when he was alone in the heart of the forest.

FED-UP WITH LIFE

A middle-aged man got fed-up with life, gulped down a pint of carbolic
acid and died at the Connaught Hospital on Sunday, leaving a list of Cred-
itors with a request that his brothers and friends pay his debts.

TOO MANY SAUSAGES!

A man chocked to death during a sausage-eating contest in Frankfurt, W.
Germany, last weekend according to a police report. Details were not
available.

In the garden a crow made the desolate sound of England in win-
ter: *aaaaark.*

Still clouded by sleep, Pauline came through from the guest room.
"You're back!" she said. "What have you got?"

"Just newspapers. Do you want to read them?"

"Not particularly. They depress me. Did you manage to get any
books?"

"I went to the British Council library and got *To the Lighthouse* if
you want to re-read it. Otherwise, *The Eye of the Storm.*"

"I've read them both," she grumbled, "twice."

"I also bought you a joke card."

"A what?"

"Outside the British Council this old guy came up to me grinning
impudently, hands me a set of these cards, then asks if I'm married. I
said yes and he picked out this one for me."

Pauline read: "We prefer married women, they already know how
to take orders, ten cents."

"Soupsweet land," she commented.

"And not so sweet. Look at this." Michael passed Pauline a note

198

that a deaf-mute boy had thrust into his hands outside the law courts that morning: "Good morning/I am no hable to spick and I can not find chob/Please will you help me/Tanka God pless."

Pauline put the note down on the newspaper and pointed at a headline. "The government's going to be spending millions on the O.A.U. conference facilities for next year." she said. "Maybe your 'chobless' friend can find work building the conference center."

At that moment Abu and Kelmansa ran into the room, followed by their mother, her arms full of schoolbags and parcels. Heidi soon appeared with the older girls, who went to their room to change out of their school uniforms. While Rose, Michael, and Pauline exchanged small talk about the humidity and the downtown traffic, Abu and Kelmansa whizzed around the carpet with their matchbox cars.

"I'll make some tea, Rose." said Pauline.

"Ask Ahmadu, Pauline. Don't you do it."

"It's all right." Pauline said, knowing Rose was now reconciled to her guests' awkwardness with servants.

When the tea was made they sat facing one another from three sides of a square formation of armchairs in the middle of the room. Rose had drawn the curtains, and the room was dark and cool. The children had gone out to play in the garden, but their voices drifted into the room with a breeze that vaguely touched the curtains.

"Do the boys remember much about the year Sewa was detailed?" Pauline asked, leaning forward to pour the tea.

Rose waited until Pauline had handed her the cup, then said slowly, "Well, Kelmansa was born a year after S.B.'s release. Abu was too young at the time to remember anything."

Unsure if Rose wanted to rehearse these painful memories, Pauline fell silent. But Rose suddenly set down her cup and saucer on the polished mahogany table. "For myself, though, I can remember everything. The day they arrested him . . . even now I shudder to think of it.

"We were living in Wilberforce at the time. You remember our house there, Mike? When S.B. was working for Alitalia? You used to come and see us. It was 1972, wasn't it?"

"Yes."

"One morning, after S.B. had left for his office, the men from the Criminal Investigation Department came. They ransacked the house from top to bottom, looking for arms and dynamite and ammunition. I don't know what else. Of course they found nothing, and left. But later in the morning they came back. S.B. was with them, but we weren't allowed to talk to him. They stayed a few minutes and left. I was completely confused. I phoned his office over and over again, until at last his messenger answered and gave me a number to ring. It was C.I.D. headquarters. I spoke to him there for a few minutes. He urged me to bear up and look after the kids. And that was it. We had no contact with him for the whole fourteen months he was detained in the Pandembu road prison. His mother came and lived with us. She wept every day. But we were powerless to do anything, and there was no way we could get in touch with him."

"No legal . . ." Michael began.

"Oh my," said Rose smiling. "There was no crime! He was supposed to have been part of a plot to blow up the houses of the two vice-presidents. But you know, Mike, how he kept away from politics all those years. In fact I'll never forget the time some former S.L.P.P. men tried to persuade him to join them. He lost his temper with them completely. There was no way he was going to get mixed up in politics again. That's why he ignored it when someone phoned him from the president's office and said he was on a list of people who were going to be detained. He didn't see any reason why he should be arrested. But the cook, or someone at the house in Murray Town where the plotters apparently met, claimed that S.B. had once given him some money to arrange transport to the house. That was the only incriminating evidence! Of course it would have been demolished in court. But there was no way to plead for the detainees, no way we could appeal. Even when we heard he was seriously ill, there was nothing we could do."

"That was about the time Noah wrote to me and told me what had happened," Michael said.

"African politics," said Rose with bemused resignation. "My sister's husband in Ivory Coast is talking of going into politics. S.B. has warned him against it. But S.B. is a politician. His life is not his own—it belongs to ferensola."

Rose looked sorrowfully at the tea she had not drunk. "I've talked so much," she said, "I'm sorry." She got up and went to the window, where she brushed aside the curtain and called the boys: "Abu, Kelmansa, come now!"

When the boys appeared, Rose ushered them off for their afternoon nap, and Pauline and Michael quietly cleared away the cups.

It was dark when Sewa arrived home from the ministry, and a group of villagers had been waiting several hours to see him. Michael had been talking to them about the rice famine they expected that year.

Sewa glanced at the visitors and muttered "Inwali" as Kelmansa ran up and embraced his legs.

"Papa, papa," the little boy cried, his face tilted back and beaming. He began tugging at his father's trousers.

"You want to fight me?" Sewa drawled. "You want to fight me? Eh, Kelmansa?"

Laughing, Sewa looked across at Michael. "His name is not warlord for nothing!"

SEWA DISTRIBUTED CELLOPHANE packets of biscuits and pistachio nuts among the older children who were busy with their school homework at a corner table. Then he sat down to hear what the villagers wanted.

They represented a political faction in Neya, and had come down to Freetown to enlist S.B.'s support in their bid for the chieftaincy.

As Sewa listened his face hardened, and no sooner had the Neya spokesman said his piece than Sewa exploded in anger: "You expect me to represent you! You expect me to represent ferensola! Do you even know what ferensola means? Why, even this tubabu here knows that it means unity. And yet you come to my house with this talk of petty differences. Do you want my disgrace? Do you know what the president would make of this if he got to hear about it? Huh? It would confirm his worst suspicions. Do you understand?"

He banged down his hand on the table, and the villagers, already awkward and abashed in the grand ministerial house, looked down at the carpet.

"You destroy ferensola with your wrangling," Sewa went on, his voice calmer. "Do you think I suffered for this? Eh? Power is a force for bringing people together, not dividing them!"

"Well said," murmured the Neya spokesman.

"It is true," another added meekly.

Ahmadu set down bowls of rice and okra sauce on the table in front of Sewa.

"Mike, have you eaten?" Sewa asked.

"Thanks."

"You should eat more you know. Put on a bit of weight while you're with us. Where's Pauline and Heidi?"

"Rose's taken them over to Wilberforce to meet a friend."

As Sewa ate, the Neya men peered diffidently at the TV. The children were playing a video-cassette that a family friend had brought

201

back from London: against the backdrop of an alkaline desert a man in a poncho snarled, then squinted at another man in a grubby greatcoat.

But their audience was over, and the Neya men got up, made respectful noises in the minister's direction, and dawdled out of the room.

Sewa shoved his dinner, unfinished, away from him. "Mike, come outside," he said.

In the garden a cicada went *dzitt, dzitt, dzitt,* and beyond a frail screen of casuarinas Michael made out the distant floodlit tourist hotels on the coast, isolated by a tidal inlet from the dark enclave of Kru Town, crossed by a single ribbon of dull orange street lights.

Sewa gripped the concrete balustrade of the terrace and looked sidelong at Michael.

"You see how tough it is, Mike. Every day I'm under pressure to explain away rumors and false reports. I'd like to come home to Rose and the kids in the evenings. Not to more problems. After what they've been through, they deserve all I can give them."

"But those men depend on you too. You can't really blame them."

"Pah! It's a matter of proportion, Mike. You know what we say: better to be in the hands of someone you know than in the hands of a stranger. And who does a person know better than himself? We have to begin with ourselves or we are lost."

"But how can anyone be expected to choose his own fate, when history overwhelms him and sheer hunger destroys his will?"

"We must do what we can. That's all. Each one of us. Unless we do, how can we ever hope to narrow that gap between ourselves and the world?"

"I know that gap. In my writing. In the way I've made Kuranko life intelligible but at the expense of the sensible. . . . I sometimes feel . . ." Michael at once felt embarrassed by this irrelevant confession.

"You underestimate what you've done, Mike."

"Maybe my real worry is what can I do now, how can I be of use, here," Michael struggled, but still sounded ingenuous. Or dishonest.

"You worry too much about what you can give. It's what you can learn and how you can change that matters. If we can't change ourselves, how can we expect to change the world?"

"Do you think that was your father's view too?"

"Yes."

The cicada had stopped trilling. The men's conversation might have been merely a distraction from the silence in the garden. As if by tacit agreement, they let the quietness envelop them.

IN THE SHALLOW DAWN, Michael and Pauline woke to the vapid clanging of the night watchman's kettle as he washed before prayers. Outside their window a mat scraped on the path, then came the monotonous call:

Allahu Akbar, Allahu Akbar,
Allahu Akbar, Allahu Akbar,
Ashhadu an la illah illa 'llah,
Ashhadu an la illah illa 'llah . . .

The prayer was soon drowned out by jangling hi-life from a radio in the kitchen, and the shouts of children running through the house searching for clothes and schoolbags.

Everyone breakfasted together, Sewa and Rose hurrying to finish their coffee as the children tumbled out of the house and into the Mercedes, which the family driver had brought round to the gate. Sewa and Rose would drop the children off at their various schools on their way to work.

But first, Sewa had something he wanted Michael to do.

He gave Michael forty leones. "Here, Mike, I want you to buy some ferensola cloth, so that you'll have something to take away with you, to remember us."

Michael demurred. "You and Rose have been generous enough, Sewa. Please. Let us pay for it."

"Ah, Mike," Sewa sighed. "You still have to learn to think like an African! We are one family now. You, Pauline, Heidi Aisetta. And weren't we saying last night that it's a changing world, that we've got to change too?"

Michael accepted the money.

"By the way," Sewa called as he hastened after Rose, down the lane to the waiting Mercedes, "Noah's sent word that he'll be in Freetown in a few days to see you off."

That afternoon, Michael, Pauline, and Heidi went downtown and bought the cloth—russet dyed and bearing the decorative indigo imprints of a cogwheel. From the cloth market they took a taxi to Lumley Beach.

The hills had been weighted with rain clouds all morning. Now, as the clouds dispersed, whisps of mist snagged the tops of huge trees. The air smelled of rain and vanilla.

They wandered along a near-deserted beach.

Sunlight shone through the green curve of a breaking wave before it collapsed with a clap and hiss, and licked up the white beach, effervescent.

Toward Cape Sierra, inshore fishermen were preparing to haul in a seine net, whose cork floats made an arc across the water, anchored at one end by a beached canoe and tied at the other to a solitary coconut palm.

As the fishermen hauled in the net, they folded and laid it down across poles to make it easier to carry away. And when the net was finally in, they plucked small fish from the mesh, tossing them back up the sand where they flicked like silver leaves until a boy collected them in a chipped enamel basin.

Michael strolled on up the beach alone. In the distance, on the headland, were the white tiers of the tourist hotel, which had been named after the highest peak in the Loma Mountains, the peak he had failed to climb nine years earlier. Behind him he heard sea gulls calling above the catch. The beach smelled of salt and oil and oranges.

Moving along the tide line he looked down into a film of water that reflected pale gray clouds in a cocoa-colored sky and now began to slide and sail under him so that he felt he was upside-down, or treading air, bound to nothing.

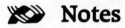 **Notes**

Chapter I

Notes to pages 3–8

The account of the settlement of Barawa by Yamisa is based on an oral history of the chiefdom by Yeli Maliki Kuyate, recorded at Firawa, February 3, 1979. Another tradition, recorded by C. Magbaily Fyle (*Oral Traditions of Sierra Leone*, Niamey, 1979:33), states that the first Barawa chief was Kankan, but according to Tina Kome Marah's written account of the Barawa succession (dated December 22, 1946), Marin Kankan was the second chief of Barawa.

The story of Marin Tamba is based on Tina Kome Marah's notes. Marin Tamba's repudiation of Islam is also mentioned by Major A. G. Laing in *Travels in the Timanee, Kooranko and Soolima Countries*, London, 1825:405–6. The account of Marin Tamba's suicide is based on Yeli Maliki Kuyate's oral history.

Details of the Sulima Yalunka State during the early to mid-eighteenth century and of the Fula jihad are drawn from E. F. Sayers, "Notes on the Clan or Family Names Common in the Area Inhabited by Temne-speaking People," *Sierra Leone Studies* 12(1927):60–61.

The account of Barawa in the late eighteenth century is based on Tina Kome Marah's notes, Laing's *Travels* (p. 195), and Sayers's "Notes" (p. 61).

The clan name, Marah or Mara, derives from the verb *ka mara*, "to keep under one's command or control." The praise-word of the Marah is *nomor*, a contraction of *noe*, "force," and *morgo*, "person."

The name Yilkanani is probably a corruption of the Arabic *Dhul Quarnein* ("two-horned"), referring to Alexander the Great.

Chapter 2

Notes to pages 9–14

Details of Laing's travels in Sierra Leone are given in E. W. Bovill, *Missions to the Niger*, vol. 3, Cambridge, 1964–66, and in Laing's own *Travels*. For a description of the Niger source, I have drawn on Sanche de Gramont, *The Strong Brown God: The Story of the Niger River*, 1977.

Chapter 3

Notes to pages 14–22

Primary sources are again Bovill and Laing. The description of Tripoli is from *The Modern Traveller: a popular description, geographical, historical, and topographical, of the various countries of the Globe: Africa*, vol. 1, London, 1829. Material on Timbuktu is drawn from E. Herbert, "Timbucktu," in B. K. Swartz and R. E. Dumett, eds., *West African Cultural Dynamics*, The Hague, 1980.

Chapter 4

Notes to pages 22–25

Historical data are drawn from oral accounts by Yeli Maliki Kuyate and Salia Kamara (Firawa, February 3, 1979), from written notes by Tina Kome Marah (December 12, 1946), and from C. Magbaily Fyle, *Oral Traditions*.

Chapter 5

Notes to pages 26–37

Sources are W. Winwood Reade's two works on Africa (*Savage Africa*, 2 vols., London, 1863; and *The African Sketch-Book*, vol. 2, London, 1873), and F. Legge, Introduction in W. Winwood Reade, *The Martyrdom of Man*, London, 1924.

Chapter 6

Notes to pages 38–43

The account of the Sofa seige of Falaba and of Sewa's death is based on C. Fyfe, *A History of Sierra Leone*, London, 1962:448; and C. Magbaily Fyle, "Sewa" in *Dictionary of African Biography*, vol. 2, Algonac, Michigan, 1979:144. E. F. Sayers ("*Notes*," p. 70) states that it was Manga Dinka who blew himself up with the powder magazine when the Sofas sacked Falaba. Sayers gives 1892 as the date. This is probably an erroneous attribution; according to C. Magbaily Fyle, Manga Dinka ruled from 1888 to April 1895 and Manga Sewa between 1862 and 1884

("The Origin and Integration of the Solima Yalunka State," *Africana Research Bulletin* 6[I], 1975:7).

The story of Manti Kamara Kulifa Marah (Yira) is based on Tina Kome Marah's notes (December 22, 1946) and on information supplied by Noah Marah.

The account of the expedition to the Niger source is based on two publications by Lieutenant Colonel J. K. Trotter ("An expedition to the source of the Niger," *Geographical Journal* 10[3], 1897:386–401; and *The Niger Sources and the borders of the new Sierra Leone Protectorate*, London, 1898).

Chapter 7

Notes to pages 43–48

Stories about white men: the first was narrated by Noah Marah and recorded in Kabala, May 1970; the second is drawn from W. Winwood Reade, *African Sketch-Book*, vol. 2, p. 424. I have recorded other similar Kuranko tales in Firawa and Fasewoia, and Ruth Finnegan has published a comparable Limba story (*Limba Stories and Storytelling*, Oxford, 1967:261–67).

Stories about skin color: the story told here is based on a narrative by Noah Marah. Comparable tales are recorded in Mary Kingsley, *Travels in West Africa*, 2d ed., abridged, London, 1904:287–88; and B. G. Dennis, *The Gbandes*, Chicago, 1972:216.

The two tales attributed to Karifa are from my collection of recorded Kuranko *tilei*.

Chapter 8

Notes to pages 48–53

Details of the British administration in Kabala are from C. Magbaily Fyle ("The Kabala Complex: Koranko-Limba Relationships in the Nineteenth and Twentieth Centuries" in Arthur Abraham, ed., *Topics in Sierra Leone History: A Counter-Colonial Interpretation*, Freetown, 1976).

The account of Tina Dondon is based on information supplied by Noah Marah. According to Noah's mother, Aisetta Mansaray, Tina Dondon was older than Tina Kome and younger than Tina Kaima. They had another brother, Sewa, who was killed in the war, and another sister, Mera. Tina Dondon had two children, a boy and a girl.

Material on Warren's administration is drawn from an oral history of Kabala by Mamina Yegbe Marah (recorded in Kabala, December 1969), and from Warren's own records (Koinadugu District Intelligence Diary 1900–1925; Decree Books 1901–35).

Chapter 9

Notes to pages 53–60

For material on the Cameroon campaigns, I have referred to Tina Kome Marah's letter (December 22, 1946) to the commissioner, Northern Province, Makeni, submitting his name as a candidate for the Barawa chieftaincy, and have expanded Tina Kome Marah's account of the war with the aid of the following books: F. J. Moberly, comp., *Military Operations, Togoland and the Cameroons 1914–1916*, London, 1931; A. H. W. Haywood and F. A. S. Clarke, *The History of the Royal West African Frontier Force*, Aldershot, 1964; M. Crowder, "The 1914–1918 European War and West Africa" in M. Crowder and J. F. A. Ajayi, eds., *History of West Africa*, vol. 2, London, 1974; and M. Crowder, *The Story of Nigeria*, London, 1962.

Details of the Nigeria incident are drawn from Tina Kome Marah's letter and from M. Crowder, *West Africa under Colonial Rule*, London, 1968; and Sir Alan Burns, *History of Nigeria*, 7th ed., London, 1969.

Chapters 10–29

Pages 60–204 are based on the author's field notes and journals, Sierra Leone, 1969–70, 1972, and 1979.

Sources

Apart from references already cited, the following books and articles contain detailed ethnographical material on the Kuranko.

Drummond, D. B., and Kamara, K.
   1930 Some Kuranko Place Names. *Sierra Leone Studies*, old series, 16:27–34.
Jackson, M.
   1974 The Structure and Significance of Kuranko Clanship. *Africa* 44(4):397–415.
   1975 Structure and Event: Witchcraft Confession among the Kuranko. *Man* 10:387–403.
   1977 Sacrifice and Social Structure among the Kuranko. *Africa* 47(I):41–49 and 47(2):123–39.
   1977 *The Kuranko: Dimensions of Social Reality in a West African Society.* London: Hurst.
   1978 An Approach to Kuranko Divination. *Human Relations* 31(2):117–38.
   1978 The Identity of the Dead: Aspects of Mortuary Ritual in a West African Society. *Cahiers d'études Africaines* 66–67(2–3):271–97.
   1978 Ambivalence and the Last-Born: Birth-Order Position in Convention and Myth. *Man* 13:341–61.
   1979 Prevented Successions: A Commentary upon a Kuranko Narrative. In *Fantasy and Symbol: Essays in Honour of George Devereux*, ed. R. H. Hook. London: Academic Press.
   1982 Meaning and Moral Imagery in Kuranko Myth. *Research in African Literatures* 13(2):153–80.

1982   *Allegories of the Wilderness: Ethics and Ambiguity in Kuranko Narratives.* Bloomington: Indiana University Press.

1983   Knowledge of the Body. *Man* 18:327–45.

n.d.   The Migration of a Name: Reflections on Alexander in Africa [MS].

n.d.   In the Thrown World: Destiny and Decision in the Thought of Traditional Africa. In *Choice and Morality: Essays for Derek Freeman*, ed. G. Appell and T. N. Madan. Forthcoming.

Kamara, K., and Drummond, D. B.

1930   Marriage Customs amongst the Kurankos. *Sierra Leone Studies*, old series, 16:57–66.

Kamara, K.

1932   Notes on Some Customs of the Kurankos. *Sierra Leone Studies*, old series, 17:94–100.

1933   Kuranko Funeral Customs. *Sierra Leone Studies*, old series, 19:153–57.

Luke, J. F.

1939   Some Impressions of the Korankos and Their Country. *Sierra Leone Studies*, old series, 22:90–94.

Sayers, E. F.

1925   The Funeral of a Koranko Chief. *Sierra Leone Studies*, old series, 7:19–29.

Glossary of Kuranko Words

amina (Arabic der.)	amen
awa	expression or exclamation meaning "let's go," "all right," "well"
bambedon	"crocodile mouth"—an embroidered cap mainly associated with the Marah.
baraka (Arabic der.)	blessedness, good fortune
bese	medicine, magical medicine
besetigi	medicine-master
danke	curse
ferensola	"town of twins"—the Kuranko area as a whole; nation
gboye	a type of magical medicine
hake	retributive justice; "guilt" (cf. Arabic *haqyqun:* "consequence")
han	exclamation of surprise, often connoting difficulty
in sene	"you are welcome"
inwali	term of greeting or acknowledgment (lit. "you work")
jeliba	praise-singer, xylophonist
kandan li fannu	protective medicines
karamorgo	Islamic teacher, imam
kitabu (Arabic der.)	book
koli	a type of magical medicine

211

kome	a species of bush spirit; also, a men's cult
konke	mountain; also, a men's cult
konne	a four-stringed harp lute
korte	a powerful magical medicine
lakira	abode of ancestral spirits (cf. Arabic *al-akhira*)
luiye	courtyard, compound
ma'bon	the house where neophytes spend their last night before initiation (lit. "to hit repeatedly")
ma sogoma	"see you tomorrow," "goodbye," "goodnight"
m'berin	my mother's brother, "uncle"
m'bo	my age-mate, my companion
miran	container, vessel; presence, dignity, self-possession, bearing
musu gbe	pale-complexioned woman
nomor	praise-word of the Marah rulers (lit. "power person")
nyenkafori	a type of magical medicine
segere	a women's cult (perhaps derived from French-speaking Guinea where *segere* means secret)
sumafan	cult association or secret society (lit. "germinal thing")
sundu kunye ma	backyard; rubbish heap; marginal domestic area
sunike	non-Muslim, pagan; ruler
tubabu	white man, European (diminutive is *tubabune*)
tutufingbe	a species of bush spirit or djinn (lit. "the black-white *tutu*")
yati	exactly
yimbe	a small drum carried by neophytes during initiation